● ● ● ● ● ●

When his attention returned to Nya, her smile seemed different. It reminded him of the glances they exchanged at the pizza restaurant. He wanted to ask about that night, but he wasn't sure how to broach the subject. He couldn't deny that she was intimidating, possibly because of their age difference.

"Have you baked any cakes lately?" he asked instead.

She got a chuckle out of that.

"What?" he asked, grinning.

"Nothing. Do you like cakes, Coach Berry?"

Hell, yes, I do!

"You can call me Marquis."

She shook her head. "No. That wouldn't be a good idea."

"Why?"

"Because you're my daughter's teacher."

He couldn't tell if that was a rejection. He decided to keep pushing, until she made her position more clear.

"Will you make me a cake?"

His eyes were daring. Hers were surprised and then skeptical.

"Don't you have enough Tupperware piled up in your kitchen? You take a dish home every week."

He laughed at that. It almost sounded like she was jealous. "I didn't ask for any of those," he said. "Yours would be different."

She smacked her lips quietly. It was a slight movement, but it made Marquis want to kiss her. He wasn't sure if he'd get slapped in return, so he kept his lips to himself.

"My cake would be different?" she asked.

She was taunting him now. He liked it.

"Of course it would be."

"Why, because you asked for it?"

"Because I've been wanting it for so long," he said.

He wasn't smiling now, and she knew he wasn't referring to dessert. Marquis thought he had a fifty-fifty chance of getting shut down. But his eyes were confident. Nya had to look away.

● ● ● ● ● ●

1

ONE ON ONE

I0589233

ONE ON ONE

KEITH THOMAS WALKER

KEITHWALKERBOOKS, INC
This is a UMS production

ONE ON ONE

KEITHWALKERBOOKS

Publishing Company
KeithWalkerBooks, Inc.
P.O. Box 331585
Fort Worth, TX 76163

For information write
KeithWalkerBooks, Inc.
P.O. Box 331585
Fort Worth, TX 76163

Copyright © 2015 Keith Thomas Walker

ISBN-13 DIGIT: 978-0-9882180-9-3
ISBN-10 DIGIT: 0988218097
Library of Congress Control Number: 2015909802
Manufactured in the United States of America

Second Edition

Visit us at www.keithwalkerbooks.com

This book is for Shelee Stevenson

MORE BOOKS BY
KEITH THOMAS WALKER

Fixin' Tyrone
How to Kill Your Husband
A Good Dude
Riding the Corporate Ladder
The Finley Sisters' Oath of Romance
Blow by Blow
Jewell and the Dapper Dan
Harlot
Plan C (And More KWB Shorts)
Dripping Chocolate
The Realest Ever
Jackson Memorial
Sleeping With the Strangler
Life After
Blood for Isaiah
Brick House
Brick House 2

NOVELLAS

Might be Bi (Part One)
Harder

POETRY COLLECTION

Poor Righteous Poet

FINLEY HIGH SERIES

Prom Night at Finley High
Fast Girls at Finley High

Visit keithwalkerbooks.com for information about these and upcoming titles from KeithWalkerBooks

ACKNOWLEDGMENTS

Of course I would like to thank God, first and foremost, for giving me the creativity and drive to pursue my dreams and the understanding that I am nothing without Him. I would like to thank my wife for being my first and most important critic, and I would like to thank my mother for always pushing me to be the best I can be. I would like to thank Janae Hampton for being the best advisor, supporter and little sister a brother could ever have. I would also like to thank (in no particular order) Beulah Neveu, Deloris Harper, Denise Fizer, Shelee Stevenson, Melissa Carter, Cathy Atchison, Lanita Irvin, Ramona Weathersbee, Jason Owens, Sharon Blount, BRAB Book Club, and Uncle Steven Thomas, one love. I'd like to thank everyone who purchased and enjoyed one of my books. Everything I do has always been to please you. I know there are folks who mean the world to me that I'm failing to mention. I apologize ahead of time. Rest assured I'm grateful for everything you've done for me!

ONE ON ONE

CHAPTER ONE
THE RECRUITER

"Girls? I thought it was the boy's team..."

Marquis couldn't hide his displeasure as he leaned back in the padded chair. Across from him Phillip Kennedy, a recruiter for Overbrook Meadows school district, sat behind a large desk that was remarkably neat. He shuffled through a few papers in a file folder he'd created for Marquis. When he found the print-out he was looking for, his eyes narrowed as he read it.

"Uh, no. It's definitely the *girl's* team..."

The recruiter was middle-aged. He was tall and handsome, and he appeared to be in great shape. He wasn't what Marquis expected when he spoke to him on the phone earlier that week, but of course expectations change. Marquis, for example, never expected to use his education degree for real-live *teaching*, but now he was glad that he had it.

Even still, he shook his head.

"What's wrong?" Phillip asked him. He was all smiles.

"I don't think I want to coach a girls' team," Marquis said honestly. "I could've sworn you said it was the boys' team."

"Honestly, I don't think you asked," Phillip stated, still smiling. "But I could've been more specific."

Marquis thought back to the conversations he had with this gentleman and decided he might be right. Phillip said there was a coaching position available for "Finley High's varsity basketball team." Marquis mistakenly assumed it was for the boys.

"This is already getting further away from what I want to do," he revealed with a sigh.

"I understand," Phillip said. "You want to coach football."

"I think I'd be better at it."

"But we don't have any openings right now, and you agreed to coach *basketball*," Phillip reminded him.

"Yes, but I thought–"

"What do you have against coaching the girls?" the recruiter asked with a smirk.

Marquis frowned. Technically this meeting was part of his job interview, so he didn't want to sound too negative. But he couldn't think of a way to answer that question without negativity.

"Let me guess," the man said. He leaned forward with his long forearms on the desk. "They're too slow. They don't hustle enough. They miss all their shots. They cry when they fall down, and no one comes to their games..." His grin was bright and sunny.

Marquis felt like he was being set up, but he nodded. "Yeah, that's about right."

"Man, that's wrong," Phillip chided him.

Marquis grinned slightly. "Hey, those were your words."

"But you agreed with me," Phillip said. "I was just fishing, trying to find out what your complaints were. I don't agree with any of that. I think this position would be very rewarding."

"Have you coached girls' basketball before?" Marquis wondered. "You sound like you might have a little experience."

"Oh, no," Phillip replied. "I've never coached or played any sport professionally. I didn't even play in high school."

"Really?" Marquis asked, raising an eyebrow.

"I know. People see a tall, skinny black guy and assume he can ball."

Marquis shrugged. "I did think that."

"No, I'm just a fan of the sport," Phillip said. "All sports, really. I have a few sons who did pretty good in high school. One of them got a basketball scholarship to TCU. He's not a starter, but he does get some playtime. All of my boys went to Castleberry..."

Marquis couldn't hide his interest. "I went to Castleberry."

"Yes, I know," Phillip said. "Class of 2007."

Marquis knew the recruiter got that information from his application, but he was surprised that he remembered such a small detail.

"You played basketball all four years," Phillip went on, "varsity for the last three..."

Okay, that information wasn't on his application. Marquis' expression was now guarded and curious.

The recruiter laughed. "I remember you!" he explained. "My oldest son came out of Castleberry in '09. You played with him your senior year. His name's Barry."

Marquis' eyes lit up. "Oh, wow. I remember Barry! How's he doing?"

"Great!" Phillip said. "He got a nursing degree from Texas Lutheran. Lives in Weatherford now. Married with two kids."

"That's awesome," Marquis quipped. "I always knew that guy would end up helping people one day. He was one of those kind of people you could always count on."

"Yes," the recruiter said. "He is. But my point is you have a strong basketball background, so I think coaching the girls' team would be a good move for you."

Marquis was not thrilled to get back to that subject.

"I know you went to LSU on a football scholarship," the recruiter said. "And everyone knows how great you played for the Cowboys."

"Yeah, right. I didn't even finish my first season."

"Through no fault of your own," Phillip added. "If you had been healthy, you'd be on a Gatorade bottle by now. Those numbers you were putting up had every defensive line in the league shaking in their boots when they saw you on the field."

Marquis' mind drifted back to his glory days in the NFL. But some of his memories were not as pleasant as the recruiter's.

"I also know about the rough patch you had when you returned to Overbrook Meadows in 2012," Phillip continued. For the first time during the meeting, his smile went away. "I know about the partying," he said. "I know about the fights, and I know about the *arrest...*"

Marquis suddenly had a sinking feeling in his gut. The *rough patch* the recruiter was referring to didn't last long, but it was memorable. Marquis was somewhat of a celebrity at the time, so his few bad deeds made it to the local papers. One had even made it to the national news.

But, "Those charges were dropped," he said in his defense.

"Yes," the recruiter said, all smiles again. "I know. I don't think you would've made it to this interview, if you were convicted of aggravated assault."

Marquis took a deep breath and blew it out slowly. He thought the recruiter's office was too chilly when he first arrived. But now it was much too warm in there. He was glad he didn't wear a tie with his long-sleeved shirt. It would've been choking the life out of him by now, and he'd look supremely guilty when he reached to loosen it.

"You know," Phillip said, leaning forward with a conspiratorial tone, "a lot of people still think you paid the victim off, and that's why he stopped cooperating with the police."

Marquis was glad he didn't ask him to respond to that. He felt like perspiration was blossoming on his forehead. But he didn't want to reach up and wipe it. He didn't expect this interview to be an emotional minefield.

"But, as you mentioned, the charges did get dropped," Phillip said, leaning back in his seat again. "So your background check should be clean. I'll send you down the hall to check when we get through here. That is, if you still want the job."

Before Marquis could respond, the man said, "I think you should take it. Given your *questionable behavior*, since you moved back to Overbrook Meadows, a lot of people view you as a stereotype; a former NFL player who doesn't know what to do with his money... A rich black man with a hood-mentality who hangs with thugs, can't hold his liquor or watch his temper."

"I'm, I'm not rich," Marquis told him.

"I know you're not," Phillip said. "You only played half a season in the NFL. And that was three years ago. You've been through a messy divorce. I understand that you're trying to get a fresh start."

Marquis didn't like that this man had so much dirt on him. But all of it was true, so he couldn't get upset. He knew that a lot of people in the community had a similar opinion of him.

"Coach the girls' team," Phillip suggested. "There aren't a lot of schools or school districts that would be willing to take a chance on you. Plus it's late July. Classes start in exactly one month. Teaching positions are few and far between. And there are no other coaching positions available in this district.

"Everman's head football coach is retiring next year, and they will have an opening then. If you do well at Finley High, prove that you have your head screwed on right, I will do my very best to get you that Everman spot next year. If not there, I'm sure I can get you a football position somewhere else in the district. All you have to do is put your two grievances aside for one year."

"My two grievances?"

"Yes: You don't want to coach basketball, and you don't want to coach girls."

"I got over the basketball part before I got here," Marquis told him.

"Good," the recruiter replied. "Then we're halfway there. So what do you say? Will you lead the Lady Grizzlies?"

"The *Lady Grizzlies*?" Marquis shook his head. "I'm pretty sure that name is the toughest thing about them."

"I think you'd be surprised."

Marquis wasn't buying it. In his mind's eye he saw a gym full of long hair, sparkling fingernails and makeup ruined by tear-stains every time one of them fell down. But hell, the recruiter was right about one thing: He did have to start somewhere.

"Okay," he said. "I'll take the job."

"Great!" Phillip stood to shake his hand.

Marquis stood too. He and the recruiter were roughly the same height, but Marquis outweighed him by at least fifty pounds. Finley High's newest teacher had rich dark skin, serious eyes and a light moustache. Even with a collared shirt on, Marquis' neck and shoulder muscles were prominent.

He wasn't in as good a shape as he was during his glory days in the NFL, but he hadn't totally abandoned his fitness regimen. Running was one of the things that kept him sane when he returned to his hometown and had to contend with his shattered dreams and an expected but still painful divorce.

"I'm going to get your paperwork finished up," the recruiter told him. "Mr. Walters is your new boss at Finley

High. He's hard on the kids, but most of the teachers I've spoken to love working for him. You can meet him on August 17th. That'll be your first staff development day."

Marquis nodded. "Alright."

"The sheriff liaison's office is down the hall on the left," the recruiter said, pointing. "You'll have to fill out more paperwork for him, let him get your fingerprints. Once he gives the green light, you're good to go. Stop by my office again before you leave, and I'll give you a welcome packet."

"Are they still looking to start me at fifty thousand?" Marquis asked.

"Fifty-two, five," Phillip corrected him. "You're only getting that much because you're teaching a core subject *and* coaching. Sorry, I know that's a big drop, compared to your NFL salary."

"Eh. I don't need a million dollars to be happy," Marquis told him.

"That's the spirit!" The recruiter walked him to the door and gave him a pat on the back as he exited the office.

● ● ● ● ● ●

Marquis had four weeks to come to terms with the fact that he was going to coach a girls' basketball team. He had also gotten over the realization that teachers don't make very much money at all.

He arrived at Finley High at 9 am for their staff development day. He entered the main office and was greeted by a short, slender woman who couldn't wipe the smile off her face.

"Wow. It's really you!" She reached across the counter to shake his hand.

"Hi," Marquis said. "I'm here to meet with Mr. Walters."

"Yes, he's expecting you," the woman said. "He's here. He just stepped out for a moment. My name's Sophia. I work here in the office."

"Nice to meet you," he said, still holding her hand. "I'm Marquis Berry."

She grinned. "Oh, I know *all* about you, Mr. Berry."

Marquis wasn't sure if that was a good or bad thing. "You can call me Marquis," he said.

She let go of his hand but didn't back away from the counter, so he didn't either.

"I can't believe you're going to be coaching here," she gushed. "I remember when you played for the *Cowboys*. Why aren't you coaching football?"

Sophia was fair-skinned, with nice, plump lips and a 100 watt smile. She had a slim waist and a nice figure. Marquis didn't check to see if she had a ring on her finger.

"I wanted to coach football," he admitted. "But there were no openings —not when I applied. I probably should've filled out an application sooner."

"They start looking to fill holes in the staff right at the end of May," the clerk said. "When did you apply?"

"Middle of July."

"Oh, well that's probably why," Sophia said. "Did you want to coach football here?"

"I wasn't particular about where, so long as it was football."

"We already have a football coach," the clerk told him. "His name's Donovan Mitchell. He used to play in college, but he didn't make it to the NFL, like you..."

Marquis wasn't sure if the woman was being friendly or flirty. He decided to give her the benefit of the doubt. He preferred to maintain a private lifestyle, as any normal person would, but he hadn't found much of that since his return to Overbrook Meadows. A lot of women he met knew about his divorce and assumed he was still a millionaire. That led to a lot of unwanted attention.

"Is your football team any good?" he asked her.

"Ummm..."

Sophia leaned on the counter, which brought her boobs closer to him. Her blouse wasn't very revealing, but Marquis had been single for quite a while. He instructed himself to maintain eye contact.

"They have their ups and downs," she told him. "You know how it is when you're coaching high school." She caught herself and giggled. "Wait, you don't, do you?"

Marquis smiled and shook his head.

"You can have an all-star team one year," the clerk told him, "and you lose all of your starters when they graduate. Or sometimes you have a really good player, then his parents move in the middle of the year and transfers him to another school. You just have to do the best you can with what you have."

Marquis nodded. "What about the girls' basketball team? Are they any good?"

"They are," Sophia said. "I think they won half their games last year."

Marquis chuckled. He thought a fifty/fifty season was *okay*, rather than good.

"They had one girl who was really talented," the clerk told him. "I don't remember her name, though."

"Let me guess, she graduated already."

"No." Sophia shook her head. "She's still here. I can tell you one thing though..."

"What's that?"

"The girls' boosters are gonna *love you*!"

Marquis was happy to get some good news. "Are they very active?"

"*Definitely.* Those ladies will do whatever they can to help the team. You should've seen them last year. Sometimes it wasn't nobody in the stands but them, but you couldn't tell by how loud they were."

Marquis grinned at that.

17

"And when they find out *you're* the new coach, you're gonna have to beat them off with a stick," Sophia warned.

Marquis raised an eyebrow.

"I ain't lying," Sophia continued. "Big, strong, tall, former NFL player coaching high school..." She giggled. "Boy, I can see them now."

Marquis laughed at that. He decided that he liked Sophia. But then she raised a red flag by asking, "Are you married?"

He shook his head.

"Oh, don't worry about me," she told him. "I've been married for ten years. *Happily* married. I'm just saying, with you being single, you will have to watch out for some of those ladies. A lot of the parents, really. And some teachers too.

"We had a cute guy teaching Algebra a few years back. He was only here for a year, but he got caught up in *two* affairs. They didn't fire him, or anything like that. But it got tense up here for a while. He quit at the end of the year."

"That's crazy," Marquis muttered. Out of all the reservations he had about teaching, that type of trouble had never occurred to him.

"But I'm sure you'll be fine," Sophia said. "Just keep telling them no, and they'll eventually back off. Unless you find yourself liking one of them back, then, you know, be discreet – and make sure she's not married."

The secretary laughed. Marquis found himself laughing, too.

CHAPTER TWO
COACH BERRY

Mr. Walters was a tall man, though not as tall as Marquis. His skin was dark brown. He wore thick glasses with bold, black frames and a neatly trimmed moustache. Marquis was impressed with the way he spoke and carried himself. He was surprised to find that Mr. Walters was impressed with him as well.

"I didn't think you'd take the position," he told him.

The two men sat facing each other in a large office that wasn't too cluttered. Several degrees hung on the wall above the principal.

"I was a little hesitant," Marquis acknowledged.

"I'm glad you gave us a shot," Mr. Walters said. "I think you'll do well here. We have a great athletic program. Our girls' basketball team is really good."

"Is that right?" Marquis didn't tell him that he had already heard the girls were only average.

"Oh yes," Mr. Walters said. "They'll have you thinking you're coaching the boys. One of them – I forget her name – but she's the real deal. She's a senior this year. I'm sure she'll get a few scholarship offers."

"I think I heard about her," Marquis said.

"I take it you still have your eye out for a football position," the principal said. "You may not stay with us next year..."

Marquis already had the job, but he didn't think it would be wise to tell his boss he would only be there temporarily.

"That's fine," Mr. Walters said before he could answer. "I won't make you cop to it. But I'm sure you know it's much too soon to be thinking about next year."

Marquis wasn't sure how to respond to that.

"Son, are you aware that you've got red flags all over you?" the principal asked him.

Marquis shook his head slightly.

"First let me say that I'm a fan," Mr. Walters said. "I've been impressed with you ever since you were running folks over at *Castleberry*. I kept up with you a little bit when you were over at LSU. I knew you'd make it to the NFL. You had that speed, son. Watching you run..." The principal shook his head, momentarily lost in a memory. "Thing of beauty. When you got drafted by the Cowboys, I told my wife, 'That boy is gonna be *great!*'"

"Thanks. But I guess it didn't turn out that way," Marquis said. He was still reeling from the principal's *red flags* comment.

"No, it didn't," Mr. Walters conceded. "But you know, God has a plan for all of us. I hated that you had to quit, but I know you made the best decision for yourself and your family."

Yeah, my family, Marquis thought. His ex-wife Paula didn't think he made the right decision by leaving football. Sadly, they would probably be together now if he was still playing. They'd be living the dream and living a lie.

"But the trouble you had when you came back," the principal continued, "you need to know that's on a lot of people's minds. They know about your drunk partying. They know about the messy divorce. They know about your arrest. Any kid at this school can google you and pull up your mugshot."

Marquis sighed silently. He wondered if he would ever get past those dark, infamous nights.

"As you can imagine," the principal continued, "a lot of parents don't like the idea of someone with your background teaching their kids. I can go on and on about all of the great things you did in high school and college and during your time with the Cowboys. But they'll continue to ask, '*What about the things he did when he came home?*'

"I'm going to have to answer that question a lot this year," Mr. Walters said. "And that's no fun. The last thing a principal wants is to have to convince a parent that their child's teacher isn't as bad as they've heard. So it looks like we're both taking a chance this year. Lucky for you," he said with a smile, "I'm a man who believes in second chances. I believe you'll love your job so much, you'll forget all about coaching a boy's football team."

Marquis was on edge, but the principal's smile and his honesty was disarming.

"I don't think I'll forget about football. But you might be right," he replied with a smile of his own.

"I hope I am," the principal said and rose from his seat.

Marquis stood too. They reached across the desk to shake hands.

"Welcome to the team, *Coach Berry*," Mr. Walters said.

That was the first time anyone ever used that title officially. Marquis liked the way it sounded.

"Thank you, sir. Glad to be here."

● ● ● ● ● ●

Mr. Walters didn't have time to give him a tour of the school, but he showed Marquis where his classroom was and introduced him to four teachers on the floor who would be part of his "team."

After meeting with them, one of Marquis' new colleagues took him to the athletic center. There he found a state of the art gym and an impressive basketball court. Marquis would rather be on the football field, but there were obvious perks to playing and practicing indoors.

Before he headed back to his classroom, he was stopped by another new co-worker.

"*Marquis Berry!*"

He turned and saw a strikingly fit gentleman approaching from the weight room.

"Welcome to Finley High!" the man said as he drew near. He reached to shake his hand. "I'm Donovan Mitchell, the football coach.

"Oh." Marquis offered him a quick smile as they shook hands. "Good to meet you, man. I heard a lot about you."

"Probably not as much as I've heard about you," Donovan stated. "I can't believe you're here. A *real live Dallas Cowboy* at my school!"

"Nah, not anymore," Marquis said good-naturedly. "Haven't been a Cowboy since 2012. I'm just regular old Marquis now."

"Man, get off that." Donovan's smile was ear to ear. "Three years is not that long ago. For a hardcore football fan like me, it seems like it was just yesterday. I remember when you ran for 189 yards against the Eagles. Two touchdowns that game. You were on pace to break Dickerson's record."

Marquis had heard that before, but he always downplayed it. Eric Dickerson was the greatest running back of all time, in his opinion. As good as Marquis was, he didn't like to be compared to the greats.

"I doubt it. I only played seven games," he told him.

"C'mon," Donovan said, shaking his head. "You got a thousand yards in those seven games. There's no way you wouldn't have broken that record. I look up to you, man. Even though you only played half a season, I think you're one of the best to ever carry that pigskin – that's taking your high school and college games into consideration."

Marquis continued to shake his head. "I don't think so, man. Not even."

Donovan sensed their new coach was not comfortable talking about his past, so he let it go for now.

"Well, you're here now," he said. "But I gotta ask: Why aren't you coaching *football*? I mean, not that we don't want you here..."

"I wanted to," Marquis revealed. "That was my goal. But I was dragging my feet all summer. Wasn't sure if I wanted to teach, even though I majored in education. By the time I made up my mind, it was slim pickings. I could've taught science at a few schools, but this is the only one that still had a coaching position available."

"And you knew it was a *girls'* team?"

Marquis found his new friend easy to talk to, so he was honest with him. "The recruiter said I could coach basketball, and I *assumed* he meant the boys. I think he knew what I was expecting, and he went on letting me think that." He chuckled. "I guess I could've backed out at the last minute, but I figured it wouldn't be so bad."

"It's won't be," Donovan said right away. "They had a pretty good team last year."

"Yeah, I heard they lost half their games."

"No, they *won* half their games," Donovan corrected him. "It's all about prospective, my brother. Plus you've got one of the best athletes in the school on your team."

"I keep hearing that. But no one knows her name."

"It's Lisa Edmonds," Donovan told him. "She's a point guard. That girl can shoot the lights out. And she's as tall as a giraffe. You don't get that too often; tall girls who got handles."

"Oh yeah?" Marquis said, feeling a little excited about his team for the first time.

"No doubt," Donovan said. "She's good for at least twelve points a game."

"*Twelve points?*" All of his hope quickly faded. "And that's my *best* player?"

Donovan laughed. "I take it you haven't been to a girls' basketball game in a while. A good game for them might end with a score of 48 to 55, in which case twelve points is a lot."

Marquis laughed. "Okay. I don't think my expectations can get any lower."

"They're gonna surprise you. Watch." Donovan had a twinkle in his eye. "Unless you're expecting all of them to dunk, then yeah, you can lower that expectation..."

CHAPTER THREE
THE NEST EGG

Marquis spent his first staff development day getting acquainted with the school and the teachers he'd be working with for the next ten months. Most of his new colleagues were aware of his glory days as a rookie running back for the Dallas Cowboys. Many of them didn't know why he quit the sport, and if they knew about his bad boy antics after returning to Overbrook Meadows, they were too polite to mention it.

With so much talk about football, it was easy to forget that he was also the school's newest biology teacher. Marquis met with the head of the department, a portly woman named Mrs. Pace. She gave him the official curriculum along with an armful of folders and notebooks and miscellaneous supplies.

She followed him to his room and gave him a run-down on everything he'd need to get through the first six-weeks of his teaching career. Marquis was soon overwhelmed with instructions, but he needn't worry:

"I have all of this written down in the folder I gave you," she said, referring to the one on the top of his pile. "I started making those notes after my first year teaching. I had such a horrible time. I didn't want to make the same mistakes the next fall.

"Since then I've upgraded and refined my little welcome packet over the years. I always keep an extra copy for any newbie who might come to the science department. Welcome aboard!"

She giggled. Marquis thought she was as cute as a cherub. She looked to be in her sixties, which meant her welcome packet was filled with knowledge and know-how; the kind of stuff you only learn from trial and error. Her notebook would probably be the most important manual he'd receive.

"Thank you very much!"

● ● ● ● ● ●

By the time he left the school, Marquis worried that he might be in over his head. But he was excited about the prospect of molding young minds in the classroom as well as on the basketball court. He met with his brother Omar at a taco shop on Magnolia. At 29 Omar was older by a few years. He was an accountant for a law firm in Killeen, married with three kids.

Marquis ordered what turned out to be a big enough plate of nachos for two people. Omar couldn't offer him much help because he had a hot plate of his own.

"Why'd you order so much?"

"I didn't," Marquis told him. "I only ordered nachos."

"That thing was piled a foot high. I thought you ordered the *double*!"

"Why would I order a double nachos?" Marquis wondered.

"I don't know, but you're getting chunky," his brother said. "And now I know why."

Omar smiled. After shaking his head, Marquis did too. The brothers' eyes were nearly identical. They both had strong facial features. Omar didn't look any older, and contrary to his comment, Marquis definitely had the better physique. He wore a golf shirt with Dockers that day. His shirt wasn't tight, but he knew his pythons were nearly bursting from the sleeves.

Omar asked him, "You think you'll like it at the school, *Mister* Berry?"

"No, they call me *Coach Berry*."

"Yeah?"

Marquis nodded.

"You think you'll like the girls' team?"

"No sir," Marquis said, shaking his head. "I don't think so."

"How come?" Omar asked, chuckling.

"What you mean how come? Have you ever seen a *girls'* basketball game? Not the WNBA – although that's bad enough – but a *high school* girls' basketball game?"

His brother couldn't stop cracking up. "You're the one who took the job!"

"Yeah, at your *insistence*."

"You had to work somewhere. You've been unemployed for the past three years. I know your savings won't last much longer."

"No," Marquis agreed, his smile fading. "They won't."

His savings once consisted of 1.7 million he'd received for seven games of service with the Cowboys. Marquis bought a house in Irving prior to his injury, when he and his ex-wife Paula were living the life. He never would've thought they'd be divorced three years later. She got the house and half of the money in his accounts.

On top of that, Marquis was ordered to pay child support and spousal support. It was no wonder he went a little crazy when he returned to Overbrook Meadows with his tail tucked between his legs; beaten on the football field and in the courtroom.

"How much you got left?" his big brother asked.

"About a hundred thousand," Marquis reported.

"How much you giving Paula?"

27

"Ten thousand a month."

Omar winced. "I don't have to count on my fingers to see where this is going."

"Me neither," Marquis said. "I'll be broke in ten months."

"You gotta take her back to court," Omar said. "You have a job now. How much you making? Sixty thousand?"

"I wish. More like fifty-two."

"Damn." Omar winced again. "Nigga, you broke."

Marquis shook his head, grinning.

"So, M.C. Hammer," his brother said, "how does it feel to go from being a millionaire to living off a teacher's salary?"

If anyone else said that, Marquis would've taken offense. But his brother's love was never in question.

"I didn't blow thirty million. It was only two. And I didn't *blow* it," Marquis argued. "I bought a little mansion in Irving. I bought my own house in Overbrook Meadows. I gave Paula half of what was left, and I had some fun with the homies."

"Lord, help him," Omar said.

Marquis' *fun* nearly landed him in prison after a bar fight left a man with significant injuries. Marquis spent a lot of money on attorneys and even more on a secret settlement that was sweet enough to make the victim conveniently come up missing when the district attorney tried to put a case together.

"I own my truck, too," Marquis said. "It's brand new."

"I know where your money went, little bro. I'm getting you ready for the questions *they're* gonna ask. People think everybody who plays a few games on TV should be set for life."

Marquis nodded. He knew what to expect.

"You need some money?" Omar asked.

"Nah."

"Not my money, I mean *your* money."

Marquis continued to shake his head.

"I think it's up to four hundred thousand now," Omar informed him.

Marquis' eyebrows rose, but he wasn't ready to touch his nest egg.

When he handed the Cowboys his letter of resignation in 2012, they sent his final wages in the form of three checks. He gave the last one to his brother. He didn't suspect his marriage would sour at the time. Rather, Marquis understood that he wasn't accustomed to so many commas in his bank account, whereas his brother was a seasoned accountant.

He signed the check over to him, saying, "Hold this for me, so I'll have something left in ten years."

Omar thought it was a good move.

Two years later, when Paula decided she wanted a divorce, the three-hundred thousand Marquis stashed away became a huge and very illegal secret.

"Has she asked about it?" Omar had asked him.

"No," Marquis replied. His eyes were wide with panic. "It never hit our account, so I don't think she knows about it. She's been spending money so fast, I know she lost track of how much we started with. It's been two years since I quit playing. She's all over the accounts, especially since she filed. If she thought we were missing three hundred thousand, she would've said so by now."

"Then agree to whatever she wants," Omar had advised him.

Marquis had found that suggestion ludicrous. "She wants the house!" he complained. "And half of everything I got left!"

"She'll probably get it any way," his brother said solemnly. "But if you want to keep the money I have for you – which is *illegal*, so I won't advise that – but if you want to keep it, you have to agree to whatever she wants. She knows what you have in the bank now, and she's not requesting pay

29

stubs from the Cowboys. Agree to her terms, and hopefully she'll never know what I'm doing for you over here."

It was a huge risk, one that could've landed both of the brothers in hot water. But Marquis took his advice, and everything worked out just like Omar said. Paula thought she took Marquis to the cleaners. She didn't know that his nest egg was thriving, thanks to Omar's smart investments.

Marquis didn't want to eat another soggy nacho, but he couldn't resist. Omar frowned at him.

"Anyway, if you're taking her to court soon, I guess I'd better sit on your stash a little longer."

"I didn't ask for it," Marquis stated. "You're doing a great job. You can keep whatever interest you get off it."

"No, that's all yours," Omar said. "Your money made that."

"You deserve something for your troubles."

"If I need anything, I'll let you know. Just don't ever let that bitch get her hands on it."

"*Hey*," Marquis said. "That's the mother of my children."

"That's also the gold digger who wanted you to get back on the field after you broke your neck."

"Yeah," Marquis conceded. "That bitch did want that..."

● ● ● ● ● ●

On Friday Marquis paid a visit to a beautiful Irving neighborhood he once called home. As he pulled into the driveway of a majestic, five bedroom mini-castle on Windsong Court, he recalled the days when he wore a #23 jersey and was the talk of the town.

He would never forget when he and Paula toured the home for the first time. She had squealed with delight, from room to room, making glorious decoration plans as she assigned rooms to the twins, the glowing couple, and "Ooh, Marquis, my office can go in here!"

He referred to that time period as the *glory days*, but there were plenty of warning signs, even before his injury. He had turned a blind eye to them because Paula married him during his senior year of college – *before* the money or the fame. Shortly after they graduated in 2011, she gave him two wonderful twin boys.

He rang the doorbell at his former home and waited for what felt like an enormous amount of time for his ex-wife to answer. Before she did, he heard one of the twins approach the door and fiddle with the knob.

"*Who is it?*" a small voice shouted.

Despite the inner turmoil this home brought him, Marquis' features softened at the sound of his son. He even knew which one it was. This was Omar, named after his uncle.

"It's your daddy," Marquis responded through the door. His chest swelled with pride as he uttered those words. He was still *Daddy*. That was one thing Paula couldn't take away from him.

"Hold on, I can't..." More fumbling with the doorknob.

"Go get your mama," Marquis instructed him. He didn't like the idea of his four and a half year old son opening the door for a random voice who claimed to be his father.

"*Okaaay,*" the boy replied, and then there was silence again.

Marquis sighed as he looked out onto the beautifully manicured lawn that a portion of his spousal support financed. There was a good amount of upkeep required to care for a home that size, but with no mortgage payments, it wasn't that much. He guessed his ex-wife was pocketing at least half of the ten thousand he paid her each month, which, interestingly, was more than he would be paid as Finley High's newest coach and biology teacher.

Paula finally opened the door. She wore a sport's bra and yoga pants along with a pair of sneakers. A coat of sweat glistened on all of her exposed skin.

"Sorry, I was working out," she said as she turned and left him standing on the porch.

"Good afternoon to you, too," Marquis replied as he followed her inside.

• • • • • •

Paula studied dance as a child. She was a natural beauty with long, slender legs, perky bosoms and beautiful, silky hair that was all hers. A Louisiana native, she parlayed her high school cheerleading into college cheerleading. It didn't take long before she caught the eye of LSU's star running back when Marquis was a sophomore. The couple dated for a year and a half and married in 2010, the year Paula graduated.

They lived off campus during Marquis' senior year, and Paula had a bun in the oven in no time. An ultrasound later revealed there were actually two precious lives growing in her womb, and Marquis couldn't have been happier. Carl was older by ninety seconds, but Omar had always been slighter bigger.

The twins rushed to their father in the foyer of his former home. He knelt to interact with them on their level. He hugged them, swallowing them up in his big bear arms. As they chatted incessantly, he took them to the living room and parked them in front of the TV, while he went to speak with the head of the house.

Paula had converted one of the spare bedrooms into a rather impressive gym. Marquis entered and found her on the treadmill, walking up an incline. Her body was toned to perfection. She had her hair pinned away from her caramel colored face. He still thought she was stunning, despite all that had happened between them.

"I started my new job this week," he said as he stepped closer. He walked to the front of the treadmill, so she wouldn't have to turn to look him in the eyes.

"Great," she said, slightly winded. Her strong arms sliced the air rhythmically with her steps.

Marquis noticed a sweat stain in the middle of her sports bra, where the perspiration settled between her breasts. He remembered the first time he saw her in a cheerleader outfit, with a similar amount of cleavage on display. Her boobs grew bigger after she had the twins, but Marquis didn't find her curves as enticing as he once did.

"The money's about what you'd expect for a teacher," he continued.

Paula looked away from him for a moment and snorted. "I already know where you're going with this, and I'm not trying to hear it."

Marquis didn't react. Arguing was woven so deeply into their relationship, he could hardly remember a time when they did get along. But they didn't have to bicker today. He simply wanted to cut out four-fifths of her income. No biggie.

"I only make fifty thousand now," he told her. "Fifty-two, five, to be exact."

"We already talked about this," Paula said.

The treadmill hummed as it kicked into another gear. The pace of her padded footsteps increased along with it.

"I know we talked about it," Marquis said. "I told you what kind of money I was looking at, if I started teaching."

She cut her eyes at him. "Marquis, I don't want to hear it."

She was confident. He'd give her that. And plenty stubborn. But the math was on his side now.

"You know it's impossible for me to pay you ten thousand a month, if I only make forty-five hundred," he stated.

She didn't bat an eye. "That's not my problem."

He kept pushing. "It's gonna be your problem when they try to draft from my account, and the money's not there."

"You still have money," she said, not missing a beat or a stride.

Marquis shook his head. "You know it's not gonna last."

"We can deal with that when it's all gone," Paula told him.

Marquis felt his temper rising. He stomped the hot coals before they flamed up.

"What do you wanna do, Paula? Bleed me till I'm dry? And then what?"

Her soft features were hard and unmoving. *"This is not my problem, Marquis. All I want is for you to do what the judge ordered you to do."*

"Those payments were based on my *football* salary," he reminded her, though she knew this full well. "I don't make that kind of money anymore."

"No one told you to quit football."

Marquis sucked air between his teeth as the floor disappeared beneath him. He caught himself before he tumbled down a pit of despair and loathing; a dark cave where a succubus named Paula was free to reveal her true form, with red eyes, glistening fangs and dark, scaly skin that reeked of spoiled fish.

You didn't have to quit football.

Those words never failed to hurt him. And haunt him. The first time she uttered them was in 2012, after *The Big Hit* laid Marquis out in his last professional game against the Cardinals. He had gained three yards on the play before a linebacker stepped into his path. Marquis lowered his head and bowled him over, gaining two more yards. But when he hopped up after the tackle, something went *tingly* down his side. His right leg stopped working properly. Eighty thousand horrified fans held their breath as the superstar rookie fell again and had to be carted off the field.

X-rays revealed a hairline fracture on his C4 vertebrae. By all accounts, it wasn't a horrible injury. Marquis regained his ability to walk within an hour, but the season was over for him, that much was certain. After surgery and physical therapy, the team physicians thought he could be ready for practice the following summer.

Except one doctor didn't feel that way.

His original surgeon told him plainly, "If you ever get hit like that again, at the same angle, I don't believe you'll get up like last time. I don't think you'll walk at all. Maybe never. I know my opinion is unpopular in your camp."

The physician's expression was apologetic. His tone sincere.

So Marquis made what he thought was the most obvious decision. The very first thing Paula said after he told her was, "But they said you would be alright. You don't have to quit."

"Or I could end up paralyzed," he had told her.

"Or you could be just fine," she countered. "The team thinks you should keep playing, and I do too."

Thinking back, Marquis would have to say that was the beginning of the end for them.

"Listen," he said.

Paula seemed to stare over his shoulder as she marched on the treadmill. She was looking his direction without making proper eye contact.

"I'm going to get some papers drawn up. If you don't want to sign them, we have to go back to court."

"I'm not signing anything," she stated. "I can't afford to pay my bills on anything less than what the court ordered you to pay."

"That's a lie, and you know it. And you could always get a job," he offered. "You are a college graduate."

She met his eyes then. "I could always go home. How about that? Me and the boys."

Marquis didn't let on how much that shook him. The threat was like a shotgun blast to his heart, but he wore the same poker face she donned. He hated that their relationship had become a cesspool of manipulation, resistance, resentment and intimidation.

"You're not taking my boys out of state. You can try if you want. That'll be one hell of a fight."

"Alright," she said. The treadmill kicked into another gear, and so did she. "Take me to court, and see what happens," she panted. "Have a nice weekend."

That was his cue to leave.

Marquis didn't want to call the mother of his children a *coldhearted bitch*, even in his mind, so he left the room and left the argument simmering, as it always was.

When he returned to his sons, they put a quick smile on his face.

Rather than head home when he got them secured in his truck, he stopped by his mother's house. She missed the twins as much as he did. She promised to have her world-famous spaghetti casserole waiting for them.

Marquis couldn't wait to get his paws on that.

CHAPTER FOUR
NYA AND LISA (AND DARYL, TO A LESSER EXTENT)

I bless the tiny cells that made you
When your mother's womb embraced you
The day we met, my dreams came true
You'll always be my little girl

On Monday, August 24th, Nya Edmonds stopped by her daughter's room at seven a.m. and turned on the lights.

"Time to get up."

Later in the school year, or even as early as next week, Lisa would roll away from the light and try to ignore her wakeup call. But today was different. This was the first day of school, which always carried a bit of excitement for a student, no matter their age.

Lisa sat up and stretched and smiled at her mother, who was already dressed in the blue scrub suit she needed for her job as a trauma nurse at Jackson Memorial.

"You gotta work today?" her daughter asked groggily.

"Yes," Nya said. "I told you that yesterday."

"I forgot," Lisa said as she rubbed her eyes.

"Don't start this already," Nya said good-naturedly.

Between her daughter's extracurricular activities and Nya's work schedule, the two were constantly scrambling to make sure Lisa got picked up from practice and made it to her basketball games on time. Nya was happy that her daughter was a senior this year. She planned to get her a car, so she could transport herself.

On the other hand, it was hard to watch her baby grow up so quickly. By this time next year Lisa would be in college. She hoped to obtain a scholarship that would allow her to live on-campus, possibly out of state. Nya knew these seven a.m. wakeup calls were numbered, and they were precious.

Lisa yawned and placed her bare feet on the floor. Nya marveled at how big they were. Lisa also had oversized legs and Stretch Armstrong arms that made her appear lanky. Sometimes she was. Though on the basketball court, she was anything but. She was fair-skinned, unlike her mom, whose skin had a beautiful, burgundy tone.

"Do you wanna ride the bus today?" Nya asked. "Or you want Daryl to take you?"

"When are you leaving?" Lisa asked her.

"Thirty minutes. I got time to make you breakfast."

"I'll ride with Daryl," she decided. "Did you call him already?"

"No, I'll call him now," Nya said and backed out of the room.

She pulled her cellphone from her pocket as she headed for the kitchen. As the phone rang, she wondered if her and Daryl's situation was peculiar, or if other women in her shoes made similar concessions when there was a child involved. Her ex-boyfriend answered immediately.

"Morning." He sounded alert and anxious.

"Hi," Nya told him. "Did you want to–"

"How you doing?" he asked her.

"I'm fine," she said. "Do you want to–"

"Have you thought about what we talked about?"

She approached the refrigerator and took a deep breath before she continued with the conversation. She almost said something rude to him. But she could hear the hurt in his voice, and she still had a good deal of sympathy for him.

"Daryl," she said calmly, "I'm not calling to talk about that. I only want to talk about Lisa right now. You said you wouldn't do this."

"Alright," he said right away. "I'm sorry. I didn't mean to."

"That's fine. Do you want to take her to school today?"

"Yes. Of course."

"She'll be ready to leave at eight."

"Okay," he said. "I'll be there."

"Alright, thank you," Nya said and disconnected.

● ● ● ● ● ●

Nya only had a few minutes to spend with her daughter over breakfast. She was dieting (*again!*) so she ate a grapefruit with Cheerios while Lisa devoured sausage patties with toast and juice.

"Do you know when practice starts?" Nya asked.

She wore her hair in braids that were currently tied behind her head. She had dark, brown eyes and an easy smile.

"It usually starts in October," Lisa told her. "I know the first game is in November."

"You have a schedule already?"

"No, but I'll try to get one today."

For her first day of school, Lisa wore skinny jeans that made her long legs look even longer with a tee shirt and a pair of Chuck Taylors. She never wore makeup, not even lip gloss. Her earrings were studs, rather than hoops or dangles.

Despite her fashion sense, Lisa didn't like to be referred to as a tomboy. She felt there were too many stereotypes about female basketball players. At school the term *tomboy* was only a hop, skip and a jump away from *stud* or *gay*.

"I know you're excited about your last season," Nya said.

Lisa shrugged, which was surprising.

"What's wrong?" Nya checked her watch. She had to hit the road in five minutes.

"Because Coach Chisholm isn't coming back."

Nya was familiar with her coach. Chisholm had led the girls through three great seasons. Well, *great* may have been a stretch, but they were certainly good seasons. The Lady Grizzlies never finished with a losing record.

"She's having a baby, right?" Nya asked.

"Yep. And she quit teaching."

That was news to her mother. "Really? How come?"

"She said she's going to be a stay-at-home mom after the baby gets here."

"Oh, well that's a good thing. A lot of women wish they were in a position to do that."

"Yeah, but I don't know who our new coach is gonna be," Lisa griped. "I hope they don't make one of the football coaches do it or throw the volleyball coach out there, like she knows what she' doing."

Nya grinned. "You don't think they hired someone new?"

Lisa shook her head. "I doubt it."

"I think you'll be fine," her mother said with a smirk. "They could put y'all out there with one of the assistant principals, and you'll still shine."

"Probably. But this is my last year. I want us to go to the playoffs this time."

Nya didn't mention that her daughter's team had *never* been good enough to accomplish that feat. She stood and approached her. She placed a hand on her shoulder and then smoothed her hair. Lisa looked up at her with a smile.

"That's better," Nya said, returning the grin. "Don't forget, you go to school to learn. Basketball is *extra-curricular*."

"No, Mama. I go to school for *basketball*. Math and science is extra-curricular."

"Let me find out you really believe that, and it won't matter who your new coach is. You'll be watching the games from the sideline, just like me."

She bent to give her a kiss on the cheek. "Be good, ladybug."

"I will," Lisa promised. She watched her mom exit the kitchen before she continued with her meal.

● ● ● ● ● ●

Daryl rang the doorbell at eight a.m. sharp. Lisa was ready and waiting. She opened the door and gave him a hug as she stepped out onto the porch.

"Hey, Daryl."

"Hey, baby," he said and returned the affection.

He looked over her shoulder and paused, as if he wanted to be invited inside. But Lisa turned and locked the door. Her mom never specifically told her *not* to let Daryl in the house, but Lisa sensed that's what Nya would tell her, if she had asked her.

"Your mama already gone?"

Lisa found that question odd.

"Yes, you know she's gone." Her tone was upbeat, and she wore a smile for him. "That's why you're taking me to school. *Remember?...*"

Daryl smiled too. He turned and followed her to his truck. He wore baggy jeans, which looked to be a little soiled already, along with a pair of work boots that had seen better days. His tee-shirt was clean, and it bore his company's logo: TEXAS BUILDERS. The thin fabric stretched over his chest and shoulders.

Daryl wasn't musclebound, but he was stout. His torso was strong and sturdy, like a tree trunk. His large hands had plenty of old cuts and bruises and dark callouses on the palms.

His truck was clean. Lisa saw that he had moved his hardhat and safety vest to the back to clear up the front for her.

"Did your mom say anything about me before she left?" he asked as he took a seat behind the wheel.

"No," Lisa said. She put her backpack on the floorboard between her feet and buckled her safety belt. "Just that you were picking me up. I appreciate it. I hate riding the funky bus." She offered another daughterly smile that made his heart flutter.

She would never understand how much he loved her.

"How's she been?" he asked as he backed out of the driveway. "How's everything at the hospital?"

"Fine, I guess," Lisa said, feeling a little uncomfortable about his line of questioning. "You didn't talk to her?"

"Yeah, but she said she was in a hurry. We didn't really have time to..." He trailed off.

Lisa wasn't sure if he even knew that he didn't finish the sentence.

Daryl wore his hair short all around. He was clean-shaven. He had a pudgy nose, but it didn't detract from his looks. Lisa always thought he was handsome, and she knew her mom thought so, too.

"I don't think we should talk about her," she said as honestly and compassionately as she could.

Daryl looked over and saw the worry and conflict in her eyes. "I'm sorry. I didn't mean to."

"It's okay. I understand." She wasn't just saying that. She truly did.

• • • • • •

As far as daddy/daughter relationships go, Lisa knew her situation with Daryl was uncommon. He and her mom started dating when she was six years old. Daryl moved in with them seven months later. Since then, he'd been the only father Lisa had ever known.

Her sperm-giver, Kareem, had been a bad apple since grade school. He knocked Nya up when she was sixteen and went to prison for murder two years later. Lisa wrote her father occasionally, certainly not as often as he wrote her. She always ended her letters with "I love you," but she didn't mean it.

Daryl was a different story. He was imprinted on all of Lisa's childhood memories; from the first bike she learned to ride to the first time she shot a jump shot. Daryl was there every time a boy broke her heart in grade school, middle school and high school. Their relationship grew even stronger when she began to excel at basketball in the seventh grade.

But he was not a perfect man. The most obvious proof of this was the fact that he'd never proposed to Nya throughout their twelve year relationship. He was quick to point out their "common-law marriage," but as she grew older, Lisa understood that was not the same thing.

Another thing Lisa didn't pick up on until her teenage years was Daryl's drinking. Throughout her life she had known him to go through a six-pack after a hard days' work. That seemed totally normal to her. He never shuffled around the house drunk, and he was always bright-eyed and happy to get to work the next morning.

But one day Nya sat her down and told her that drinking a six-pack after work every day was not normal behavior. She told her one beer was okay, maybe even two. But six beers a day (*every day*) was more than a form of relaxation. It was a bad habit and maybe even an *addiction*.

Lisa was glad for the lesson, because up until then she'd looked forward to bringing her husband a six-pack a day, whenever she did grow up and find the man of her dreams.

After the talk, Lisa became aware of negative aspects of Daryl's drinking. She noticed how moody he became and how he didn't get along with Nya as well. Lisa would never forget the time she went to the kitchen before bed and saw Daryl about to take a piss in the refrigerator. He had looked up at her with a confused expression, and then he looked inside the fridge and zipped up his pants.

"Hell, this ain't the bathroom," he had told her with a laugh.

Lisa was fortunate not to see his penis (ever), and the story was more funny than disheartening.

But it wasn't just the drinking that got him evicted. Daryl messed up when he combined it with his insecurities. Towards the end, Nya stopped telling him about her new co-workers and the strange things that happened at the hospital. She got tired of hearing Daryl bitch.

"If everybody up there is having affairs, what about you? Who you fucking on your lunch break?" Or, "Why it's so many men nurses? I know they be trying to talk to you. Which one of them likes you? Tell me."

But Lisa never saw that side of Daryl, so her opinion of him was not the same as her mom's. She'd cried like a baby when Nya kicked him out of the house three weeks ago.

"I know this is hard, baby," Nya had said. "You love him, and he loves you too. That's why I won't put him out of your life completely. He's been your father for twelve years. He raised you as much as I did. You can see him whenever you want to. And I'm gonna try to work it out with him. I just need him away from here, until we get this figured out. Me and Daryl, we'll date a little, see how it goes..."

Lisa's eyes had brightened, but her mother was quick to tell her, "Don't get your hopes up. There's a lot Daryl has to do to make things right between us. To be honest, I don't think he can do it. But after twelve years, he says..." She looked pained for a moment before saying, "I owe him a chance."

And so it was that despite not being her sperm-giver or ever proposing to her mom, Daryl maintained his position as Lisa's (sorta) father. He even got to be there for her for (sorta) special occasions, like the first day of her senior year.

● ● ● ● ● ●

After having his attempts to gather information about Nya thwarted, Daryl settled down and focused on the other important lady in his life.

"You excited about this season?" he asked as they drove the short distance to Finley High.

Lisa told him about her coach dilemma.

"It don't matter who they put out there," Daryl said. "They could let the *janitor* coach y'all, and you'll still get your numbers."

Lisa giggled. "That's what Mama said – except she said *principal.*"

She regretted her comment, thinking Daryl would jump at the opportunity to ask about Nya again. But he didn't.

"Tricia's back this year, right?" he asked instead.

Tricia was the second best player on their team last year. She wasn't as tall as Lisa, but she had always been the team's center.

"Yeah, she's back. I talked to her over the summer. She's excited too. She thinks we can both get scholarships this year, if we do good."

Daryl frowned. "Don't worry about that mess. You know the odds aren't in your favor. You need to focus on your school work. Keep up your grades in math and science. Get yourself an *academic* scholarship, and then you'll know you done did something."

Lisa agreed that academics should be her primary focus, but she didn't think a basketball scholarship was chump change. After having a baby while still in high school, her mom busted her tail to get through college while working a fulltime job. If Lisa's hooping skills got her a free-ride to a university, it would be a blessing.

Daryl pulled to a stop in front of her school a few minutes later.

"When do you think you can get me a copy of your basketball schedule?"

"I don't know," Lisa said as she gathered her things. "As soon as I find out who our new coach is, I'll ask her for one."

He nodded. "I wanna give it to my boss, so they'll know not to try to keep me past five on your game days."

His comment warmed Lisa's heart. It let her know that despite the recent shakeup in their home, she was still his priority.

"Thanks." She leaned over and kissed him on the cheek.

"I love you," he said as she exited the vehicle.

"Love you, too, Daryl." And with this dad, she meant it.

He was surprised to find himself misty-eyed as he watched her meet up with a couple of friends in the courtyard. He had the same lump in his throat when he and Nya dropped her off for the first day of school in the second grade. It reminded him of something his mother always said.

The more things change, the more they stay the same.

CHAPTER FIVE
LARGER THAN LIFE

The first day of Lisa's senior year went exceptionally well. Unlike some of the freshmen who seemed to have a dazed look in their eyes most of the time, she had plenty of friends on campus. It didn't hurt that she was the star of the girls' basketball team. Her popularity was off the charts.

Students went out of their way to greet her in the hallway. So many people wanted to walk and talk with her, she had trouble dividing her attention amongst them. By lunchtime she felt like the queen of the school, even more so than the prettiest cheerleader. She sat at a table with other girls from the basketball team and picked at a chicken fried steak meal while they discussed a mystery that was becoming more curious by the second.

"I heard he used to play for the Cowboys," Pam Young reported. She wasn't on the team last year, but her best friend Latavia was.

"No, he didn't," Tamika Brown said. "That's stupid."

"No it's not," Pam countered.

"Why would a football player coach *basketball*?" Tamika wanted to know.

"Why would somebody who played for the Cowboys wanna be a teacher?" Michele asked. "They're millionaires."

"Maybe he went broke," Pam offered.

"That's stupid," Michele decided. "You stupid."

47

"Forget you! You stupid."

"He did used to play for the Cowboys," Monica told them.

"How you know?" Michele asked her.

"Because I had him for science class this morning. He told us hisself, so I think I know what I'm talking about."

"Y'all talking about Coach Berry?"

A newcomer approached their table; a boy named Jared Shaw.

"Nobody said anything to you," Monica snapped with a good helping of attitude.

"Damn, girl, why you being so mean?" Jared asked her. He found an empty chair and made a spot at the head of their table.

"You can't sit there!" Monica yelled. "Ain't no room!"

"You the only one tripping," he noticed.

He was right about that. Jared was a star player for the boys' basketball team. Most of the girls at the school thought he was a dreamboat. Monica used to feel that way herself, but their love affair fizzled over the summertime. Rumor had it Monica's 19 year old sister took a liking to him, and Jared couldn't resist her charms.

"Anyway," he said, "I heard he was gonna coach *football*, not basketball."

"You don't know what you talking about!" Monica barked, sneering at him. "This morning he told us he's the new coach for the *girls' basketball team*, so why you over here lying?"

"But he used to play *football*, not basketball," Jared maintained.

"He really played for the Cowboys?" Lisa asked. She couldn't hide her intrigue.

"Yeah, you wanna see his picture?" Jared asked. He removed his cellphone from his pocket.

"You took his picture?" Rochelle Burns asked.

"Naw," Jared told her. "I googled him. Don't y'all know nothing?"

Lisa leaned closer to get a look at his phone, while most of her friends looked him up on their own devices.

"What's his first name?" Cheri Bearfield asked.

"Marcus," Monica said.

"No, it's not. It's *Marquis!*" Jared told her.

"I can't stand you! Get away from our table!" Monica pouted.

But Lisa didn't want him to leave, not just yet. The image search he did for Marquis Berry made her eyes bulge.

"That's him?" she asked.

"Yeah," Jared said. He clicked one of the pictures to enlarge it. "See, this is him when he was with the Cowboys."

Lisa took the phone from him and pressed the back button. She found another picture she'd rather enlarge. This one appeared to be from football practice. It was summertime, and Marquis Berry was sweating. And he was *topless*. And he was HUGE! She didn't realize her mouth hung open until Jared pointed it out.

"Close your mouth," he said with a chuckle. "You gon' let a fly in."

"Oh my God, look at this!" Lisa said, showing the pic to her friends.

They all gathered around her. Latavia was the furthest away. She nearly crawled over the table when she saw the nice chunk of man meat in the pic. Her friends laughed at her.

"Girl, quit playing!" Latavia said. "That is not our coach!"

Lisa was in a state of disbelief as well, though she saw it with her own eyes. She turned to the one person at the table who had been to science class already.

"This is Mr. Berry?"

Monica nodded. "Yep. That's him."

"He still looks like this?"

"Mmm hmm," Monica said. "He fine."

"I don't know why y'all getting excited," Jared said, taking his phone back. "He a millionaire. He don't want none of y'all."

"You just mad 'cause don't nobody want your ugly ass!" Monica snapped.

"Bitch, don't nobody want yo funky ass!" Jared replied, growing irritated with her.

That was a bad move. The girls could be as catty as the next clique, but when it came time to defend one of their own, they would come together in a heartbeat.

"Who you calling a *bitch*, ol' dumb ass boy?" Pam growled.

"You need to get the hell away from our table, is what you better do!" Monica added.

"Why you still here?" Cheri asked as she threw an empty milk carton at him. "Gone, boy!"

"Hey, watch out!" Jared shot to his feet and checked to make sure none of the liquid in the container spilled on his new shirt. "Man, if that shit woulda got on me..."

Cheri grabbed another milk carton from Tamika's tray. "This one still got a lot in it," she warned as she hoisted it in the air.

Jared retreated without another word.

Lisa watched the wild scene, but she didn't pay attention to what her friends were doing. Her mind was stuck on the pictures she'd seen. Despite what everyone said, she wouldn't believe there was an NFL player working at the school until she saw it for herself.

● ● ● ● ● ●

In seventh period Lisa finally got a chance to meet the world-famous Marquis Berry. She wasn't merely impressed to see that all of the pictures on the internet were accurate. She was spellbound. Awed even.

50

Her new coach was tall. At six-foot-one, Lisa was accustomed to looking down at people, even her teachers. But Mr. Berry had a couple of inches on her.

He was big. He wore a long-sleeved shirt that wasn't clinging to him, but she could see how massive his chest and arms were. He looked like he could put a bear in a headlock.

Lisa had never seen any videos of him playing football, but she could picture it. She imagined him hurdling a defender with a football in his hand, tucked closely to his body. In her vision he wore the slacks and loafers he sported today, but that didn't slow him down one bit.

She took a seat in the middle of the classroom and had to remind herself what Mrs. Seabrooks said about a teacher crush going awry. Avoiding a crush on this man was going to be a tall order, because she was eighteen years old, and he didn't look to be older than twenty-five. His hair was short and trimmed perfectly. He had a slight moustache and a little hair on his chin. His skin was dark chocolate.

Lisa had a teacher crush before, but never one that started on the first day and never one that felt so overwhelming. She shook her head, laughing at herself. She knew this would be a very interesting year.

When her teacher spoke, Lisa felt a spattering of goosebumps sprout on her arms.

"Good afternoon." Mr. Berry rose from his seat and stood in front of his desk.

The room was completely silent. This was the last period on the first day of school. Everyone was anxious to go home or connect with friends they didn't expect to see in that class. But not one person spoke. Every eye watched the former Dallas Cowboy, who truly was larger than life.

"As I'm sure some of you have heard," he said, folding those powerful arms over his chest, "my name is Mr. Berry. Since I will be coaching the varsity girls' basketball team, you can also call me *Coach Berry*. You're all seniors, so you probably know each other pretty well. But I'm new here, and I know you're curious about me."

The students were unblinking.

"I'm from Overbrook Meadows," he said. "I graduated from Castleberry. I've played basketball and football since I was little. Science has always been my favorite subject, so that's what I majored in when I got to college. I went to Louisiana State University. I was their starting running back. Almost won the Heisman. After I graduated, I was drafted by the NFL. I was the starting running back for the Dallas Cowboys my rookie season."

Most of the students knew he played for the Cowboys. The few who didn't gasped in surprise.

"I didn't finish my first season with the Cowboys," Coach Berry continued. He didn't sound remorseful about it, so Lisa didn't think it was something that haunted him.

"I broke my neck during a bad tackle," the teacher said. He kept talking, before the wide-eyed seniors had a chance to react. "I know that sounds bad, but it wasn't a terrible injury. I was never paralyzed. Never had to use a wheelchair. But it was enough to make me worried about continuing to play, so I quit. *Retired*, I supposed.

"But thankfully I didn't waste the opportunity I had in college," he told them. "Even though I was a star player at LSU, I took my studies seriously. At the time, I never thought I'd use my education degree. But as it turns out, I'm your new teacher. And for some of you, I'll be your basketball coach."

The students began to applaud when he finished speaking, which was something Marquis didn't expect. It didn't happen in any of the other classes. A wistful smile parted his lips as he held a hand up to quiet them.

"Okay, so one of the things I told you isn't true at all," he said. That shocked and engrossed the students once again. "I have a prize for whoever can tell me the false statement I made." He reached into his pocket and produced a coin. "Here it is," he said. "A shiny quarter."

The students laughed at such a paltry offering, but they found the game enticing.

"You didn't play for the Cowboys?" Barbara Smith guessed.

Coach Berry told her, with a serious voice, "We will always raise our hands before we speak in here."

Barbara's hand was one of four to shoot up.

He acknowledged her with a nod. "Go ahead."

"You didn't play for the Cowboys," she repeated.

"Sure I did," Marquis said. He looked around and pointed at another student. "What you got?"

"You didn't go to LSU?"

"I did," Marquis stated. "Excellent school. I highly recommend it."

The game continued for a few minutes with over ten students attempting to poke a hole in his story and each one coming up short. Towards the end, it appeared everything Coach Berry told them was true; asking them to find the lie was a trick question.

"Y'all give up?" he asked.

They looked around. No one raised their hand.

"I did *not* almost win the Heisman," Coach Berry revealed. "I wasn't even in the running."

The students laughed at his cunning.

"Alright," he said. "Now all of you will get a chance to pull one over on us. We'll go around the room. Each of you will state your name and tell us three things about yourself. One of those things will be a lie. We'll see if your peers can pick it out."

The students were delighted to participate in his activity.

● ● ● ● ● ●

After class, which involved nothing more than getting to know each other, Coach Berry stopped two girls before they filed out of the room. Lisa was thrilled to hear him call her name.

"Hey," he said, leaning back on his desk. "I hear you two are on the varsity basketball team."

Lisa and Tricia were all smiles. They nodded.

"You're a point guard, right?" he said to Lisa.

"Yes, sir."

"They say you're pretty good."

Lisa's eyes danced with delight. She blushed, rather than respond to that.

"You definitely got that height," Marquis noticed. "How tall are you?"

She could barely find her voice. "Six-one," she managed.

"And you're the center," he said to Tricia.

She too was thrilled by this special attention.

"You got a reputation of being a big shot blocker," he said. "That's good. We need that."

The girl almost squealed.

"It's nice to meet you both," Coach Berry said. "I got our schedule for the year. Our first game is November 9th, and we're not allowed to practice until October 21st. Is that how it usually goes? We only get a couple of weeks to practice before the first game?"

The girls nodded.

"Yes," Lisa said. "That's the way it usually is."

"That seems crazy to me," Marquis stated. "I don't know anything about the team. Your old coach managed to whip you into shape that fast?"

"That's why we always lose our first game," Tricia said.

"No we don't," Lisa countered, with a flash of annoyance.

"I don't want to lose our first game," Marquis told them. "I hear both of you are team leaders, so I would like for you to do what you can to get people interested in playing. Do y'all have tryouts?"

"We'll take whoever wants to play," Tricia replied. "Sometimes it's hard to get enough people."

Lisa shot her friend another look. She didn't want the new coach to think they were a band of uncoordinated misfits, even if that was the case sometimes.

"That's cool," he said. "But I think it would be better if we actually had tryouts this year. The more girls we get, the better chance we have to put together a good squad. Does that sound like something you ladies could start working on?"

They readily agreed. Lisa knew of at least two of her friends who would do great on the team if they managed to keep their grades up. Maybe Coach Berry could be the incentive they needed.

"Alright," he said. "That's what I wanted to hear. I know we're gonna have a lot of fun this year. I can't wait till October."

Me neither! Lisa thought. She wished they could go to the gym that very moment, so she could show him her skills.

● ● ● ● ● ●

She rode the school bus home and had to wait until her mother returned from work before she could tell her the great news. Nya barely had a chance to put her purse down before Lisa bombarded her.

"Calm down," Nya said with a giggle. "This morning you were upset about Coach Chisholm not coming back."

"Who?"

Lisa laughed when her mom gave her a look. "Nah, I'm just kidding, Mama. I do miss Coach Chisholm. But our new coach is better!"

"How do you know he's *better*?" Nya wondered.

"He used to play for the Cowboys."

"That doesn't, what do you mean he played for the Cowboys?"

"He was a football player. Come here. Look!"

She led her to the computer and did a search for *Marquis Berry*. Before Nya could scrutinize any of the websites, her daughter clicked on "Images," and the screen was filled with photos of a very handsome football player. Some of the pictures were from football games, where Marquis wore an LSU or Cowboys jersey. There were a lot of live-action shots, in which his sprinting and cut moves were forever immortalized.

Nya frowned with confusion. It was obvious this man was a football player, but what in the world was he doing at Finley High? She sat quietly while her daughter gushed over her new teacher and explained his new career choice as best she could. Nya couldn't deny that she felt a little uncomfortable looking at the pictures with Lisa, because Marquis was topless in some of them. She could tell her daughter was greatly enamored.

"Okay, baby," she said, pushing away from the computer. "This is, kinda strange," she admitted. "But it's pretty cool, too. I think I remember him, from when he played with the Cowboys."

"Latavia said there's some videos on here," Lisa said, reaching for the keyboard again.

"What kind of videos?"

"His football videos. What did you think?"

Nya was surprised to find herself frowning and a bit leery. "Nothing," she said as she vacated the seat in front of the computer. "Go ahead."

When she got to her room, Nya closed the door and turned on her tablet. She did another image search for Marquis Berry and found the picture she saw a moment ago. Towards the bottom of the page was a mugshot. It was definitely him. Nya didn't want to click on it while her daughter was watching, but she was very interested.

The picture led to an article from the *Overbrook Meadows Telegram*. Nya's nostrils flared when she read the blaring headline: **Former Cowboy Arrested for Assault**.

She sat on the bed and worked to keep her breathing steady as she read the article. It revealed how Marquis frequented many of the city's night spots after his football career ended. There were multiple incidents of him and his drunken crew being disruptive or violent. His bad boy antics culminated with a man being seriously injured in a bar brawl. Marquis was arrested, but Nya couldn't confirm that he was ever convicted of the charge.

She was none too pleased when she completed her research.

Did Marquis lose all of his money after his catastrophic fall from grace? Is that why he had to fall back on teaching? Why would the district hire someone who had done so many bad things? Were they that hard up for teachers, or were they blinded by the fact that he was somewhat of a celebrity? What bonehead looked at Marquis' application and said, '*Oh yeah. That's the one!*'?"

Nya planned to get answers to those questions first thing in the morning. She was glad that Lisa was excited about basketball again, but at what cost? Wasn't her daughter's safety the school's number one priority?

Simmering, she went to the kitchen to get started on dinner. She hoped she was overreacting, but the facts spoke for themselves. And the fact was a criminal was not who she wanted as an example for her daughter. Marquis had ruined his life and was trying to get a second shot at it at her daughter's expense.

And that, Nya decided, was unacceptable.

CHAPTER SIX
THE HYPE

Shine on, black athlete on TMZ
With the model type
Check out her physique
Rolling with the homies
Those boys look mean
Chilling with Drake in the VIP
Cops pulled him over
Found some pills and weed
Snapped the handcuffs on
That's the new bling!

The next morning, Nya waited until after nine before she tried to reach the principal. A clerk took her number and said he'd call her back, which he did around one.

"Good afternoon," she told him. "Thanks for returning my call."

"No problem, Mrs. Edmonds. What can I do for you?"

"I, um..." Nya was fired up last night. Now she wondered if her complaints were premature. "I would like to ask you about one of my daughter's new teachers."

"Which one?" he asked. "What's your daughter's name?"

"Lisa Edmonds. The teacher is Mr. Berry."

"Oh. Okay." He didn't sound like this was the first time someone had questioned his bold move. "What's going on? Is there a problem?"

"Uh, no, not exactly. Lisa told me about him yesterday. This is the same Marquis Berry who played for the Cowboys a few years ago?"

"Yes. One in the same. We're excited to have him here."

"Oh, well I may be overreacting. But I did a little research on him last night, and I found some things on the internet that, you know, show him in a very negative light."

"Yes," the principal said right away. "I'm aware of Mr. Berry's past."

Nya expected him to elaborate on that, but he didn't.

"So, he's been arrested?" she said.

"Yes, but he was never convicted of a crime," Mr. Walters stated.

"He didn't get charged with assault?"

"I understand there was a fight at a bar, and someone was injured. A witness said Mr. Berry was involved, and the police made an arrest. But, as I mentioned, he was never convicted of that crime."

"Was he innocent?" She didn't want to be pushy, but *Coach Berry* would be spending an enormous amount of time around her only child. She had the right to get a straight answer.

"Honestly, Mrs. Edmonds, I don't have the answer to that. Trust me, I understand your concerns. I'll tell you a true story," he said.

Nya didn't have time for a story, but what the hell.

"When I was in college," he said, "I was very poor and rather irresponsible. Paying for my car's inspection stickers was nowhere near my priority list. I wasn't responsible with my insurance payments, either. I accumulated dozens of traffic tickets. When I graduated, I applied for my first teaching job, and I was arrested in the administration building because, unbeknownst to me, several of my tickets had become warrants for my arrest."

Nya was surprised to hear that.

"I begged my parents to bail me out," the principal continued. "I set up my tickets for payment plans and community service, and I went back to the admin building the following week. The same sheriff who ran my background check the *first* time was disgusted to see me back in there. He couldn't believe it when he ran my record again and found it *perfectly clean.* Since getting arrested for a traffic ticket is not a felony, I got the job I applied for and have continued to excel from there.

"The point I'm making is, people make mistakes. If they turn their lives around and try to move on, we should let them – as long as they haven't committed a felony."

He chuckled.

Nya did too.

"I believe Mr. Berry has moved past his mistakes," the principal said, "and he is well-qualified for the position I hired him for. So I couldn't, in good conscious, deny him the job because of his one arrest that was never prosecuted."

Nya wanted to hold on to her grievances, but she agreed with his thinking. "Okay," she said. "Sorry to bother you. Thank you for your time."

"Are you sure there's nothing more?"

"No. You're right. I appreciate you calling me back."

• • • • • •

Over the next two months Nya remained vigilant in regards to her daughter's new coach, while Lisa became increasingly enamored. She constantly gave updates on what was going on in biology class. She never liked science before, and Nya was pretty sure she didn't like it now. But if Lisa was willing to go the extra mile to impress her new teacher, there was no harm in it.

Whether or not Mr. Berry would be a successful basketball coach remained to be seen, but everyone was optimistic. One day, towards the middle of October, Lisa stayed late after school to hang posters that invited students to try out for the team.

When Nya picked her up, she told her, "I love to see you fired up. But don't expect a miracle. This is the first time Mr. Berry has ever coached a game."

"We're gonna win," Lisa said without question.

"Win what?" her mom asked. "Your first game?"

"Yes. Maybe all of them."

Nya was startled by the bold prediction. "He hasn't even put the team together yet," she cautioned. "Didn't three of your starters graduate last year?"

"Yeah, but we got a whole lot more people trying out this year. Coach Berry got everybody excited."

Nya never hoped her daughter would lose a game, but she wouldn't have been upset if Marquis lost *his* first game (that wasn't the same thing). Maybe that would take a little shine off him. She smiled at her awful thought, rather than feel guilty about it.

● ● ● ● ● ●

October was also a month of trial and tribulation for her decade long relationship with Daryl, which was moving closer to the brink of extinction. Nya didn't mean to be dismissive or discount his feelings, but their time apart hadn't brought them any closer – which is what Daryl had told her from the beginning.

On Tuesday, October 20th, they met for dinner at The Capital Grille downtown. The high end restaurant was a little too expensive for Nya's tastes. But Daryl was going out of his way to impress her. It gave him an opportunity to wear a sport's coat and slacks, rather than the jeans and work boots she was accustomed to seeing him in.

Nya wore a blue evening gown. She was shorter than her daughter, and much more curvaceous. She was impressed with Daryl's attire and his demeanor, but it would take a lot more than a pair of Stacy Adams to make her forget about the arguments and all of the beer cans she had to dispose of each morning before she woke her daughter up for school.

"Been thinking long and hard about everything that happened between us," Daryl said after the waiter delivered their entrées. "You know, you were right about everything. I see that now."

Nya nodded politely as she nibbled her herb roasted chicken. How many times had he said that before? She guessed at least twenty.

"I cut down on my drinking," he said. "I'm not like I was before. I mean, I wasn't no alcoholic to begin with. But I drink even less now."

Nya hoped that was true, for his sake.

"So, I think I'm ready to come home," he continued. "You wanted some time, some space to get your head together. And I gave you that. I moved out – no problem."

She almost commented on that. While Daryl did move out at her request, it was *a very big problem*. He fought her decision for over a week. When he finally did leave, he returned late in the night several times reeking of alcohol, begging her to open the door.

"No, I don't think I'm ready for that," she told him.

His nostrils flared as he stared at her over the expensive meal. His eyes were glossy.

"Wha, why not, Nya?"

"Because I don't know if I want to get back with you."

"You said we needed some time apart," he reminded her. "It's been two months. I haven't been able to see Lisa–"

"You see her every week. Several times a week."

"It's not the same," he complained. "I don't get to see her at night. We don't get to eat dinner together."

"You can pick her up for dinner anytime you like. Just give me some heads up."

"I wanna eat dinner with you, too. I wanna come home."

She sighed and put her fork down. She rubbed her hands together nervously. "I have a lot of bad memories, Daryl. A lot of stuff happened."

"And I said I was sorry for all that."

"Apologizing doesn't make it go away."

"Neither does living in different houses. You said you wanted to see if I could change."

"No." She had to call him on that. "I said I didn't wanna be with you anymore. *You* said you could change, and *you* asked me to give you a chance to prove it. So that's what I'm doing."

"But how can I prove it?" he wondered.

Nya understood his dilemma. She sighed. "Daryl, you're right. What's happening between us is unfair to you. I never asked you to change. I don't wanna hold you or your heart hostage. I think you should move on."

His lips trembled, and he lost a good deal of his composure. Things would've gotten even more uncomfortable if he started to cry, but thankfully he held it together.

"I don't want to move on," he breathed. "I wanna prove to you that I can be the man you need me to be. We've been together for *twelve years*, Nya. I know you're not ready to throw it all away."

She wanted to stand her ground, but they did have a lot of history together. The things he'd done for Lisa were phenomenal. She could never forget about that.

Sensing he was getting through to her, Daryl reached across the table and placed his hand on hers. He squeezed it comfortingly. Despite his suit and grooming and the lotion and cologne he wore for their dinner, Daryl's hand was rough to the touch. Rather than turn her off, the calluses on his palm had the opposite effect. She appreciated a hardworking

63

man, especially one who had worked his fingers to the bone for over ten years to provide for her and her daughter.

"Give me a little more time," he begged, "before you decide. Don't give up on us."

Nya had a ton of misgivings, but her heart was touched, so she nodded.

• • • • • •

By Wednesday, October 21st Marquis had been on the job for two months. He was happy to say that he enjoyed teaching, for the most part. But there was *way* too much paperwork. On most nights he got home at five and worked a few more hours grading papers, inputting scores in his gradebook and working on his lesson plans. He also accumulated lots of notes and packets from his team and faculty meetings.

It was the kids that made teaching worthwhile. Once his newness started to wear off, and he got down to the serious business of science, Marquis marveled at how bright some of his students were. They were like sponges, quick to soak up as many facts as he could throw at them. Sure, there were slackers in every period, but they were greatly outnumbered.

Marquis would never forget the first time one of his students made an A on a difficult exam. It felt like he had taught his own child to ride a bike. He looked forward to experiencing that warm sense of pride many more times throughout the six weeks and semesters and hopefully the years to come.

But as rewarding as teaching was, it was sports that *really* got his blood flowing. He counted down the days to his first practice with the girls. When that morning arrived, he sat up in bed with a smile, five minutes before the alarm went off. He hopped out of bed wearing only a pair of boxers. His muscles and dark skin were delectable, even before he dropped to the floor for the first of three sets of pushups.

He did not need a cup of coffee, and he was quick to smile throughout the day. In seventh period, he was as anxious as some of his students who watched the clock all period, praying 3:30 would get there sooner.

When the final bell rang, his heart drummed as he dismissed the class. His two team members didn't hurry out of the room like their peers. Practice didn't start until 4:00, so they had plenty of time.

"Y'all ready?" Marquis asked as they approached his desk.

They both said they were. Their confidence was off the charts.

"I can't wait till you see my fadeaway, Coach," Lisa told him.

"Fadeaway?" Marquis said, looking up at her. "Is that your secret weapon?"

"Yep. Wait and see." She shot an imaginary ball towards the windows, fading away as she did so. "I'm nice with mine."

"Alright," Marquis said. "You know I'll be watching. What about you?" he asked Tricia, who was the team's center for the last couple of years. "Whose style are you more like, Kareem or Shaq?"

The girl looked confused as she asked, "Who?"

"Kareem Abdul-Jabbar?" Marquis said. "He was one of the best centers of all time. But that was a long time ago," he conceded.

Tricia shook her head. "No. I don't know that dude. What is he, a Muslim, or something?"

"Yeah, I think he was," Marquis said with a chuckle. "He used to wear goggles, invented the sky hook."

Still shaking her head, Tricia asked, "What's a sky hook?"

Marquis didn't like the idea of any center, girl or boy, not knowing what a sky hook was. He had to remind himself that these girls were born in the nineties. "What about Dwight Howard?" he asked.

He couldn't hide his surprise when Tricia shook her head again.

"Well, who do you play like?"

"I play like myself, Coach."

Marquis almost asked if she ever watched basketball or studied the craft outside of their games at school, but he didn't want her to think he was disappointed.

"I guess we'll see what you're working with in a few minutes. If you're a starter, I'm expecting you to crash those boards."

Again Tricia didn't look like she knew what he was talking about.

But she said, "Yeah, Coach. You know it!" and the girls left the room.

• • • • • •

Thirty minutes later the school gym was humming with activity. Marquis and his group were assigned to the "old" gym, because the boys' basketball team took priority. But the old gym was new to him, and he didn't get any complaints from the ladies. Twenty-five girls showed up for tryouts. There weren't enough practice uniforms, so they all wore the shorts and tee shirts they brought with them.

He told them to gather around as he introduced himself as their coach. Since the beginning of the school year, Marquis got several *looks* from fast-tailed girls that could be considered flirtatious. At that moment, he was bombarded by them. He felt like a rock star surrounded by groupies.

Donovan Mitchell, the football coach, gave him a little advice on this subject:

"Ignore them. Don't smile back. Don't compliment their clothes or makeup – especially if you think they're trying to flirt. If they ever come right out and say something inappropriate, shut them down immediately. You don't have to be rude, but you do have to be firm."

"Do you still have that problem?" Marquis had asked him, noticing Donovan was not much older than he was.

"Yes. Every year. And they know I'm married. The worst ones are the girls who've turned eighteen or *nineteen*. They think they're grown for real. I'm sure you remember how it was when you were in high school. Did you have a crush on any of your teachers?"

"Yeah, Miss Houston," Marquis had said, musing. "My hands started sweating every time I talked to her. But nothing ever came of it."

"Exactly," Donovan replied. "The only way anything could've come of it is if Miss Houston initiated it."

Marquis nodded.

He didn't think any of the girls who showed up for basketball practice were taking their infatuation too far, but he wanted to wipe those smiles off their faces *immediately*, so he started them off with laps around the gym.

In addition to getting them out of his face, the conditioning exercise separated the athletes from the wannabes. The girls who had only come to ogle at the coach were huffing and puffing within minutes, complaining about their hair and feet. Marquis watched them with amusement.

After running, he let them grab a few balls for layup and free throw drills. Not surprisingly, a lot of the players were mediocre at best. A few of them looked like they had never played basketball before. *Ever*. Most of the excitement Marquis felt in the days leading up to their first practice was washed away in a big toilet bowl of disappointment. It was no wonder the team only won half of their games last year.

To make matters worse, they were not alone. Marquis was constantly distracted by strangers entering the gym and taking a seat in the stands. The visitors were adults; parents and supporters of the team. The crowd was mostly quiet and respectful of his practice, but they did talk amongst themselves.

Once the spectators grew to fifty people, Marquis pulled one of his players aside and asked, "Do these people always come to your practices?"

Latavia shook her head. "No. Maybe one or two people, but not this many."

"Why are they here now?" he wondered.

"Because of *you*," she said with a grin. "They never met a real-live *Dallas Cowboy* before. You're a celebrity."

"No, I'm not," Marquis insisted.

"Hmph. Tell them that..."

Marquis saw that many of the women in the stands were grinning at him more than their hot-tailed daughters.

● ● ● ● ● ●

Nya didn't work that day. She was interested to know how her daughter's first day of practice was going, so she headed for the school a few minutes early. When she got there, she was surprised to find dozens of vehicles in the parking lot of the old gym. She checked her watch, thinking she was late for something, but it was 5:45. Practice didn't end until six.

Her eyes widened when she entered the gym and saw all of the people in the stands. The girls' team *never* got that much attention – sometimes not even on game days. She took a seat among them, and soon the mystery was solved. Every conversation she overheard was about Marquis. The ladies thought he was *super fine*. They wondered if he was still a millionaire and why they were fortunate enough to get such a superb specimen of a man at Finley High.

Bridgette Young, the organizer of the Lady Grizzlies Booster Club and mother of Dalia (a mediocre player), was the most vocal. She seemed to know everything about Marquis. She told the ladies about his football injury, the bad press he got when he returned to Overbrook Meadows, and his divorce last year.

"He's single y'all," she cackled, her smile big and toothy. "But don't try to make a move – 'Cause I already got my sights on him. I'm bringing him a casserole *tomorrow!*"

Nya knew these horny women would be throwing themselves at her daughter's coach all season. It was disappointing. And Marquis obviously liked it, since he was letting them sit there. She already had misgivings about him. This spectacle didn't help his case.

She ignored the women and focused her attention on the court instead. When she spotted her daughter, a smile replaced her frown. Lisa was the tallest girl on the hardwood. She was tall enough to play center, but she was the best ball-handler, and she loved her role as the team's point guard.

Nya's attention moved to the rest of the team. She was glad to see that Tricia was back. And so was Latavia, who was one of their best defensive players. Dalia was still as uncoordinated as ever. And Tamika hadn't practiced her free throws over the summer break.

Nya didn't realize she was avoiding the man of the hour until Marquis jogged by her field of view for a second time, and she found herself looking away. She sighed with annoyance and forced herself to at least look at the man.

She rolled her eyes in disinterest when her gaze fell upon his chocolaty skin, his serious features and strong jawline. His lips were – she hated herself for not coming up with anything milder than *perfect*. His neck and shoulder muscles were breathtaking. His arm muscles were well-toned. His back fanned out like a giant cobra.

As her inspection continued down his frame, she skipped over Marquis' butt as he shuffled down the court to catch an errant rebound. She decided she might as well look at that too, but she didn't ogle. Yes, those buns looked nice and squeezable under his shorts. Big whoop. His legs were powerfully built. Nya could imagine him charging down the football field, outmaneuvering defenders on his way to pay dirt. She realized her mouth was open. She snapped it closed and looked around to see if anyone noticed.

Okay, do you wanna go over there and sit with Bridgette? she thought and inwardly laughed at herself. She already knew Marquis was a strong, muscular man. None of this should come as a surprise. He did look a lot better live and in action, but she would not allow herself to become mesmerized.

But then he moved closer to them. He briefly turned towards the crowd, and Nya's throat caught. She found his gaze compelling. He didn't look directly at her, but she wished he had.

Okay. He's attractive. Speaking that in her mind made it easier to get past whatever her heart (or more likely her hormones) were trying to do right now. Her attraction didn't change how she felt about him, and she was not going to make a fool out of herself, like Bridgette was about to do.

And that was that.

• • • • • •

At five minutes to six Marquis dismissed the girls. They headed to the locker room to gather their things before reuniting with their parents in the gym. Marquis took that opportunity to speak to the crowd, who seemed to have been watching his every move for the past hour.

"Good evening," he said, approaching the stands. "How y'all doing?"

His voice was deep and commanding. The parents happily returned his greeting.

"I appreciate all of you for coming out," he said. "It's awesome that you want to show support for the girls. But I'm afraid this can't happen every day. *Any* day. I don't want y'all to become a distraction, so practice will be closed to the public from now on."

A lot of people were disappointed to hear that. But they were so captivated by the former NFL player, they didn't question him.

"Can I have your autograph?" someone screamed.

The crowd laughed at that, while Marquis shook his head and grinned sheepishly.

"No, there won't be any of that, either," he replied. "I'm not a celebrity. I only played a few games with the Cowboys. That was over three years ago."

"You're still *Trucker!*" a male voice shouted.

The moniker tugged at Marquis' heart for a moment. His fans gave him the nickname back in college, because of his tendency to run over defenders, rather than attempt to elude them. Sadly, it was this style of play that eventually led to his neck injury with the Cowboys.

"I'm not trucking over anybody these days," he told the fan. "These girls are the only players I'm concerned with. So if y'all could focus your attention on *them*, I'm sure they would appreciate it. Don't get me wrong. I love that you remember my career. But this isn't about me. Tomorrow, if you could show up no sooner than 5:55 to pick up your daughter, that would be great."

Nya was surprised and impressed with the way he handled the situation. But she knew it would take a lot more than that to settle these people down. She didn't have to wait five seconds for proof.

"Hi, I'm Bridgette Young!" the woman said, rising to her feet. "I'm the coordinator for the Lady Grizzlies Boosters."

Marquis nodded, smiling. "Nice to meet you."

"I always take care of our girls and our coach," Bridgette said. "Ask anybody. So I gotta get you a gift, to welcome you to the team."

"Oh, no. That's not necessary," he told her.

"You like spaghetti casserole?"

Marquis couldn't deny that was his favorite dish. "Um, yes, Ma'am. I do."

"Don't call me *Ma'am*!" she said. "I'm not even *forty*. My name is Bridgette. Dalia's my oldest child."

Nya couldn't believe she was having this conversation in front of everyone. She was embarrassed *for* her.

Bridgette was fair-skinned and cute, a little chubby, but Marquis thought she was fine. He felt like she was flirting with him, but he didn't think she would do that so openly. Maybe she was just outgoing.

"Okay, Bridgette," he said, "that'd be fine." Before he turned and left the gym, he said, "Remember, everybody: Come at 5:55 tomorrow. Don't make me lock you out!"

The crowd laughed at the joke, but Nya knew he was serious. She found herself smiling at him, but that was okay, because everyone was smiling.

CHAPTER SEVEN
FIRST GAME

Marquis had two weeks to whip his ragtag band of misfits into shape before their first game. He knew it would be an uphill battle. The physical exertion he demanded from them would gradually weed out those who weren't serious about playing. One by one he watched the number of girls who showed up for practice decrease.

But losing the slackers didn't mean he was left with a gold mine. Marquis was increasingly worried about the squad he would present on November 9th. He was hit with feelings of déjà vu as he watched his team throw up brick after brick and miss easy fast break layups during practice. This was how he remembered the girls playing when he was in high school.

At Castleberry, the girls' hooping skills, or lack thereof, was laughable. Marquis and his crew only went to their games if they had nothing else to do. He and his friends would sit in the stands snickering and shaking their heads.

How many wide open shots is she gonna miss?

Watch, I bet she's gonna fall down if anybody tries to guard her.

Do they even know how to work the ball around the court?

Look! She's on the ground again!

Ha ha!

After watching Cheri set up a half-ass screen one muggy afternoon, Marquis rushed in with his eyebrows knotted together, his nostrils flaring.

"*What the hell was that?*" he demanded.

"What?" Cheri asked. The girl who breezed by her was equally puzzled.

"That was a screen?" Marquis asked. "That thing you just did, you call that a screen?"

Cheri didn't want to acknowledge it now.

"And what do you think you're doing?" Marquis turned on their center with fire in his eyes.

Tricia's eyes bugged. She couldn't respond at all.

"How are you supposed to get the ball, if you're not getting position on Rochelle?" he wondered. "And you sure as hell ain't crashing those boards!"

"*I don't know what that means!*" Tricia cried.

"Why didn't you tell me you don't know what that means?!" Marquis shouted back. "I been telling you to crash the board for over a week!"

Tricia's eyes were big and glistening.

"*What are you gonna do, cry?*" their coach shouted.

Much to his surprise, she did just that.

"I don't believe this," Marquis said. He brought a hand to his head and rubbed his throbbing temple. "All of you!" he said, looking over his pitiful team. "*You're playing like girls!*"

None of them dared to point out the obvious.

"Move out the way!" he told Cheri.

She quickly gave up her spot.

"Alright," he said to Dalia, "you guard Lisa, and I'm going to set a pick. I want all of you to pay attention to this."

There was no problem there. Trey Songz could've walked into the gym, and they wouldn't have noticed.

"Come this way, and make a cut at the top of the key," he told Lisa.

"Which way do I cut?" she asked.

"It depends on which way I set the pick," he said. "You gotta pay attention."

She nodded, hoping not to let him down.

Marquis moved to the shooting guard's position and told her, "Alright, come on."

Lisa started dribbling, and Dalia backed up as she guarded her.

"Get low, Dalia," Marquis said. "And keep your hands out. She can go between your legs any time."

Dalia bent her knees more and spread her arms as instructed. When Marquis saw that Lisa had her full attention, he stepped forward and created an immovable wall a couple of feet away. Lisa cut in his direction, and Dalia ran into him when she tried to keep up. The pick was perfect. It was so perfect, Dalia hit the floor hard after colliding with her coach. She looked up at him with tears in her eyes.

"Damn, coach. *Whyyyy?*" she cried.

Marquis fought to keep a straight face as he helped her up.

He asked her, "You alright?"

She nodded, but her scowl was deep and serious.

"That's how you set a pick," Marquis told the team.

"I thought it was a screen," someone commented.

Marquis would've been disappointed to know who had asked the question, so he didn't try to figure it out. "A *screen* and a *pick* are the same thing," he said calmly. "They're synonymous. We're running a pick and roll drill for the rest of the day, so divide up into groups of three. One ball per group.

"And you," Marquis said to their center as the girls began to select their partners, "you better show me something, if you expect to be a starter next week. And stop crying! You think Joakim Noah cries every time his coach yells at him?"

"Wh, who?" she sniffled.

"What, you..." Marquis was mystified. "Your homework tonight is to find out who Joakim Noah is. And find out who Kareem Abdul-Jabbar is, too. I want you to write me a one page paper about why they're so good at being a center."

"Uh, okay."

"And *crashing the boards* means *getting rebounds*," he informed her. "Everything that comes off the rim or the backboard is *your* ball. Do you understand that? It doesn't matter if you're playing offense or defense. When a ball comes down in the paint, it's *yours*! Nobody else's. You got it?"

The girl nodded, but she didn't seem too sure of herself.

● ● ● ● ● ●

When practice ended that day, Marquis remained in the gym until the last of his girls got picked up. In only a week, he had gotten to know some of the parents. He knew that Bridgette, the coordinator for the Lady Grizzlies booster club, was a hell of a cook, and she was trying her best to get him in the sack. Cheri, a starter, walked home from school, which was troubling for Marquis. If he was coaching boys, he would've offered her a ride. But being alone with a female student off campus was a major indiscretion.

Marquis' best player, Lisa Edmonds, always had someone waiting to pick her up. Sometimes it was her mother. Other times it was her father. Marquis spoke to her father once. The man introduced himself as Daryl. But Lisa's mother never paid him any attention, that he was aware of.

He did ask all of the parents not to treat him like a celebrity. Maybe Lisa's mother took that to mean he didn't want to be approached. After seeing her a few times,

Marquis hoped she would stop to say hi. The woman was very attractive, and she had a calm nature that he found endearing. Sometimes she came to the school wearing scrubs, so Marquis figured she was a nurse. Even with those scrubs on, it was impossible not to notice how curvaceous she was.

So maybe it was good that Lisa's mom never spoke to him. Marquis was constantly avoiding the affections of silly seniors, pushy booster moms and even a faculty member at the school. The last thing he needed was to develop a crush of his own on a married woman.

● ● ● ● ● ●

The next day Tricia approached him at the beginning of their seventh period biology class and gave him a piece of paper. Marquis didn't assign any homework the day before, so he wore a puzzled look.

"It's my report," she said.

He skimmed over it and saw that she had written about Kareem Abdul-Jabbar and Joakim Noah. He looked up at her and asked, "What'd you learn?"

"Kareem was one of the best centers in NBA history," Tricia told him. "He's over seven feet tall, and he has long arms and legs. He wears real little shorts."

Marquis grinned at her. "Everyone in the league wore little shorts back then. Who did he play for?"

"The Lakers."

"What was his trademark move?"

"The skyhook."

"What's a skyhook?" Marquis asked.

"That's when you jump and shoot a hook while you're in the air."

"Do you ever shoot like that?"

She shrugged. "I don't think so."

"Alright," Marquis said. "Who's Joakim Noah?"

"Oh, he's *fine*," Tricia said, her eyes lighting up.

"*Ugh*. That's your opinion. What else do you know about him?"

"He's only six-eleven."

"*Only*?"

"I mean, he's not as tall as Kareem."

"Who does he play for?"

"The Chicago Bulls. He played for the University of Florida, and he won two championships with them."

"What makes him special?" Marquis asked.

"He's tough," Tricia reported. "And he's mean. He don't let nobody push him around."

"Very good. Do you think Joakim cries like a girl when his coach yells at him?"

She shook her head, grinning.

Later that day in practice, Marquis pulled Lisa aside to discuss something that had been troubling him.

"What's up with that fadeaway?"

"What do you mean, Coach?"

"Why do you shoot so many?"

"Why? You don't like 'em?"

"I don't *hate* them," Marquis said. "But I don't think you understand when and why you need them. Usually you would only shoot a fadeaway if a defender is in your face, and you're trying to avoid getting your shot blocked. But I see you shooting them with almost every shot, even if you're wide open."

"That's just my style," she said casually.

"Who taught you that?" Marquis pressed.

"My dad. Well, he's not really my dad."

Her coach looked confused, so she told him, "He was my mama's boyfriend. They were together for twelve years, but they broke up."

"Are you talking about the man who picks you up from school sometimes?"

"Yeah."

Marquis had a lot of follow-up questions, but he didn't want to pry. Instead he asked, "I think you could be a better three-point shooter. Are you willing to learn a different shooting technique, so you can save your fadeaways for when you really need them?"

"Sure," she said, all bright-eyed and bushy-tailed.

● ● ● ● ● ●

On Monday, November 9th Daryl called while Nya was getting ready to head to the school for her daughter's first game. She stopped styling her hair, so she could take the call.

"What's up?"

"Hey," he said. "You getting ready to go to the game?"

"Yeah. You going?"

"You know I'm going. What time are you leaving?"

"In about twenty minutes," she said, checking the time.

"Can I come get you, so we can ride together?" Daryl asked.

"Um, I can meet you there."

"Are you gonna sit with me?"

Nya frowned. She couldn't think of a reason to deny the request. "Yeah. Sure."

"Why can't I come get you then, if we're gonna be together anyway?" he asked. "That way I can have time to talk to Lisa for a little bit, when I take y'all home after the game."

"You can take Lisa home. I don't have a problem with that."

"I wanna talk to you, too, Nya. I know you won't talk to me at the game."

He was right about that. Nya didn't want him to pull her attention away from her daughter on the court. Plus she

79

didn't want to have a talk that could lead to an argument in public.

"Okay. You can come get me," she decided.

"Alright. I'm on my way."

Daryl showed up fifteen minutes later. Nya thought he looked handsome in his khakis and golf shirt, and she told him as much.

"You looking good too," he replied. "Them jeans got me like *dayum*."

Nya turned and locked the front door while he wolfishly admired her figure. Her jeans weren't that tight, but they fit her more loosely three months ago, hence the diet she was currently struggling with. Up top she wore one of her Lady Grizzlies tee-shirts. It wasn't tight, either, but her bosoms created two sexy bulges on her chest.

When she turned back to face him, Daryl surprised her by pulling her in for an unexpected hug. Nya wasn't sure why, but the feel of his arms around her wasn't immediately comforting. She didn't know when she started to feel that way. She expected him to reek of alcohol, but there was only the pleasant scent of his cologne.

When he backed away, he moved in for a kiss, but the look on her face stopped him.

"We're not there yet, are we?" he asked.

She shook her head apologetically.

He nodded and then turned and headed for his truck. He opened the door for her before heading to the driver's side. Nya watched him through the windshield. She thought he wore a look of defeat. She could see it in his posture as well; the way his shoulders slumped.

As he backed out of the driveway, he asked, "What happened to us?"

"I got tired," she said simply.

Daryl looked into her eyes, which, coincidentally, looked tired at the moment.

"Tired of what?"

She frowned. "Do you really want me to give you a laundry list?"

"Are you seeing someone else?"

"I'm *definitely* tired of that."

"What you mean?"

"You've been accusing me of sleeping with someone else for years, Daryl."

He didn't think that was the case. In any event, "You didn't answer the question."

"We're past the point of you forcing me to respond to your wild accusations." She watched his grip on the steering wheel tighten as he considered that. "No, I'm not seeing anyone," she stated.

He shook his head. "I'm supposed to believe that, after it took you so long to answer?"

She shrugged. "Doesn't matter. I don't care what you believe."

He blew hot air from his nostrils. The exhalation was audible, like a bull. "You sho' done got cold."

Nya continued to stare straight ahead.

After a few beats, he switched gears, "I stopped drinking."

No response.

"You hear me?"

"That's good," she said.

"I did that for you," he said. "And for Lisa."

She didn't have a reply for that.

"I'm making all these changes," he said, growing frustrated. "What does it get me? You not treating me no better. I thought that's what this separation shit was about."

"I said I needed time to think."

"Separation don't work, Nya. I told you that. People need to work out their problems at home, in the house together. Ain't no man ever left the house for a separation and got back in. You said we'd be going out on dates. But you're always busy. I only see you twice a month. I'm trying,

81

woman. But what are you doing? *Thinking*? That's all you gotta do is *think*, while I make all these changes?"

"You know something, Daryl? You shouldn't have asked me that a minute ago; if I was seeing someone else. You want me to believe you changed, but you sound like the old you. And the way you're getting mad right now..." She looked his way. "It's *too* much like the old you. That's all I see; the same man who used to sit on the couch and try to control me. But that's fine. You gotta be you. Can't fake it."

To his credit, Daryl managed to calm himself. "Okay. So I'm losing my wife and my daughter?"

"I am not your wife."

"Twelve years together makes you my wife."

She rolled her eyes in annoyance. "That common law mess expired the moment you left my house."

"We built that house together."

"But it's in *my* name. The mortgage payments come out of my account."

He seemed to mull that over. "And Lisa?"

"She's not your daughter."

Nya's frustration was getting the best of her, and she regretted that comment. Even when they were together, Daryl didn't like to acknowledge the fact that he wasn't Lisa's father.

"After everything I did for her. All the times..." His throat caught. He winced, and a tear rolled down his cheek.

It broke Nya's heart to see him like that. Technically she was right, but so was he.

"I'm sorry, Daryl. This is complicated. I know it is. Look, we're almost at the school. If you don't pull yourself together, I don't think you should go in. You'll be a distraction, if Lisa sees you like this."

She felt like she was being a bitch. It wasn't easy to talk to him that way, but their drama was not Lisa's problem. She didn't want it to be.

Daryl managed to stifle his tears before they arrived at the school. He even offered a smile to the woman at the ticket stand and all of the other friends he had come to know from attending Lisa's games over the years.

● ● ● ● ● ●

The Lady Grizzlies beat the Lake View Scorpions 44-35. Lisa was the highest scorer on either team with 14 points. Tricia didn't try any skyhooks, but she did crash the boards with moderate success. She pulled down seven rebounds. And she made five out of six foul shots, which was a better percentage than most of the NBA's premier centers.

Marquis was on cloud nine after the game. His mood didn't falter when he met up with his brother in the parking lot, and Omar told him, "You know that was terrible, right?"

"Yeah, it was pretty bad," Marquis admitted. His smile was ear to ear. "But you know what, it didn't *feel* like they sucked, not while I was in the midst of it."

"Do you know how many times the ball went out of bounds?" Omar asked. No smiles from him.

"Yeah, it was awesome! They were all on the floor. Hair flying." Just thinking about it got Marquis' blood going again.

"But it would be nice if your girls would *catch* the ball, instead of letting it go out of bounds," his big brother insisted.

"Yeah, yeah. We're working on that," Marquis said. He gave him a side-to-side hug. "Thanks for coming, bro."

"Wouldn't miss it for the world. Congratulations, Coach."

CHAPTER EIGHT
HARD SELL

The team only had two days to prepare for their next game. On Tuesday Marquis gathered the squad together for a talk before practice.

"I have to say I'm proud of you ladies."

The team was seated on the first two rows of the bleachers. Marquis paced the floor before them as he spoke.

"We didn't have a lot of time to come together," he said. "We started off with twenty-five people, and now we're down to sixteen. I expect that number to get even smaller when the first six weeks' grades get posted."

The girls looked around, wondering who would be the ones to suffer from the school's no-pass/no-play policy.

"Even if I do get to keep all sixteen of you," their coach continued, "I can't say that I'm happy about the way we played yesterday."

They were surprised to hear that.

"We didn't set one single pick," Marquis continued. "We didn't have enough people trying to get open, when Lisa brought the ball down. Anybody can defend you, if you don't move your feet. I didn't see enough ball rotation before we took our shots. A lot of you didn't look around to see if anyone was open. You didn't even wait to see if *you* were open. You just turned and threw it up there, like a prayer."

Nearly everyone was guilty of this. Their eyes fell to their sneakers.

"But what bothers me the most is your lack of *cohesiveness*," he said. "We're not gelling together as a team. What I saw was a bunch of people playing one-on-one. You did manage to win. But if you go against a good team playing like that..." He shook his head. "You're gonna get beaten. *Badly*. It'll be embarrassing, and I'm not gonna let you embarrass me on that court.

"So today we're gonna work on a few drills; the 5 on 5 fast break and the five man weave. And since some of you don't catch well – yes, that's very concerning – we'll be doing the 5 on 5 no-dribble *every day*. Any questions?"

The girls had none. They had no idea what those drills entailed, but they were ready to get started.

"Alright, let's get our stretches done."

● ● ● ● ● ●

On Thursday, November 12th the Lady Grizzlies improved their record with another win. This time it was an away game at Kennedy High. Granted, the Kennedy girls didn't put up much of a fight, but Marquis thought his team played a little better than they did earlier that week. The final score was 53 to 31. Lisa led all players again with 12 points, three steals and five assists.

After practicing with her for a few weeks, Marquis was aware of Lisa's ball-handling skills, but he was increasingly impressed when he watched her play. It was rare to see such a tall player move the rock like that. The girl threw amazing passes. Unfortunately her teammates were rarely ready for them. If they were, Lisa's assist numbers would be much higher.

During their ride home, the girls were hype and wild. They taught their coach a team fight song that he'd never heard before. He couldn't say he approved of the lyrics, but there was no denying the sense of comradery that came over the team as they belted the rhyme:

We comin' to your town!
Yah! Trick! Yah!
We gonna shut you down!
Yah! Trick! Yah!
We from the dirty south!
Yah! Trick! Yah!
Grizzlies all in yo mouth!
Yah! Trick! Yah!

A few of the booster moms rode the bus with them. They were as spirited as the girls. Bridgette, the most outspoken of the bunch, sat in the front of the bus near Marquis.

Before they reached the school, she leaned over the aisle and asked him, "Did you like my casserole?"

"I did," he said with a grin. "Sorry. I thought I told you."

"You should tell me what other kind of dishes you like," she said. "Or dessert. I can make you some sweets."

The look in her eyes made it clear that the sweets she was offering didn't have to come from her kitchen. But Marquis was not interested. She was a nice enough lady. A cutie with nice proportions. But there was nothing about her that made his heart sigh when he looked her way.

Besides, he didn't want to get involved with any of his students' parents. There was nothing illegal about it, but he sensed things would change at school and with the team if it didn't work out.

"I can't have you cooking for me," he told her. "People might get the wrong idea."

"Maybe they'll get the *right* idea," Bridgette quipped.

"Ah, man, you're trying to get me in trouble," Marquis said with a chuckle. "It would probably be better if I focused on my job. This is my first year teaching. No offense, though. I think you're a special lady."

Bridgette smiled, and it didn't look like she took offense to that.

Marquis thought that was the end of it, but she brought a plateful of cookies after practice the very next day.

"I made too many," she told him. "I promise I wasn't thinking about you when I put them in the oven."

"Thank you," Marquis said as he accepted the plate. "You're too kind."

● ● ● ● ● ●

At practice on Friday, the girls were surprised to find a dozen traffic cones set up strategically in the gym. Marquis was anxious to move on to more advanced strategies, but pushing the ball down the court was still a weakness for his team. He taught them a dribble enhancement drill, and they repeated the passing drills they learned earlier that week.

Lisa, who was by far the best ball-handler, felt special when Marquis pulled her aside.

"What's up, Coach?"

"That fadeaway," he said. "We gotta work on that. You need to attack the basket sometimes, instead of backing away from it. I know you're good, but your shot can be better. Do you want to play in college?"

She shrugged. "I want to, but I haven't got any offers or anything."

"I think you could do it," Marquis said. "But they're not gonna want you, if you're a one-trick-pony. You need to learn how to follow-through with your shots – that way you can shoot more three's."

Lisa didn't look comfortable with that. Three-pointers were not her forte.

"You can do it," Marquis assured her. "First you have to believe in yourself. Then you have to be willing to learn and change."

She nodded and offered a guarded smile. "Okay, Coach. I'll try."

● ● ● ● ● ●

For the next two hours Marquis split his time between Lisa's shooting technique, Tricia's post-up moves and the rest of the team's passing and dribbling. When practice ended at six, he was not surprised to find his star player frustrated and unsure of herself. He watched her interact with the person she said was "not really my dad" when he came to pick her up.

The man looked in Marquis' direction. He spoke to Lisa again, and then he began to walk towards the coach. Marquis met him halfway.

"Evening," he said, reaching to shake his hand. "You've got one hell of a player there."

Daryl shook his hand, but his expression was less than friendly. "I'm Daryl."

"Nice to—"

"What issue you got with Lisa's shot?"

Marquis was wary of the vibes he was getting. But he remained polite and professional. "Lisa's got a great shot. She's our top scorer."

Daryl nodded. "Yeah. I taught her everything she knows."

Marquis' eyes widened for a moment. It only took a second to evaluate the situation and realize what he was up against.

"You did a great job," he said. "I guess I should be thanking you for the good start we're off to."

If Daryl took that as a compliment, it didn't show.

"But I think Lisa should learn different techniques," Marquis offered.

"Different like what?"

"Well, you know, like a regular jump shot. I don't think everything she shoots should be a fadeaway."

"You played *football*, didn't you, Coach?" Daryl asked.

Again Marquis was confused by the hostility. It had been his experience that most parents would want their child to listen to their coach.

"I played basketball as well," he said. "But, yeah, I did focus on football when I got to college."

"So you probably know more about football than you do about basketball," Daryl surmised.

At that point Marquis wondered if he was being set up. Surely this was a joke. If he reacted the wrong way, Daryl would start laughing as he pointed out all of the cameras hidden around the gym. Either that, or this was his first experience with an overbearing helicopter parent. Despite his training, Marquis realized he wasn't prepared for that scenario.

"Do you have some experience playing basketball?" he asked.

"As much as you," Daryl replied.

This is some weird shit, Marquis decided. Were they arguing? If so, why? They both wanted the same thing; for Lisa to be successful.

"I think she has a good chance of getting a scholarship," he said. "Right now her shooting is one dimensional. But if she learns..." He trailed off because Lisa's *not really my dad* was shaking his head.

"She needs to focus on her *studies*," Daryl told him. "Her reading and her math. Basketball is a hobby."

"Yes, of course. But sometimes a hobby can turn into something lucrative, if you play it right. I went to college on a football scholarship, but I majored in education, and it paid off."

"Kids are different these days," Daryl argued. "You tell them they can get a hooping scholarship, and that'll be their only focus from then on. That's why I would never tell her that."

Despite being an inexperienced teacher, Marquis knew when to back down. "You're right," he said. "Lisa should focus on her studies."

Daryl nodded and said, "Thanks," before he reunited with his step-daughter and they left the gym together.

When they got in his truck, she asked him, "What were y'all talking about?"

"You," Daryl told her.

"I know that," Lisa said. "What about me?"

"I wanted to know why he's trying to change up your shot all of a sudden," Daryl told her as he rolled out of the parking lot. "You been the best player on the team for four years, and he wants to come in and shake things up."

Lisa didn't like the idea of altering her shot either, but, "I don't think he's trying to shake things up. He just wants me to get better. He said I might be able to get a scholarship."

Daryl frowned at that. "You're smart enough to get a scholarship with your *grades*. Don't ever forget: Your mind is what's most important. Sports come and go. They can never take away your smarts."

Lisa knew that was sound thinking, so she didn't argue.

"What's it like in practice with him?" Daryl asked after a few beats. "You his new project?"

"What do you mean?"

"Does he focus on other girls, or do you feel like he singles you out?"

Lisa thought that was an odd question. "He, um... I know he works with Tricia a lot, too."

"Don't forget who taught you how to play," Daryl told her. "I'm sure your coach would like to swoop in at the last minute and try to take credit. But he wasn't there practicing with you for the past five years, through the rain, sleet and snow."

Lisa didn't remember ever practicing with Daryl in the rain, sleet or snow. His comment made her feel uncomfortable. After thinking about it for a few moments, she understood why:

He sounded jealous.

She remembered how he would have similar conversations with her mother whenever there was a new male in her life, be it her boss or a coworker. Lisa often heard him speaking disparaging about men, saying things that would make Nya not like them, just because he didn't like them.

But he had never been controlling with Lisa. More than likely he was still reeling from the breakup with her mom. In his depressed state, he was worried that he would soon be forgotten. Maybe Daryl was trying to safeguard against that. Lisa decided to express sympathy rather than annoyance.

"I won't ever forget what you taught me," she promised him. "You don't have to worry about that."

He smiled, and Lisa felt better about the conversation, too.

● ● ● ● ● ●

The following Monday, Marquis was happy to see Nya come to pick up her daughter after practice, rather than Daryl. He wasn't sure why, but he found Lisa's mother intriguing. He didn't think it was because she tended to ignore him. At least he hoped that wasn't the case. It seemed a little childish to be attracted to the one woman who wouldn't give him the time of day.

He saw that she wore a black thermal under her scrub top that evening. She had deep, dark skin, beautifully shaped lips and serious curves. She was shorter than her daughter by at least a foot.

Nya didn't wear a lot of makeup or do anything special to her hair. Marquis knew she wasn't trying to catch his attention, but she had it just the same. He longed for her to look him in the eyes. He didn't realize how badly he wanted her to speak to him until she entered the gym unceremoniously, and then left with Lisa by her side.

Dammit, Marquis thought to himself, and he felt his legs moving in their direction. He didn't have a game plan in mind as he pushed through the double doors and was greeted by a cool, November sunset. The truth of the matter was Lisa was his star player, and it was plain, old *odd* that her mother hadn't said so much as Hello to him in four weeks. He knew he couldn't tell her that, but he felt like he had to say *something*.

He spotted the mother and child as they slipped into a new sedan that was parked near the gym's entrance. Marquis felt unexpectedly inadequate when Nya looked up at him over the steering wheel. He grinned foolishly as he approached the car and waved at her.

She frowned and awkwardly waved back. She closed the door, but Marquis didn't walk away. He waved again, and Nya narrowed her eyes in confusion. She turned and said something to her daughter and then opened her door and leaned out slightly.

"Hi. Is there something you need?"

Yeah, I need you to acknowledge me, woman!

"Uh, yes," Marquis said. "I've tried to meet all of my girls' parents, but I don't believe I've had a chance to touch bases with you..."

He thought that was both lame and brilliant. He was offended when Nya's eyes registered annoyance before she got out of her car. Marquis found her reaction to him perplexing. He wondered if Daryl had told her about him trying to change up Lisa's shot, and if she disagreed as well.

He was grateful when Nya closed the car door before she approached him. He sensed she might say something that wasn't for Lisa's ears.

"Hi, Coach Berry. It's nice to meet you."

He reached to shake her hand, and she complied. The feel of her small mitt in his made Marquis' heartbeats stutter. He guessed that was because she was so elusive, rather than any chemistry they might have had.

"You have a very special daughter, Mrs. Edmonds," he told her.

She smiled curtly. "Thank you."

"I spoke with her, um, *Daryl* last week. I told him I think Lisa could get a basketball scholarship, if she tightens up a few fundamentals."

If she was happy to hear that, it didn't show.

"Is there a problem?" he had to ask. "I feel like I'm getting a chilly reception."

Nya appeared to debate whether or not she would say. She walked past him, heading back towards the gym. Marquis looked into her car and locked eyes with Lisa before he followed her. The girl didn't have an explanation for any of this. She shrugged.

Nya stopped at the gym's entrance and turned to face him. They weren't very far from her car, but she figured they were a safe enough distance to keep Lisa from hearing their conversation.

And even though her demeanor conveyed irritation at the moment, Marquis was glad that she was finally looking at him. Her deep brown eyes were not inviting. He wasn't sure why he found her so damn sexy.

"I was not comfortable with the idea of you coaching or teaching my daughter," she told him.

His jaw dropped. "You, why?"

"I heard about you," Nya told him. "I read about you. I know about your arrest, the drinking, the fights. I'm sorry, but that's not the type of behavior I'd expect from a school teacher."

Marquis was stunned. He wasn't surprised that people felt that way about him, but he didn't expect to hear it from her. Or maybe he just didn't want to. Out of all of his students, he wanted Lisa's parents to like him. She was his star player. It was depressing to know that both Nya and Daryl were against him.

"I'm sorry," he told her.

"Why are you apologizing?"

"Because I don't want to be a cause of concern for you. You should feel comfortable about everyone your daughter spends time with. Those things you read about me, that was a bad time in my life. I was going through a lot. I'm not like that."

"You don't owe me an apology," she said. "You've been teaching for a few months, and nothing bad has happened. The team is winning, too. I know it's only been a couple of games, but still... I should probably be the one to apologize to you."

Marquis foolishly thought she might do that.

Instead she told him, "You have a nice evening, Coach Berry," and abruptly returned to her car.

Marquis sensed that would be the only time they ever spoke. He tried to convince himself that was no big deal as he returned to the gym.

CHAPTER NINE
U MAD, BRO?

Over the next month Marquis continued to find success as he acclimated himself to his new assignments. He worried that he'd grow weary of the task of teaching, but there was constant excitement as he reignited his love affair with science. Passing down his knowledge to a younger generation was rewarding, especially when the students showed serious interest.

In the meantime, the Lady Grizzlies continued to thrive on the basketball court, despite being down to twelve players by mid-December. Marquis was proud to say the remaining twelve were all die-hards. His heart thumped with delight when he watched them give their all in practice and heed his instructions during the games.

He didn't want to take credit for their early success. He had never coached before and was reluctant to believe he was better than any of the other coaches in the district who'd been on the job for years.

"You already had a good squad when I got here," he told the principal when the Lady Grizzlies won their seventh game.

"We're lucky, that's all," he said to his brother when the team's record shined at 10-1. "It's not like we played anyone with a *spectacular* record."

"Nobody's that lucky," Omar countered. "And remember, I saw your first game. Those girls didn't learn how to catch on their own."

"I didn't teach them how to catch," Marquis laughed. "They were nervous that first game. And I had a bunch of players out there who didn't know what they were doing. They're gone now."

"I guess your team comes up with their own plays, too," Omar said sarcastically. "All of that yelling you do during the games doesn't matter at all..."

"I don't yell. I speak *forcefully*."

"You're one modest SOB."

"It's not me," Marquis insisted. "It's the girls."

But there was no denying his coaching prowess when the Lady Grizzlies got a second place trophy in the Nazareth Tournament on December 5th and third place in the Dimmit Tournament on December 12th. Marquis was surprised to get a call from the Overbrook Meadows Telegram. The sports' editor wanted to set up an interview. Marquis invited him to the school and met with him after practice.

"Coach Berry, I gotta know, what led such a prominent football player as yourself to coach a girls' basketball team?"

The reporter was a well-fed man with rosy cheeks and a handlebar moustache.

"Everyone knows it wasn't my first choice," Marquis told him. "Football has been my focus since I graduated high school. But I was pretty good at basketball, too. There weren't any spots available to coach football when I applied for a teaching job. But they told me I could coach basketball, and I jumped on it."

"You jumped on the opportunity to coach a *girls'* team?" He was rightfully skeptical.

"I prayed on it," Marquis said with a chuckle. "I was more worried about me being successful as a coach, than I was about it being a girls' team."

"Looks like you are successful," the reporter said. "Your team is 11 and 1. You brought home another trophy last weekend."

"The girls are playing their hearts out. I'm very proud of all of them."

"Lisa Edmonds is having a phenomenal year under your tutelage."

"She's outstanding," Marquis acknowledged. "But I'm new to the team. I can't take credit for the things she's done out there. Lisa's a born leader."

"How has life been for you since quitting football?"

Marquis knew the question was coming. "It's completely different. I'm in a good place right now."

"Do you ever miss the Cowboys?"

The question brought with it bright flashes of stadium lights, the tumultuous roar of seventy thousand fans.

"I do miss it," he admitted. "I knew football wouldn't last forever, but I expected it to last for more than seven games." He grinned wistfully. "But life is good at throwing curveballs. You gotta be ready for change. I'm glad I have my health, and I'm happy to be at Finley High."

"You've got a lot to be happy about," the reporter said. "So how about it, Coach? Are the Lady Grizzlies going to the playoffs?"

"*Way* too soon to be talking playoffs," Marquis said with a chuckle. "Right now we're only thinking about our next game."

● ● ● ● ● ●

During the month of December, Marquis found that he was acutely aware of Nya when she came to the games or picked her daughter up from practice. He didn't attempt to speak to her again, but he felt her presence, even when he had his back to her and was instructing the team.

He decided that he did not like Daryl – not only because of the way the man spoke to him, but also because he sat with Nya at Lisa's games. If they broke up, why did they continue to sit together? Marquis understood how foolish it was to be jealous of a man who was spending time with a woman he had no chance of being with. It was just as foolish as the silly crushes some of his students had on him.

But he couldn't stop his mind from thinking about Nya and wondering. He always noticed when she wore her hair down and when she wore street clothes rather than scrubs. His throat caught when he saw her sporting bold-rimmed glasses one day. He didn't know she wore contacts. The glasses gave her a sexy, nerdy look that made Marquis stare a second longer than he meant to. Not that she noticed. Since their talk, Nya never paid him any attention. He knew it was best if he responded in kind.

So he ignored the curiosity and allure that beckoned him to look her way whenever they were in the same room. Just when he thought he had things under control, Nya approached him after their victory against the West Carroll Panthers. Marquis was so stunned to see her walking his way, he looked around, thinking she was coming to speak to someone standing on his right or left.

But there was no one there. And her big, brown eyes were clearly focused on him. Best of all, they weren't filled with spite or judgement. They were soft and excited. Her smile was the same.

She said, "Good job, Coach."

A lot of people told him that after a win, but it felt special when she did. He wasn't sure why her approval was so necessary.

He told her, "Thank you. Lisa's killing 'em."

She smiled before walking away. It wasn't a huge encounter, but it was enough to get his crush going again.

You're a fool, he thought. *You don't know anything about her, other than the fact that she doesn't like you.*

Yes, it was certainly a foolish venture, and a complicated one, given the Lisa and Daryl factor. So he worked to reduce his interest yet again. Maybe he was ready to pursue a new relationship, but it wouldn't be with her.

● ● ● ● ● ●

On Friday, December 18th, the hallways at Finley High were decked out in red, green and silver, along with festive wreaths and cut-out snowflakes. All of the students (and teachers too) were excited about the winter break, which would keep them out of school until after New Year's.

The Lady Grizzlies didn't have any games scheduled during the holidays, but Marquis didn't cancel practice that Friday. He knew his players were going to lie around and get fat off pecan pies during their vacation. If he had it his way, they would still meet at the school every day for conditioning at the very least.

Before practice, Marquis was surprised to hear a group of girls engaged in a heated argument outside of the gym. When he stepped outside, his eyes widened at the sight of his star player in the middle of a brewing fight. Lisa and a girl Marquis didn't know were chest to chest, threatening to kick each other's ass, while six other girls gathered around and urged one of them to throw the first punch.

Marquis rushed to the center of the fracas. He pushed Lisa away and yelled at the girls.

"What the hell's going on here?"

His booming voice shut the argument down immediately, but no one offered an explanation for what was about to go down.

Marquis fixed angry eyes on his point guard. "You're supposed to be getting ready for practice!"

Lisa's fair skin was red with embarrassment and fury. Her chest heaved up and down. She looked past her coach and continued to shoot daggers at the girl she was arguing with.

"Hurry up and go change!" Marquis ordered her. "You can start off with twenty laps."

Despite her anger, Lisa was obedient. Her nostrils flared as she bottled her fury. She turned and disappeared inside the gym.

Marquis looked at the other girl. "What's your name?"

She stared at him but didn't respond.

"If I have to find out the hard way, you're getting two days in ISS."

Some kids didn't mind in school suspension, but it was a decent deterrent for popular students who loved to socialize.

"Tania," she said sneering at him.

"I suggest you fix your face," he told her, "or we're gonna have to get administration involved in this."

She sighed roughly and then rolled her eyes. Marquis wanted to follow through with his threat to escalate the incident, but he didn't know what was going on, and he didn't want to get Lisa in trouble. Plus the girl did stop sneering at him, which was good enough for now.

"You wanna tell me what's going on?" he asked her.

"She started it."

"What are y'all arguing about?"

"I don't know what her problem is."

Marquis knew she was lying. "I don't ever wanna see you starting trouble again," he told her sternly. "Why you still here anyway? School's out. Go home. All of you."

The girls shuffled away, and Marquis headed back inside.

• • • • • •

He ended practice ten minutes early. He didn't attempt to talk to Lisa until she gathered her things from the locker room and returned to the gym to wait on her ride. Marquis sat next to her on the bleachers and fixed disappointed eyes on her.

"I'm sorry," she told him.

The two hour practice had changed her looks. She wore shorts and a tee shirt, rather than the skinny jeans and tight tee she had on earlier. Her hair was a little messed. The collar of her shirt was dark with sweat.

"What were y'all arguing about?" Marquis asked her.

His disappointment deepened tenfold when she told him the fight was over a boy.

"Are you kidding me?"

"She started it."

"It doesn't matter who started it. I can't believe you're fighting over a *boy*. You're better than that. Who is it, anyway?"

"Who, the boy?"

"Yeah."

"LeMarshall."

"*LeMarshall*? What the hell kind of name is that?"

She giggled.

"You need your butt whooped, just for that," Marquis said. "*LeMarshall*." He shook his head. "So who's he cheating on, you or her?"

"Neither," Lisa said. "He started talking to me this week. He already broke up with Tania. She's the one who can't get over it."

"And that was worth it to you; almost getting kicked out of school, just so you can say that's your man?"

"She started it, Coach," Lisa insisted. "I was just trying to come to practice."

"It doesn't matter. If y'all started throwing blows, you'd be outta here. You would've been off the team, for at least a few weeks. That's worth it to you?"

She sighed. "No, Coach."

"I hope not, because you got a lot of people counting on you. You can't be out there making stupid decisions, like you're the only one who's affected by them. It's not only about being able to play basketball. It's about being a responsible person."

"Alright, Coach. But what am I supposed to do if she keeps messing with me?" She leaned forward with her forearms on her knees.

"Go tell it."

"You want me to snitch?"

"Hell yeah," Marquis said. "Whatever it takes to keep you out of trouble. If people give you a hard time about snitching, you can snitch on them too!"

He grinned. Lisa returned his smile.

"Who's picking you up today?"

Marquis hoped it was her mom, but she said, "Daryl."

He noticed she didn't seem excited about that. He considered whether he wanted to get involved in another one of her conundrums before he asked, "Is everything okay?"

Lisa shrugged and said, "Not really."

He didn't think she wanted to talk about it, but she went on to tell him how complicated things had gotten, ever since Daryl and her mother broke up. Marquis felt a little awkward listening to the tragic tale. But he understood that kids will pick who they're comfortable talking to. The adults in their lives were given the great task of being open-minded and understanding and offering the best advice they could.

"My mom says they were trying to work it out, but it's not working," Lisa revealed. "She thinks it's going to get even worse when she tells him."

Her story shed light on a few things Marquis was curious about, like why Daryl and Nya looked like they were together when they attended Lisa's games. Inwardly he was happy to know that Nya was not reuniting with her ex, which was reason enough not to offer any advice. But Lisa had poured her heart out, and he had to say something.

"That, that's a hard one," he mused. "I think you know that whatever's going on between them is not your fault."

"I know, but I feel like I'm stuck in the middle of it."

"Having two people in your life who love you and want to be around you is not a bad thing," he told her. "As a matter of fact, you should consider yourself lucky. A lot of kids don't have a father – or even a father-figure in their lives."

She nodded. "Do you think–"

"Hey, you ready to go?" a voice interrupted.

They looked up and were surprised to see Daryl standing there. Marquis didn't hear him enter the gym. Daryl's expression was curious, as if he knew they'd been talking about him.

"Yeah," Lisa said and rose to her feet. "See you later, Coach," she said as they headed for the exit.

"Alright," Marquis told her. "Y'all have a Merry Christmas."

Daryl didn't respond to that, but Lisa told him, "You too, Coach!" and then they were gone.

● ● ● ● ● ●

On the way home, Daryl noticed his little girl was quiet and contemplative.

"What's wrong? I thought you'd be happy about your Christmas break."

"I am. Just thinking about some mess that happened at school," Lisa said. She gazed out of the passenger window.

"What was it?" Daryl asked. "Your coach still complaining about the way you shoot?"

Lisa shook her head. "No. It didn't have anything to do with basketball."

"You don't wanna talk about it?"

"I already talked to Coach," she said. "I don't wanna talk about it anymore."

Daryl didn't think she was being rude, but her comment cut him deep. His time with her was so limited. She didn't always tell him everything that was going on in her life, but now that they weren't living together, the times she didn't want to talk seemed more significant.

He didn't want to blame her new coach for the rift, but how could he not? Not only did Coach Berry force her to alter a shot Daryl spent three long years perfecting, but now Lisa was confiding in him.

Daryl fumed silently. He sensed he was overreacting. But he couldn't shake the feeling that he was being slighted. Coach Berry was a has-been, a thug and a screw-up. If anything, Lisa was responsible for the team's record this year, not him. And if she needed a mentor, she should come to her father, not him.

Daryl felt like he should do something to counter Coach Berry's invasion into their lives, but at the moment, he couldn't come up with a solution.

CHAPTER TEN
'TIS THE SEASON
(FOR HEARTACHE)

My wretched soul's depleted
My heart pumps grief
You're gone
I'm stained
Dejected
Somehow alone
I mourn and pray for sweet relief
But none entreats
Alone I sleep
And think of you

On Monday, December 21st, the Christmas season found Marquis in great spirits. This was the first time he experienced one of the sweet vacation perks that came with his job as a teacher. During the summertime he would get a whopping two months off and never miss a paycheck. That wasn't enough to make him forget about the paltry salary the school district was paying him. But it was enough to make him call his brother and gloat.

"Hello?"

"Hey, bruh. What you up to?"

"On my way to work," Omar said.

"Oh. Shit. That sucks."

"Uh huh. I guess your little vacation starts today."

"Yup. Two weeks off. Two weeks and a couple of days," he clarified. "We're off till after New Year's."

"Lucky you. Y'all don't have any games during the break?"

"Nope. No practice, either. Nothing but chillaxing."

"Did you call to see how I'm doing or to rub it in?"

"Both."

"Little brothers never stop getting on your nerves," Omar noticed.

Marquis got a chuckle out of that.

"What are you doing with yourself this week?" his brother wondered.

"I'm picking up the twins today. Want me to bring them by this weekend?"

"Yeah. I'll throw something on the grill. You keeping them all week?"

"I'm keeping them for two weeks."

"She let you have them for Christmas?"

"One thing I can say about Paula is she never told me I couldn't come get the boys. Even if we're arguing, she lets me have them whenever I want."

"I wonder why."

"I'm sure they can be a handful," Marquis guessed, "especially with her not working. She never gets a break from them, unless they're with me."

"Knowing her, they're cramping her style," Omar thought. "Kinda hard to do all of that shopping, if she's gotta worry about the boys every time she ducks into a fitting room."

Marquis knew his brother was probably right about that. Paula was still getting ten grand a month from him. What she was doing with all of that money was a huge source of contention.

Not wanting to bum him out, Omar moved the conversation back to the twins, who could brighten any gloomy day.

"What are you doing with the boys today?"

"We're putting up my tree," Marquis said with a smile. "I've been waiting for them to get here before I set it up."

"You haven't put your tree up yet? It's damned near Christmas already, you slacker."

"No, it's not that," Marquis told him. "It's just, you know, the kind of thing a guy should do with a family, not by his lonesome..."

● ● ● ● ● ●

He made it to his former home in Irving at noon. Paula answered wearing jeans and sneakers. She had her keys in hand and three pieces of luggage piled by the door.

The twins rushed Marquis like they hadn't seen him in months, though it had only been a week. They wore matching Nike apparel. They dressed more fashionably than Marquis did when he worked out.

"Dad, we're spending Christmas with you!"

"That's right!" Marquis said as he knelt to hug them.

His babies were caramel colored beams of sunshine. They were happy and well-fed. Paula may have squandered the majority of the monthly income Marquis provided, but he could never complain that she didn't spend enough on the boys.

"You taking off?" he asked, noticing her suitcases.

Paula wore her hair down. It was full and flowing, raven black. He thought she looked amazing, even in her travel wear.

"Yes, could you take those to the car for me?"

She offered no smile as she pushed a button on her key ring that made the Lexus in the driveway chirp.

"And then could you come back in here for a moment," she added. "I need to talk to you. You can leave the twins in your truck."

Marquis' eyebrow rose. He figured she wanted to argue, if she was worried about the boys hearing what she had to say. And he already knew what it was about. He was served with a court summons on Wednesday, and Paula had no doubt received the same paperwork. She knew that Marquis had followed through with his plans to take her to court to reduce the amount of his child and spousal support payments.

"Come here. Give Mama a kiss goodbye."

The twins hugged and kissed their mom while Marquis took her three bags to the car. He returned for the twins and got them secured in his truck before heading back inside. Paula stood waiting in the foyer.

"Taking me to court is a bad idea," she told him.

No pretense with this one.

"I told you I can't afford to keep paying you ten thousand a month," Marquis stated. "You left me no choice."

"And I told you that's not my problem. The judge ordered you to pay it. You agreed to pay it. So pay it."

He shrugged. "Ain't no sense in arguing with each other. We'll let the judge look at my check stubs and decide how much I can afford. I already looked into it. The most they can take is half my check. If you're not happy with half of every dime I make, then I don't know what to tell you."

"I'll move back to Lake Charles," Paula said matter-of-factly.

The threat didn't buckle Marquis like it did the first time she told him. "You can't take my boys out of state. That's in our original agreement."

"If you want to start changing things, what makes you think I can't?"

"Because what I want to change doesn't affect your ability to see your children. You're crazy, if you think a judge is gonna let you take my boys to Louisiana."

"I don't think so," Paula said. She was full of sass this afternoon. "You said I should get a job. Isn't that what you suggested? Instead of me depending on you, I should get a job."

Marquis did say that, but the way she was asking made him hesitant to agree.

"I found a job," Paula announced.

"Great." Marquis was guarded. "What's that got to do with–"

"My dad wants me to be a manager at one of our restaurants."

He shook his head, partly relieved that that was the best argument she could come up with. "That's not gonna work."

"I think it will," Paula said. "I didn't have the twins in Texas. They were born in Baton Rouge. That's their hometown. We moved here to be with you, and now we're not with you anymore. I can't afford to pay the bills here by myself, but I will have plenty of family support in Lake Charles. I also have a job there waiting for me. And I have my own home in Louisiana, fully furnished."

The blood drained from Marquis' face as he listened.

"You said I'm sucking you dry, right?" Paula asked. "Okay. I'll leave, and you won't have that problem anymore. You can send me your regular child support payments – whatever it is on your current salary, and we're good."

Marquis realized her disgusting logic made sense, and it shook him to the core. But would a judge agree with her? He couldn't be sure. He tried not to let on how upsetting the news was. He failed.

"You're not taking my boys out of state," he growled. His eyes were low and fierce.

Paula wasn't fazed. "Take me to court, and we'll see what happens."

"I have to take you to court! I can't afford to pay you ten grand a month."

"Then don't. All I know is, I'm going to live how I want to live. I don't care if it's here or in Louisiana. You're not going to dictate my lifestyle, Marquis. I am. Now if you don't mind, I have a plane to catch."

He felt sick to his stomach. His whole body broke out in a thin coat of sweat. The twins were safely locked away in his truck, but he felt like they were gone already.

"If you take my kids to Lake Charles, I'll buy a house within twenty miles," he promised. "You're not putting me through that long distance shit."

"I'm not putting you through anything. You're the one taking *me* to court," she coldly reminded him. "Now if you don't mind, I have to get going."

Marquis could do nothing but exit the house, as she demanded.

● ● ● ● ● ●

As upset as he was after the argument, the twins always managed to put a smile on his face. Marquis took them out to lunch and marveled at a playground tale they told almost simultaneously.

When they got to his home, he made cocoa and put on a holiday CD, like his mother used to do. The twins weren't much help hanging lights or garland on his Christmas tree, but they were happy to assist with the ornaments. Marquis had to lift them one at a time, or everything they hung would've been knee high.

After supper he called his brother, as he always did when life started to get chaotic. Omar listened to the news about Paula's latest threat and told him, "It sounds like she's been talking to a lawyer."

Marquis suspected that too, but he asked him, "Why do you say that?"

"Everything she's telling you is a warm-up for the courts," Omar said. "She knows she can't just up and leave with the boys, so she has to come up with mitigating circumstances that would make a judge agree with her."

"You think she has enough?" Marquis asked, his stomach tightening again.

After a pause, Omar said, "I hate to say it, bro, but yeah. I think she might."

Marquis couldn't believe it. He was startled to find his eyes watering.

"She says she can't afford to live here," Omar stated. "You can't afford to keep her here. Obviously she can get a job, but she wants to work at her family's business."

"She doesn't wanna work."

"It doesn't matter. That's her story, and it's a good one. Plus she has no family in Texas. She has no support system. She could say that she doesn't have any friends, either. Everyone she knows is in Louisiana. So with her marriage over, there's no reason for her to stay in Texas – other than the fact that you need to be close to your kids."

"You think a judge would let her leave?"

It broke Omar's heart to hear the quality of his little brother's voice. He knew Marquis loved the twins more than anything.

"I don't know what a judge would do," he said honestly.

"What if, what if I don't take her to court?"

After a few beats, Omar asked, "And then what? Keep paying ten grand a month?"

"Ye, yeah."

"With what money?"

"The four hundred grand. You could give me my money back."

Marquis was glad that he couldn't see his brother's reaction to that. Omar didn't respond for what felt like a long time.

"First of all, she knows you don't have enough money to keep up with those payments. What are you going to tell her next year, when she asks where the money's coming from? Are you gonna come clean, and admit that you hid it?"

"No."

"Good, because your ass would be in major trouble. Mine too, probably. But more importantly, how long do you think you can keep that up? You can't afford to give her that kind of money until the boys are 18. As a matter of fact, you'll run out of money again in less than five years. You put that money up for a reason, Marquis. What sense would it make to give it to her now?"

"*But I can't let her take my kids.*" A tear rolled down Marquis' cheek. He fought to keep from sniffling, so his brother wouldn't know how messed up he was.

"Let me, let me think on it some more," Omar said. "I'll talk to some of the guys at work. I'll let you know if they come up with something."

"If we lose, I can move down there with her," Marquis said. "She can't do anything if I move to Lake Charles, right?"

Omar sighed and said, "No, she can't do anything about that. But I don't want you to leave any more than you want her to leave. So let me get with some people and see if there's another way out."

● ● ● ● ● ●

The holiday season was also a time of stress for Nya's *situation* with Daryl. He called on Christmas Eve, wondering if he'd be included in her yuletide plans.

"I'm going to my Mama's house tomorrow," she told him.

She lay on her bed, but she was still dressed. She got off work a couple of hours ago. She was thankful to have the next three days off.

"Do you want me to come with you?"

She shook her head wearily as she said, "No. I don't think that would be a good idea."

"Why not?"

"Because we're not together anymore." She was so tired, she didn't give much thought to her words.

"I thought we were working on it," he said.

Nya closed her eyes and told him, "We were."

His breaths were now audible on the other end of the line.

"Since when were we *done* working on it?" he wondered. "I don't believe I got that memo."

"Since, now, I guess. I'm sorry."

"Sorry for what? Sorry for dragging me along with this separation shit? You knew you weren't taking me back all along. That's why you been acting all shady."

"Don't start. It's... Not today."

"What about all my changes, Nya? I quit drinking. I calmed down my temper."

She checked the clock. It was 8:45. She could pass out right now, but she promised to bring a few pies to her mother's tomorrow. Lisa didn't like to bake, but Nya was so sleepy, she would have to ask her to keep up with the oven timer tonight.

She kicked her legs over the side of the bed and sat up with a grumble. She didn't want to be mean to Daryl, but she had to cut this conversation short. He needed to accept what she was saying and move on.

"I don't know about any of your changes," she said. "If you stopped drinking, that's great. But I still don't want to be with you. I'm sorry, but that's it. I don't have anything else to say about it."

She waited a reasonable amount of time for him to let that sink in. When he didn't respond, her eyebrows bunched in irritation.

He said, "What about Lisa? I don't get to spend Christmas with my girl?"

"Daryl, look, you need to accept the fact that she's not your daughter." Before he could throw a hissy fit, she added, "Yes, you raised her for most of her life. You cared for her like a daughter. She gives you father's day cards every year. For all practical purposes, you are her father. But legally *you're not*. So don't start making demands, like we have some court papers or something."

"I don't believe this shit."

"I'm sorry."

"After all I did for her."

"People break up, Daryl." She didn't understand why he couldn't get that through his thick skull. "And life goes on. Even if there are kids involved, life goes on."

"If we were married, you'd—"

"But *we're not*. You never asked, after twelve years — you never asked!"

"I deserve to be in Lisa's life."

"I never said you couldn't see her, Daryl. You wanna give her a present? Bring it now. Or you can wait till tomorrow. I'll call you when we get back from my Mama's. I'm not pushing you out of her life, *just mine*. Now I gotta go. Are you coming, or not?"

"Coming, what?"

"To bring her present."

"No. Not, not now. I..."

She hated to hear him like that. He was heartbreak personified. But this was necessary. She told herself it was.

"Then I'll call you tomorrow, when we get back."

She disconnected. Movement in her doorway caught her attention. She looked up and saw her daughter standing there. Of course she was. Nya rubbed her exhausted eye sockets.

"Was I yelling?" she asked her.

Lisa nodded. "A little." Despite her height, the girl looked small and fretful.

"Come here," Nya said, patting the bed next to her.

Lisa came and took a seat.

"It's over between me and Daryl," her mother told her. "But just because I don't want to be with him doesn't mean things have to change with you two. Do you, you still want to see him? I know he wants to be a part of your life."

Lisa sensed the breakup was imminent, but she never thought she'd hear her mom talk to Daryl like that.

"I do want to see him. But I want him to be like he used to be. Lately he's been..." She shook her head. "Different."

"If he makes you uncomfortable—"

"No," Lisa said. "I know he's mad because you made him leave. It's fine."

Nya understood what she was saying, but she didn't like the idea of her disgruntled ex taking it out on her daughter. "I'm going to tell him not to pick you up from school for a while."

"Mama, I said I was okay. What do you think he's gonna do, kidnap me?"

She was joking, but Nya didn't think it was totally beyond the realm of possibilities.

"Just till things get a little better," she said. "He can come to your games, but I'm not sitting with him."

Lisa's eyes glistened. It really was over. The twelve years Nya had been with Daryl seemed like an eternity.

Her mother put an arm around her. "You okay?"

The girl nodded. Nya pulled her closer and held her tightly. Lisa felt safe and warm in her mother's embrace. If it was just the two of them, she knew they'd make it just fine.

When they separated, Nya asked her, "What were you doing? You busy?"

"No. Why?"

"I need you to make me some pies..."

Lisa griped inwardly, but she didn't decline the request. She saw how exhausted her mother was.

"Okay, Mama."

115

• • • • • •

That night Daryl drank a beer for the first time in forty days. Why the hell not? He wanted another afterwards, and he ended up finishing the six-pack. That was no crime, and it didn't mean he had a problem. He hadn't missed a day of work in four years. He hadn't missed one of Lisa's games, either.

On Christmas Day he went to *his* mother's house. Everyone there loved him. He never burned a bridge with any of his family members, as people with *problems* tended to do. His cousin Benny had great advice, as far as Nya was concerned.

"Man, fuck that bitch. It's bitches everywhere."

Lisa called at five and said she and her mom had made it home. Daryl showed up a couple of hours later. He had a gift for Lisa and one for Nya. Lisa got a new tablet. Nya got a cheap bottle of perfume. Initially he bought her an expensive bottle of perfume and earrings too, but those gifts went to his mother and sister. Nya didn't deserve nice things.

He got a little teary-eyed when he had to leave and Lisa walked him to the door, but it wasn't anything major. Their situation was different now. No biggie.

Nya was right; people break up. As long as she was willing to let him be a part of Lisa's life, Daryl had to consider himself blessed.

CHAPTER ELEVEN
THE CAKE LADY

School resumed on Monday, January 4ᵗʰ. Marquis was thrilled to get back to the classroom and the basketball court. He drilled the girls hard in practice that day, telling them they had gotten lazy over the holidays.

"This is no time to take it easy! Step it up! Get those feet moving! You're playing like girls!"

He sent them to the locker room early, but practice wasn't over. He had the video from their third place finish in the Dimmit Tournament. He played the film on a projector. Most of the girls had never seen themselves on film. They found it amusing, initially, until Marquis started to point out their faults.

He focused their attention on one of their opponents, who was constantly moving with or without the ball. By contrast, players on their team did little to get in position for a rebound or a pick.

"This girl ate y'all for lunch," he said. "It was the same thing every time. She comes down to the top of the key, she moves the ball around. By the time it gets back to her, she's in a different position, and no one is keeping up with her. And then she shoots…"

As he spoke, number 21's jumper hit nothing but net.

"Watch how different we look when Lisa brings the ball down…"

Marquis marveled at how the girls hung on his every word as they watched their past selves play poorly on the projector. They believed in him, which was humbling because he wasn't one hundred percent sure of himself.

• • • • • •

After practice Marquis waited to make sure all of his players got picked up, before he locked up the gym and took off. He didn't think he'd be so vigilant if he was coaching boys. He remembered that his high school coach would sometimes leave the school after dark, while some of his players were loitering in the parking lot. Marquis chuckled at the memory.

He was conscious of Nya when she entered the gym. She hadn't come inside in a while. After their last talk, she had taken to calling her daughter from the parking lot. Marquis thought she was avoiding him, which was not easy to come to terms with.

That night the sight of Nya affected him, as it always did, though outwardly he did no more than glance her way.

The glimpse was enough to reveal her hair was up and out of her face. This was the way she usually wore it when she came from work. The cool temperatures had peaked at 41 degrees that day, so she had a gray thermal under her top. He thought her scrub pants were a little tight about the hips and thighs. He wanted to get a better look, but he forced his eyes not to linger.

He noticed she was walking in his direction. It was okay to turn and face her then. Her features were soft, her eyes indecisive. She didn't wear a smile or a frown. Marquis found her features breathtaking. He wondered what it was like to be one of her patients. He cursed himself for still wanting her, after she had judged him and labeled him a menace.

She stopped within a few feet and looked him in the eyes. Marquis saw Lisa a moment ago, but she wasn't by her mother's side. He wondered if Nya sent her to the car because this was going to be another one of those mean talks; the kind that left him feeling regretful and inadequate.

"Coach, I wanted to talk to you about something."

"Okay." He tried to sound casual, as if the temperature in the gym didn't jump ten degrees. "What's going on?"

"It's about Lisa."

Marquis was disappointed to hear that. He wasn't sure why. It wasn't like she'd ever want to talk about him and her – that would be ridiculous.

He nodded.

"Her, step-father won't be picking her up anymore," Nya revealed. "Not for a while, at least."

Marquis' eyes narrowed. Okay this was serious. But he thought–

"Well, technically he's not her step-father," Nya clarified. "We were never married. But he, he helped raise her."

"Is there a problem?"

She shook her head. "No. But things have been tense since me and Daryl broke up. I told him not to pick her up. He said he wouldn't, but if he does come up here..."

Marquis saw danger signs. They were blaring.

"Have you called the police? Do you need me to–"

"No," she cut him off. "It's nothing like that. He's not violent or threatening or..." She dismissed those thoughts with a wave of her hand. "It's nothing like that."

"But he can't pick her up from practice?"

She nodded. "That's right. If that changes, I'll let you know."

"If he does try to pick her up, what do I do, call the police?"

"No. He's not going to show up. If he does, Lisa knows not to go with him."

"But if she does?" Marquis wanted to be prepared for all possible scenarios.

"If she does, I'm sure she'd be kicking and screaming, so feel free to call the police." She smiled.

As much as Marquis loved to see her lips curve in amusement, this conversation had him on edge. "I think there's some forms we should fill out..."

She chuckled, which helped to put him at ease.

"You're overreacting."

"I'm new here," Marquis said. That line got him out of a few incidents already, like when he further incapacitated one of the school's copy machines while trying to clear a jam. "I don't know what I'm supposed to do when a parent tells me not to let someone pick up their child."

"You don't have to do anything but try to be aware of who picks Lisa up after practice," she said, still smiling.

God, he liked the way she smiled at him. He liked the tone of her voice, her lips.

"I suppose if he *does* pick her up," she said, "or you get busy, and you're not sure who she left with, you can call me, not the police."

"You're gonna give me your number?"

There was nothing flirtatious about the question, but Marquis felt a little awkward when he asked.

"Uh, yeah," she pulled her wallet from her purse and found a business card.

Marquis was intrigued when he took it and saw that she was a dessert caterer.

"Nya Edmonds, the *Cake Lady*?"

"Oh, I don't do that too much now," she said. "I only do about one event a month."

"You're a *baker*?" Marquis found it hard to believe – not that she didn't look capable. But several other team moms had offered and provided him with casseroles and other baked dishes. He didn't expect it or even want their gifts in most instances. But to know they had a real-live baker among them who hadn't offered him one single cupcake was hurtful. He knew it was silly of him to feel that way, but he couldn't help it.

"Okay. I'll call you if something happens."

"I'm sure it won't," she said. "But thanks."

She walked away. Marquis was careful not to stare after her. He would certainly get caught up, if he checked out her backside. There were other students and parents in the gym. He knew their eyes were always watching.

● ● ● ● ● ●

The Lady Grizzlies lost their Wednesday game against Roosevelt by a score of 67-54, bringing their record to 11-2. It was a hard fought match. Marquis couldn't deny that his team showed a lot of hustle. They were simply out-played. One major fault he could point out was how his girls panicked in the final minutes. They passed up easy layups in favor of contested three-pointers that barely hit the rim.

As they headed for the locker room, Marquis was pleased to see the booster moms were forever supportive. They told the team, "Keep your heads up, ladies! You almost had 'em! Keep doing your thing, Coach Berry!"

Two days later Finley High demolished North Pines with a final score of 66-36. Marquis let his backup squad play most of the second half, but Lisa still finished with 17 points and eight assists. Nearly every shot she took went through the hoop that night. Marquis was increasingly impressed and happy for her.

He was happy for her mom, too, who had to be the cheeriest woman in the stands. Marquis didn't look her way during the game, but he heard her. Out of all of the voices behind him, he could separate Nya's. She was one proud mama, for sure.

CHAPTER TWELVE
A NEW PAIR OF SHOES

On Saturday, January 9th, Marquis took his brother up on an invitation for dinner with his family. The temperature peaked at fifty degrees that day, which was cool, but not too chilly to hang outside with his big brother and his humongous grill.

Omar's home in Killeen was nearly as impressive as the mini-mansion Marquis purchased with his Cowboys money. Omar built his fortress working as an accountant for a reputable law firm. He had always been the thinker in the family. If not for him, Marquis might have majored in something trivial, like philosophy, when he was at LSU.

Marquis stood next to his brother offering unsolicited grilling tips while Omar's wife Tatyana and their three kids entertained the twins inside.

"Did I ever thank you for talking me into majoring in education?" he asked.

"You're having fun teaching?" Omar surmised.

"I have some rough days," Marquis conceded. "I definitely prefer coaching. But teaching was a good move. I can see why so many people say they love it, even though they're not paid enough."

"Not *they*," Omar corrected. "You can say *we* now. You are officially one of the underappreciated."

Marquis laughed. "I don't know about that. People seem to appreciate me just fine."

"That's good."

He lifted one of the grill's heavy lids and then pulled out his phone and sent a text message. A minute later his wife appeared at the backdoor with a Tupperware container in hand. She turned away from a stiff breeze that made her eyes water. She was a petite woman, but Marquis knew she was no pushover.

"Ooh. Y'all not cold out here?" she asked as she approached the cook.

"Nah. I'm fine," Marquis said. He watched his brother gather sizzling fajita meat from the grill with metal tongs.

He deposited the chicken and beef in Tatyana's container and gave her a kiss before she hurried back inside. Marquis watched their interactions with a hint of jealousy. He knew that Omar had found a soulmate in Tatyana. Marquis thought he'd found the same with Paula, but their fairytale didn't have a happy ending.

"Did you text your wife to come out here?" he asked when she was gone.

"Yeah. What about it?"

"Just thinking about how times have changed. I remember when Pops used to grill. He'd have to send one of us to get a tray, or he'd go get one himself, if we weren't out there."

"Technology is a beautiful thing."

Marquis agreed that it was. "What did your peeps say about my Paula situation?" he asked.

Few attorneys at Omar's firm practiced family law, but they had connections all over the country.

"They agreed that she has a strong argument," Omar told him. "You have to counter it with a strong argument of your own."

"What's my argument?"

123

"I think the fact that you'll die without your boys here will suffice."

"I will."

"I know," Omar said. "And you have to get a good lawyer; someone who can drag her request out for a couple of years, if need be. I already have one on standby."

Marquis hated the idea of getting embroiled in an extended court battle with Paula. "What good will that do, dragging it out?"

"The longer she stays in Texas the better, especially if she ends up getting a job. It'll weaken her argument that she can't afford to live here."

Marquis nodded. He liked that line of thinking. "Thanks."

After a moment of silence, Omar asked, "Are you seeing anyone yet?"

Marquis shook his head.

Omar knew that his brother's marriage was rocky and void of love for nearly a year leading up to the divorce. Marquis hadn't had a serious relationship since.

"You at least got somebody you can hit up for a booty call?"

Marquis shook his head. "Not anymore," he admitted. "It's been a while."

"How come? Has Paula ruined you for the entire female species?"

"No, not at all," Marquis said with a smile. "I'm still very interested in the female species."

"What about the teachers at your school? There's at least one super fine teacher at every school."

"We have one," Marquis agreed. "Mrs. Stevens. Happily married, but you're right. She's smoking."

"Nobody else?"

"There are a few, but I'm not trying to go there with them. I gotta see 'em every day." He smiled softly. "There's this one parent though..."

"You'd rather hook up with a parent instead of a teacher? Wouldn't that create a conflict between you and the student?"

"Yeah, probably," Marquis agreed. "And she's my star player's mom, so you know I don't want that. It doesn't matter anyway, because she doesn't like me."

He told him about Nya and how she said she didn't think he should be teaching with so many negative incidents in his past.

"It's probably for the best," Omar said when he was done.

"Yeah, I know," Marquis agreed. "But I can't stop thinking about her. I can't wait to see her, when she comes to the games. Even though she usually doesn't say anything to me, I keep hoping she will." It felt good to vocalize his emotions. Omar was the only person he was comfortable enough with to share this side of him.

"Damn, bruh. Sounds like you sprung."

"Nah. How could I be? We never talk. I don't know anything about her, except that she works as a nurse, and she broke up with her boyfriend."

"How do you know that?"

He told him what Lisa and Nya said about Daryl.

"I'm sure that makes it harder for you," Omar deduced.

"How's that?"

"Knowing she's single, probably makes you feel like you got a chance."

"Yeah," Marquis said. "I probably would give it a shot if not for the part about her hating me."

"And you're teaching and coaching her daughter."

"Yeah. That too."

"And you're a first year teacher," Omar added, "who's already coming in with a dark cloud hovering over you. I would say the last thing you need is more scandal."

Marquis agreed with that, "But would it be a scandal?" he wondered. "We're both adults."

"Depends on how people take it. What if your star player finds out, and she hates the idea and up and quits the team. That would be a scandal."

Marquis didn't think that would happen. But it *could* happen, and that was reason enough not to pursue it. He was glad he brought this conundrum to his brother's attention. As usual, Omar's advice was always the best.

● ● ● ● ● ●

Marquis had a great day at school on Monday. It was interesting to watch how the popularity of the girls' team played out on the schoolyard. The Lady Grizzlies were the big men on campus. The boys' varsity team hadn't won half as many games, and they struggled for relevance.

There was a running debate among the students. Eventually the rumors made their way to Marquis. Most of the kids thought he would take over the boys' football team next year. Some of them predicted he'd be the coach for the boys' basketball team. Few thought he would stay on with the girls'.

Marquis hoped Coach Mitchell hadn't caught wind of the talk, because he was an excellent football coach, and he wasn't going anywhere. And little did they know, Marquis might not return at all next year. If Paula succeeded with her plans to flee to Louisiana, he would have to leave too. He knew that would break more than a few hearts.

After school he went to his truck in the faculty parking lot to retrieve one of his gym bags. As he returned to the school, Marquis thought he saw a familiar face in the adjacent parking lot, which was still populated with students. He moved in that direction. His heart squeezed uncomfortably when he saw that Daryl had come to pick up

Lisa. The father (figure) and daughter stood next to his truck talking. They were both smiling.

Marquis' muscles tensed. This was the worst case scenario Nya had warned him about, but she was confident it would never happen. Marquis knew that she wanted him to call her rather than the police. But she didn't tell him what to do if he was in a position to thwart the kidnapping before it took place.

Kidnapping.

Shit, is that what was happening? If so, Marquis was not prepared. And Daryl was taking his sweet time about it. He wasn't getting in the truck or trying to get Lisa to do so, either. *Wait.* As Marquis grew nearer, he realized he'd spoken too soon. Daryl moved towards the drivers' side of the truck and opened the door.

Marquis' heart knocked. His brain raced. He couldn't physically stop Daryl from taking Lisa, but he couldn't stand there and do nothing. Should he start a commotion? Should he demand that Lisa stay put and let her make the decision? He realized Nya had put him in a very difficult position. He felt like this might be the kind of thing he could lose his job over, depending on how things went down.

But Daryl didn't get in his truck. Instead he reached over and removed an item from the passenger seat. When he backed out of the vehicle and closed the door, Marquis saw that it was a Nike shoebox.

Lisa squealed with delight when he handed it to her. She opened the box and became even more animated at the sight of her new shoes.

"Ooh, Daryl! Thank you! These are *nice!*"

Daryl leaned back on the truck grinning with pride. Marquis understood that he was invading a private moment, but it was too late. By then he was within fifteen feet of the truck. Daryl looked up and noticed him. Lisa did too.

"Hey, Coach!" she said, beaming.

"Hey," Marquis said. He was guarded.

Daryl was not happy about the intrusion. Marquis could see it in his eyes. He wanted to back off, but he felt like Nya's request that this man not pick up her child still had to be honored. If that offended Daryl, so be it. He was not Lisa's father.

"How you doing?" he said to the father figure.

Daryl nodded slightly and said, "Alright."

The two men stared at each other, not aggressively. A young buck and a mature bull. Lisa didn't notice the testosterone building up around her.

"You coming to practice?" Marquis asked his star player.

Daryl's eyes narrowed.

Nope, Marquis told himself. *Not making any friends here.*

"Yeah, here I come," she said.

Marquis took a step back. He smiled and stood his ground. Lisa looked back and realized he was waiting on her.

"Oh," she said and then turned to Daryl. "Thank you! I guess I'll see you later."

He had a quick smile for her. He ignored Marquis as she gave him a hug and a kiss on the cheek. It was a lovely scene, until Lisa backed away and walked to her coach. With her back to him, Daryl was free to speak to Marquis with his eyes.

You're wrong for taking this little time away from me, Coach. Wrong, wrong, wrong, those eyes said.

Marquis ignored him and turned to walk with Lisa.

"Got you some new kicks?" he asked when they entered the school.

"Yeah!" Lisa said. "Look! He got *blue and white*, so I can wear them to our games!"

Marquis saw that the sneakers were bold and expensive. And they matched the school colors.

"That's great, but why you gotta style on 'em like that?" he joked.

"That's the last thing I want them to see when I'm breaking ankles out there; these shoes as I fly by."

He chuckled. "Daryl called you and told you he was gonna be here after school?"

She nodded. "Yeah. But it's okay."

"I know your mom said you weren't supposed to leave with him, that's why I went over there."

"It's cool," Lisa said. "She didn't say he couldn't visit me up here or come to my games. She'll probably let him pick me up again later, after things cool off."

Marquis nodded, thinking.

● ● ● ● ● ●

When Nya picked Lisa up after practice, she made sure to step inside the gym and wave at Marquis, so he would know who the child left with. She'd been doing that since their talk after Christmas break. Despite the conversation with his brother, Marquis enjoyed these brief moments of communication with Nya. It didn't matter if they were nonverbal.

She didn't seem alarmed by the box of shoes Lisa was carrying, so Marquis assumed she knew about the visit from Daryl. But he decided he'd tell her anyway. Kids could be deceitful. Plus Nya might think Marquis was slacking on his guard dog duties, if she learned that he spoke to Daryl at school but didn't tell her.

He waited until after dinner before he found her business card in his briefcase. *Cake lady.* She never offered him any of her cakes. And he really wanted a taste. He dialed her number. She answered fairly quickly.

"Hello?"

"Hello? Mrs. Edmonds?"

After a pause she said, "Yes?"

"Hi. This is Coach Berry. Marquis."

"Oh."

129

Did she sound pleased to hear from him? He hoped so.

"Hi. What's up?"

"I was just calling to tell you what happened at school," he said, "in case Lisa didn't tell you."

"About Daryl? She told me he brought her a pair of shoes."

"Oh. Okay. I figured she told you, but I wanted to call, in case she didn't."

"Thank you. I appreciate it."

Marquis was about to end the conversation when she said, "She told me you came out and walked her back inside."

"I didn't come outside for her," he said. "I just happened to be in the parking lot when I saw them. But I did wait on her."

"You went above and beyond."

Was she being sarcastic? Did she think he *shouldn't* have done that?

"Daryl, he, I don't think he appreciated it," he told her.

"Don't worry about him," she said. "He shouldn't have been there in the first place. You did the right thing."

Her approval comforted him. He imagined her face as he listened to her. He wondered if she was smiling. He leaned back in his loveseat with a wistful grin.

"I told him not to come to the school anymore, except on game days," Nya said.

Marquis felt tense again. He suspected Daryl would blame him for that.

"Are you going to get a restraining order?" he asked. "I can't stop him from showing up at the school. All I can do is tell you about it. If it's a serious problem, you should call the principal, and we can talk to the campus monitors."

"It's not a problem like that," she assured him. "I never told him not to visit Lisa at school, so he gave it a shot. He's looking for loopholes. Now that I made myself clear, he said he won't do it again. If he does, Lisa will tell me, and I'll call the police and go from there. But I don't think he will."

"Okay. I hope everything's cool."

"I was with Daryl for twelve years," she revealed. "He and Lisa are really close. He's a good man, but this is hard for him."

"That's a long time. I know it's hard for all of you."

"It is. You know, I wanted to apologize for being a butt when I first met you."

That was unexpected. Marquis' felt his heart rate increase. "That's okay."

"No, I shouldn't have come at you like that," she said. "I know how different things must be for you. You've had your ups and downs, but I shouldn't have thrown your past in your face like that. I was wrong."

Marquis was surprised by her honesty and her compassion. Getting her off his mind would be even more difficult now, but get her off his mind he must.

"Thank you," he said. "That means a lot."

"See you tomorrow, Coach."

He immediately looked forward to it. He couldn't stop smiling.

"Okay. You have a nice evening."

CHAPTER THIRTEEN
GRIZZLIES ON A WARPATH

We're down by two points
They shoot and miss
No whistle blow
I jump and grab the rebound
Push the rock
Control the flow

The Lady Grizzlies beat the Forrestville Badgers on Tuesday, February 9th to end the season with a final record of 17-5. The team qualified for the bi-district playoffs for the first time in fourteen years. The school threw them a well-received parade. It traveled 3 ½ miles, past the Chase Bank and Jiffy Lube on Dalton, where thrones of fans lined the street to cheer them on. The parade ended with a humongous pep rally in the school's parking lot.

We comin' to your town!
Yah! Trick! Yah!
We gonna shut you down!
Yah! Trick! Yah!

Coach Berry and Lisa were honored with an invitation to the local news station for an interview. When they arrived at the studio, Marquis ran into Nya backstage. He couldn't get over how nice she looked. She wore a black dress with heels. Her hair was down and layered. He had never seen her in anything but jeans or scrubs. She was gorgeous. And nervous. She doted on her daughter and ended up doting on Marquis as well.

"Here," she said, beckoning him forward.

Marquis stepped to her with a curious expression. His stomach tightened when she reached to adjust his tie. He could smell her perfume, her hair. The closeness made the hairs stand on every part of his body. Her nimble fingers never came in contact with his skin, but he wished they had.

"Sorry," she said, pulling back, catching herself. "It was just, a little..."

"I appreciate it. Thanks," he said.

"I can't believe my baby's gonna be on TV!" She grinned nervously. She brought her arms over her body to calm herself. She chuckled, then looked him in the eyes. He stared back at her with a quiet intensity. She reacted, he thought, as if she felt what he felt. Her eyes grew a bit larger as they stared at each other.

"Lisa deserves to be here," he said. "Have I told you lately how grateful I am to have her on the team? We wouldn't have made it to the playoffs without her."

She continued to smile. She nodded and then returned to her daughter's side. She looked back at him and saw that he was still watching her. Then a producer came to speak to him, and he had to turn away.

During the interview, the sport's anchor raved about Marquis' success at LSU, with the Cowboys and now at Finley High. But Coach Berry consistently redirected the attention to Lisa, who he felt needed the recognition more than he did.

He hoped he and Nya would have another *moment* someday soon, and they did. It occurred on Saturday, the 13th. The team had to travel to Dallas for their most important road game to date. They boarded the bus at ten a.m.

There was room for all six booster moms who wanted to travel as chaperones. Nya was one of them. Marquis hoped she'd sit near the front with him, but she headed to the back of the bus. He supposed that was best. Somebody had to keep an eye on the players back there.

The very single Bridgette Young sat across from Marquis instead. Since the season started, the booster mom had given him two casseroles, a pie and a platter of cookies. She had also organized a bake sale that helped fund the girl's road trips. Bridgette didn't flirt with him during the hour-long ride, but there were hardly any breaks from her incessant chatting, not even when Marquis pretended to busy himself with his playbook.

When they reached Moody Coliseum, the coach made sure the girls had all of their belongings, and he was one of the last ones off the bus. Nya wasn't too far ahead of him. She pulled along a tote bag on wheels while trying to shield her face against brisk 30 degree winds that were hitting them head on.

She wore a leather jacket with jeans and black boots. Her pants weren't too tight, but her curves were on display. Marquis took advantage of the opportunity to check out her backside, and then he noticed her looking back at him.

He thought he was busted, but she smiled and said, "How was your ride, Coach? You enjoying your time with Bridgette?"

She giggled, knowing the woman had talked his ears off. Nya wore a knitted stocking cap with most of her hair concealed beneath it.

"It would've been better if you sat up front with me."

Marquis knew that was a bold move. He had never flirted with her directly, but that comment could be taken as such. He worried that with the season technically over, he and Nya were on borrowed time. A loss in the playoffs would mean sudden death, not just for the team, but for any hope

Marquis had of initiating a conversation that would lead to him seeing her outside of school.

She appeared startled by the comment, but not offended. She looked around, gauging how close the nearest parent or student was. The rest of the team wasn't far away. But with the wind blowing and everyone focused on getting out of the elements, Nya felt safe enough to look back and ask, "Oh yeah. And why is that, Coach?"

He didn't know the type of response he expected, but he didn't think she'd match his boldness with boldness of her own. "I don't know," he replied.

He grinned, hoping to make his comment sound suggestive, but it didn't work. Nya smirked and shook her head.

"You gotta do better than that."

Marquis sucked air between his teeth. Was she flirting back? He couldn't be sure. And he still couldn't think of a snappy come back. Dammit, this was his chance! But she took all of his game away, made him feel like a little–

"How old are you?" she asked. "About twenty-five, twenty-six?"

She was reading his mind. He felt totally exposed. He nodded. "Yeah."

"Yeah," she repeated. "That's about right."

She faced forward again, and that was the end of their second *moment*. If Marquis had to call it, he'd say things didn't go well for him. His pickup line fell flat, and he couldn't match her wit, which prompted her to point out their age difference.

He didn't know how old she was, but Lisa was 18. Although she didn't look older than 35, Nya may have been in her late thirties or even early forties. If so, she'd found the fountain of youth.

Whatever their age difference, Marquis didn't think she had totally blown him off. Before she turned away, he thought her smile was beckoning. Teasing. He understood that he was dealing with a mature woman. He had to display his own maturity, or he wouldn't stand a chance.

• • • • • •

The team got a chance to check out most of the Honey Grove versus Collinsville game before they headed to the locker room to get ready for their match. Marquis had heard many pep talks over the years, and he'd given quite a few as well. Each one was different. As he looked upon his squad of twelve, all of them dressed and anxious, their muscles primed for battle, he smiled.

"Which one of you thought we would make it to the playoffs?" he asked. "Not me. The first time I saw y'all practice – I remember it, because a lot of parents showed up, and they were making so much noise in the stands..." He chuckled. Most of the girls did, too.

"The first time I saw y'all practice," he continued. "I didn't think we'd win half our games, let alone make it to this coliseum, on this day for this purpose. And yes, it can all end today. If we lose this game, we're out. Everything we worked for will be over just like *that*," he said with a snap of his fingers.

"But I wouldn't hold my head down on the ride home. Because just to make it this far is *huge*. They threw us a *parade!*" Everyone's eyes twinkled at the memory. "You've made your parents very proud, and your school, and your teammates and *me...*"

He shook his head thoughtfully. "I suppose you've made me as proud as any coach ever was. With that being said, I do expect us to win this game. If we're losing by halftime, you'll see me in a totally different mood than I'm in right now."

The girls smiled knowingly.

"But for now," Marquis said, "let's get out there and have some fun! Muenster ain't got *nothing* on you. Bring it in! I want teamwork on three!"

The girls rushed forward and placed their hands over his.

"One, two, three."

"TEAMWORK!"

"Alight! Let's get 'em! *Let me hear you, Grizzlies!*"

The ferocious roar of a dozen Lady Grizzlies filled the locker room and rumbled down the tunnel as the girls rushed towards their destiny.

● ● ● ● ● ●

Finley High handily defeated the Muenster Yellow Jackets 60-39. They advanced to the area finals, which would take place at the Will Rogers Coliseum next Friday and Saturday. Lisa led all scorers with 18 points. Tricia was not far behind with 15. The confident center impressed her coach with 10 rebounds and a clumsy hook shot that scored and drew a foul.

"Did you see my *Kareem*?" she asked as they boarded the bus after the tournament. *"Did you see me, Coach*? You see me Kareem?"

"Is *that* what that was?" he asked with a chuckle.

"Aww, Coach! Don't hate."

"It went in," he said. "I ain't mad at ya!"

● ● ● ● ● ●

On Wednesday the following week, Marquis prepared his squad for Whitney Young High, the team they'd be facing in the area finals. Based on his research, Finley High would face their biggest challenge of the season that Friday. Whitney had a better overall record, and almost half of their games were blowout victories.

He drilled the girls so hard that day, half of them looked like they wouldn't return, including a couple of starters. But they all did. On Thursday they had a light practice and watched the video from their first playoff victory. The film showed a lot of awesome play from the Grizzlies, but their Coach pointed out plenty of areas they could improve on.

On Friday Whitney Young proved to be as formidable as Marquis expected. Their point guard, a junior by the name of Shauntae Huguley, shredded the Grizzlies' defense early and often. She was shorter than Lisa and quicker on her feet. After getting burned for three shots in a row, Marquis ordered a zone defense. But Shauntae was just as good at penetrating and dishing the ball out to one of their guards.

Marquis was shocked to see his players react so slowly. The Grizzlies were unsure of themselves, stumbling over their own feet. Marquis called two timeouts to try to get their heads right. The only bright spot was Tricia, their center, who outweighed Whitney's center by twenty pounds. When they did manage to get the ball down to her, Tricia made half her shots.

At halftime the Grizzlies were trailing by twelve points. No one who watched the game from the beginning would bet on Finley High. Their glorious season had come to an end. Marquis sensed this, but he was not willing to give up on their fairytale just yet. They had come so far. But his girls were playing so poorly! He was beyond frustrated. He felt like they'd forgotten everything he had taught them.

The team sat before him on the benches in the locker room. Their coach paced the floor with a frighteningly upset expression. He didn't have a motivational speech. All he had was complaints. He grumbled to himself. His eyes were low and dark. He spun on them suddenly, and yelled.

"You're playing like girls!"

If not for the tragedy that had befallen them, the comment may have been comical. Exasperation got the best of Michele, and she was the first to say what they were all thinking.

"We are girls, Coach."

"Yes, of course you are," Marquis snapped, pacing again. "But you don't have to play like it!" He spun again, glaring at them with wide, determined eyes. "Do you know why people hate girls' basketball?"

The questioned caught them off guard.

"Don't kid yourself," Marquis said. "There are people who hate your sport. And yes, a lot of it has to do with the fact that most girls can't dunk. But more importantly it's because girls don't run as fast or catch as good or shoot as well. The sad thing about that is you can do all of those things *just as good as the boys*, if you gave it your all. *You can*! I can tell by the way some of you are looking at me that you don't believe it. You don't believe in yourself.

"Right now you're not giving it your all. You're out there playing like girls, but I need you to play like *men*! If you wanna win this game, that's what it's gonna take today. All that whining and crying and bitching and fear has to go! Get it out of your system right now! Leave it in this locker room.

"Either that, or you can go on and roll over and call them Daddy and take your spanking. It's up to you! But I'm twenty-six years old, and I'm not taking a spanking! I'm going out fighting, with or without you!"

He stormed out of the locker room wondering how many warriors would follow him. Not surprisingly, all of them did.

In addition to charging the girls with the impossible task of playing like men, Marquis made adjustments on both sides of the court. To stress the Whitney players and fatigue them more quickly, he instructed the girls to initiate a full-court press. Every ball handler was hounded. Their point guard was double-teamed. The press began to show dividends in the third quarter. The Grizzlies got several turnovers by way of steals and errant passes flying out of bounds.

On the offensive side, Marquis ran his offense through Tricia, and she continued to dominate. By the time Whitney opted to double-team her, the schools were tied in the fourth quarter. The pressure on Tricia yielded a few turnovers. But as the game wore on, she managed to kick the ball out to Lisa when the defense collapsed on her.

Nearly every spectator in the building was on their feet when Tricia shot two free-throws with 3.2 seconds left in the game. She tied the score with the first shot and gave Finley High their first lead of the game with the second one.

Whitney was able to inbound the ball cleanly on their next possession. Their fiery point guard raced down the court to the top of the key. Lisa was in her face. She jumped with her. The only thing on Marquis' mind as the girls rose in the air was the command he gave all of his players before the play started: *Don't foul! No matter what, don't foul!*

Shauntae's shot bounced off the rim, and the game clock sounded.

The ref backed away without blowing his whistle.

Finley High advanced to the regional quarter-finals.

● ● ● ● ● ●

Marquis took the team to Mama's Pizza to celebrate their victory. The restaurant staff connected several tables to make one long table for the players and team moms. Nearly everyone was seated when Marquis noticed Nya standing next to the seat directly across from him. She was looking down the table, in search of another spot, but by then it would look awkward if she walked away from an open chair.

She seemed to realize this as well. She looked at Marquis. He gave her a brief smirk. She rolled her eyes slightly and then took the seat across from him. He thought she looked amused. She wore her hair down that night. Marquis didn't think she had mascara on, but her eyelashes were long and full, drawing him into her dark pupils.

Unfortunately he and Nya were surrounded by unsuspecting players and parents. He had to be careful if he spoke to her, and he couldn't get caught staring, which happened to be the two things he wanted the most.

The Grizzlies were hype. The whole restaurant was. Their meal was buffet-style, so people were constantly moving. Except Nya. She only ate one plate. Marquis didn't get up for seconds, either. No one noticed. They also failed to notice the few glances Nya and Marquis dared to float across the table. She knew that he wanted her. Unless she was completely blind, she had to know. And he knew that she was at the very least *interested* in him. He felt she was curious about the possibility.

Their glances could not communicate whether they would agree to pursue the possibility, but Marquis considered this *moment* a positive step in his direction. She looked into his determined eyes and saw him as a man. She looked away, but her eyes returned to his a moment later. His dark orbs remained as bold as a grizzly. The hypnotizing power they exuded made her heart stutter.

And then he looked away, lest anyone notice.

● ● ● ● ● ●

When they returned to the school, it was after sunset. Most of the parents were already there, waiting to take their victorious and pizza-filled child home. But there were always a few girls who had to wait on their rides. Marquis wouldn't leave until they got picked up. Tonight he had to wait with Latavia, Cheri and Tamika.

When a pair of bright headlights pulled into the school's circular driveway, all of the girls checked to see if it was for them. But Marquis recognized Daryl's truck. The sight of it made the hairs stand on his arms. Lisa had already gone home – with her mother. Daryl wasn't breaking any law by driving onto the school's parking lot, but he had no reason to be there. Not on that day, at that hour.

Marquis was seated on the curb with his players. He weighed his options as he rose to his feet. What could this man possibly want? Marquis assumed he came to speak to him. But why? Surely nothing good would come of this.

He waved for Daryl to stop as he approached the vehicle. He wanted to keep whatever Daryl had to say or do away from the girls. Marquis wasn't an exceptionally courageous man, but he knew how to look out for his team. He'd been doing that since the peewee league.

Daryl's hulking Chevy came to a stop, and Marquis crossed in front of the vehicle, heading for the driver's side. His heart knocked uncomfortably. For a brief moment, as he was blinded by the truck's headlights, he wondered if Daryl would stomp his foot on the gas unexpectedly. It was a silly thought, but at the time it didn't seem that far-fetched.

Daryl didn't attempt to get out of the truck, which was good. Marquis didn't think he would be confrontational from a sitting position.

He maintained a safe but neighborly distance away from the vehicle as he looked inside and said, "Hey, what's going on?"

Daryl put the Chevy in park and turned his way. Marquis couldn't decipher his expression. He wasn't happy, that was for sure. Marquis looked back at the girls, wishing there was something he could do to better protect them.

"Congratulations on your win," Daryl told him. "They played a hell of a game. You got 'em in line, Coach."

Marquis doubted if he had come to the school just to tell him that. He nodded. "Thanks." He didn't know if Daryl was at the game. The coliseum was packed. If he was there, he wasn't sitting with Nya, that was for sure.

"Lisa's a force to be reckoned with." Daryl's voice was soft and reflective.

Marquis didn't like the vibes he was getting. Not at all.

"She is," he agreed. "She says she learned everything from you."

"Hmph. She said that?"

"I wouldn't lie about that," Marquis replied.

"Nya, she don't seem to appreciate what I did for Lisa."

"That's not..." Marquis shook his head. "That's not something I wanna talk about. If you got a problem with Nya, you should take it up with her."

"I'm just trying to tell you – well, hell, you probably know what's going on."

"Sir, I don't think–"

"You told her I brought Lisa those shoes," Daryl stated. "Now I can't do that no more. She won't ever let me see her."

Marquis saw so many red flags he couldn't count them all. Why was this happening to him? It was his first year. He was not equipped for this type of family drama.

"Sir, you need to talk to Nya about that. I'm a teacher, and a coach. The stuff you're talking about is way over my head. I'm feeling real uncomfortable right now. This is inappropriate."

"Naw, man. It's not like that," Daryl said with a shake of his head. "I'm not asking you to do anything about it. I'm just talking, man-to-man."

"But–"

"You know a man don't got no rights in a situation like this," Daryl rambled on. "A step-father has *no rights*. If that's not your child, then you're not guaranteed visitation or nothing like that. If she puts you out, after ten years, twenty years – you could've raised all of her kids since they were in

143

diapers, but if she say you can't see them, that's it. That's... That's all I'm saying. It ain't right. That's all."

Marquis didn't point out the fact that Daryl put himself in this situation by behaving in such a way that would cause Nya to turn cold on him. And even more disparaging was the twelve year relationship without the commitment of marriage. Why didn't Daryl ever propose to Nya? Marquis couldn't fathom treating a woman like that.

But his goal was to deescalate, so he told him, "I understand what you're going through. It sounds like a bad situation. But I have to say this again: I'm only a teacher. I can't have this conversation with you. It's not appropriate."

"I get you," Daryl said, growing exasperated himself. "I just..." He sighed. "I just came to tell you congrats on your game, coach. Your season. That other stuff, it's just me talking. Sorry to throw that at you."

"It's alright," Marquis said. "Like I said, I understand what you're going through. I got two kids of my own."

Daryl nodded and gave him a half smile. He put his truck in gear and continued through the circular driveway, past the three girls, and then he exited the parking lot and was gone.

Marquis wasn't sure what to make of the encounter as he watched another vehicle pull into the driveway. This time it was Tamika's mother.

He decided Daryl's *venting* wasn't a problem. It was misdirected and discomforting, but it didn't put anyone at risk. Even if he wanted to complain to his principal, what would he say?

This lonely guy stopped by and cried to me because he can't see his daughter that much – but she's not really his daughter.

Nah. That story was too depressing to share.

CHAPTER FOURTEEN
CHEMISTRY

By chance our eyes
Should meet and smile
Across the plains
On distant peaks
I live for your soft
Murmurs
I'll taste every whisper
Moist and sweet

The next day Marquis picked up his sons bright and early. Paula didn't bring up the court date again, which was fine with him. He hated to argue with her, especially when the stakes were so high.

The twins were excited about their plans to go to the movies. When they got back to Overbrook Meadows, they had an hour to kill before the show started, so Marquis stopped at a nearby shopping center. He spotted a Foot Locker from the main thoroughfare, and he'd been eyeing a new pair of kicks. Maybe he could get something for the twins, too. They grew out of their sneakers as quickly as he and Paula could replace them.

Twenty minutes later the threesome left the store with shopping bags in hand. Before they made it back to his truck, Marquis spied a vision so lovely he hardly believed it was real.

But it was her, stepping out of a Karate studio, of all places. Nya sported black jeans with UGG boots. She wore her hair down. Today's high was 51 degrees, and she opted for a sweater rather than a jacket.

Marquis decided this must be fate, as he led his boys in her direction, one in each hand. Nya didn't notice him as she headed for a Barnes & Noble on the same shopping strip. Marquis had to call out to her.

"Miss Edmonds!"

She turned and looked as startled as he did when he spotted her.

"Coach Berry..."

"Fancy meeting you here," he said, offering a smile.

She stared at him and looked down at the twins before her expression softened. "Small world," she agreed. "Are these your kids?"

"Yep. Carl and Omar."

"Wow. Twins." Her smile was delightful. "How old?"

"Almost five. Y'all say hello to Miss Edmonds."

The boys declined to speak, but their gazes were intense.

Marquis wore a long-sleeved tee that fit him nicely. The contours of his chest and arm muscles made Nya gasp quietly. She stared for longer than she meant to.

"You can call me Nya."

He looked into her eyes and said, "Alright." Her smile made his blood flow faster.

She knelt slightly and asked the boys, "How are you young men doing today?"

They grinned and said, "Fine," almost in unison.

Nya was tickled pink. "You guys are the cutest thing *ever*," she said before rising to her full height.

"Where's Lisa?" Marquis asked, looking around. "Is she with you?"

"Just dropped her off at karate class."

His smile broadened. "I saw you coming out of there. I was wondering if you were the one taking lessons."

She laughed pleasantly. "No. Not hardly."

"I didn't know Lisa went to Karate class."

"Really? I thought she told you everything."

"No. I guess not."

They watched each other for a moment, and then Marquis said, "Well, I don't mean to keep you."

"I'm just going in here to pass the time, until she gets out."

"How long is the class? About an hour?"

"An hour and a half. I'll probably end up going home, if I can't find a good book."

Marquis started to back away, but he wanted this encounter to last longer. He hadn't planned on telling her about Daryl's stunt last night, but this was the perfect opportunity.

"Can we go inside and talk for a moment?" he asked. "Daryl came by the school last night, after y'all left. I talked to him for a minute."

Nya's face was immediately filled with concern. "Yes. Come on, let's, go in here."

She led the way inside the bookstore.

● ● ● ● ● ●

Marquis was surprised to find Barnes & Noble filled with soccer moms and kids of all ages. They went to the children's area and caught the tail-end of a puppet show. Marquis parked the twins with fifteen other little ones who had gathered to watch. He and Nya found a table and chairs nearby.

He was able to keep an eye on the boys while he told her about Daryl's visit. He didn't think it was a big deal, but Nya was ready to move on to phase two.

"Do you think I should get a restraining order?"

147

He shook his head slightly. "I don't think so. Why? Do you think he's dangerous?"

"No," she said right away. "But I told him not to come to the school."

"But he didn't come to see Lisa. Supposedly he came to congratulate me."

"And he decided to complain about me..."

"I don't know why he picked me for that. I didn't like it, but it's not illegal. I guess if you feel unsafe around him, you should definitely get a restraining order. Don't hesitate."

She thought for a moment. "No, it's not that. But I don't like the idea of him talking to you."

He nodded. "You and me both."

They were quiet for a moment.

"What do you think," she asked, "about what he said?"

Marquis was surprised that she would ask him. "I... That's your daughter. You gotta do what's best for Lisa and yourself. He was acting weird last night. If he's acting like that around Lisa..." He stopped short of advising her one way or the other.

Nya understood. She nodded. "You care a lot about her..." She smiled.

Marquis smiled too. He loved that she was finally looking at him and talking to him. He checked on the twins. They were enthralled in the puppet show.

When his attention returned to Nya, her smile seemed different. It reminded him of the glances they exchanged at the pizza restaurant. He wanted to ask about that night, but he wasn't sure how to broach the subject. He couldn't deny that she was intimidating, possibly because of their age difference.

"Have you baked any cakes lately?" he asked instead.

She got a chuckle out of that.

"What?" he asked, grinning.

"Nothing. Do you like cakes, Coach Berry?"

Hell, yes, I do!

"You can call me Marquis."

She shook her head. "No. That wouldn't be a good idea."

"Why?"

"Because you're my daughter's teacher."

He couldn't tell if that was a rejection. He decided to keep pushing, until she made her position more clear.

"Will you make me a cake?"

His eyes were daring. Hers were surprised and then skeptical.

"Don't you have enough Tupperware piled up in your kitchen? You take a dish home every week."

He laughed at that. It almost sounded like she was jealous. "I didn't ask for any of those," he said. "Yours would be different."

She smacked her lips quietly. It was a slight movement, but it made Marquis want to kiss her. He wasn't sure if he'd get slapped in return, so he kept his lips to himself.

"My cake would be different?" she asked.

She was taunting him now. He liked it.

"Of course it would be."

"Why, because you asked for it?"

"Because I've been wanting it for so long," he said.

He wasn't smiling now, and she knew he wasn't referring to dessert. Marquis thought he had a fifty-fifty chance of getting shut down. But his eyes were confident. Nya had to look away. And then her eyes widened, and she subconsciously leaned away from the table. Marquis followed her gaze, and he did the same.

Oh hell.

"Coach Berry? Nya?"

Small world indeed.

Marquis was surprised to see another Grizzly mom headed their way. It was Tenisha Burns, Rochelle's mother. She had a look on her face like she just caught them in the

midst of a heated affair. Marquis felt that way too. He had
to remind himself that they had done nothing wrong. A
teacher running into a parent on the weekend was not
uncommon. Hell, apparently a teacher might run into *two*
parents at the same time.

"Mrs. Burns. What a surprise!" He stood to shake her
hand.

"Morning, Coach. Hey, Nya."

"Hi." Nya smiled but didn't rise from her seat.

"What you two got going on?" Mrs. Burns asked.

Marquis found the question rather audacious. If he
and Nya *had* met up for a tryst, this woman would have no
problem getting in their business.

"Nothing," he stated. "I brought my boys here for a
puppet show, and I happened to see Miss Edmonds."

"Lisa's at karate practice," Nya offered.

Marquis appreciated how she covered for his lie so
smoothly.

Mrs. Burns looked skeptical, but the puppet show
ended at that moment, and the twins returned to their father.
They were happy and lively and very corroborating.

"Oh, look at them!" Mrs. Burns said. "They look just
like you!" she told Marquis.

He stole a glance at Nya. She looked amused.
Marquis wondered if she was thankful for Mrs. Burns'
interruption or if she hated it, like he did.

"Well, I'll let you get back to whatever y'all were
doing," Mrs. Burns said, looking from Marquis to Nya.

He couldn't believe she was being so messy.

"We're on our way out," he told her. "Which way you
headed? Is Rochelle here with you?"

He proceeded to walk and talk with Mrs. Burns.
Obviously there was nothing going on with him and Nya, if
he gave all of the players' moms equal treatment. He barely
looked back to tell her, "Good seeing you, Miss Edmonds,"

before he and Mrs. Burns rounded a shelf of books and disappeared from sight.

"Good seeing you too, Coach." Nya left her seat in search of a caramel macchiato.

• • • • • •

Marquis had to command himself not to call Nya for the rest of the day. He felt like their flirting had reached a boiling point, but they had both been intentionally ambiguous thus far. Marquis felt that as a man, he should be the one to make the first move. But as a teacher, he had a lot more to lose. If he had read the signs all wrong, Nya could make trouble for him. He could hear the principal lecturing him again.

If a parent gives you their number, you can't call and ask them out on a date, Mr. Berry. How could you not know that? This is disappointing, very inappropriate.

Marquis didn't think Nya would report him, but he'd be the first to admit he didn't know her very well.

At nine o'clock she called him. At first he didn't believe it. He stared at the phone in confusion, thinking he had accidentally called her. But this was definitely an incoming call. He calmed his nerves before he answered.

"Hello?"

"Marquis."

That was the first time she ever used his first name. It sounded so good, he had to sit down.

"Guess what," she said.

Her voice was laced with excitement. Marquis was happy for her, even before hearing her news. "What's up?"

"I got a call from SMU today. They offered Lisa a scholarship! Oh my God, I'm *still* excited. We went out to celebrate."

Marquis was ecstatic. He was on the edge of his seat. "That's awesome! I knew she'd get an offer. She'll get some more, watch."

"I had to call and thank you," Nya said. "This whole season. Everything. It's all because of you!"

"No, it's not. Lisa's a great player. She would've got–"

"Stop it, Marquis. They wouldn't have made it to the playoffs without you."

He loved that she was using his first name. He wanted to ask why the sudden change, but he didn't want to spoil it.

"So I decided to make you that cake you've been asking for," she said. "What kind do you want?"

He chuckled. "You're gonna make me a cake?"

"Yes. You deserve it!"

"I can't believe it."

"Calm down. It's just a cake."

"No, it's not. It's special."

"Don't say that! You're gonna put too much pressure on me."

They never spoke this candidly. Marquis was on cloud nine.

"What's your favorite kind of cake?" she asked.

"Carrot."

"I make one helluva carrot cake!" she boasted. "I'm not giving it to you, though. I'll get Lisa to do it. The other ladies already hate me."

"No they don't. Who?"

"The rest of the boosters," Nya informed him. "They think Lisa's your favorite. They're really gonna think I'm sucking up, if they see me give you a cake."

She laughed, but when Marquis spoke again, he was serious.

"You don't have to give it to me at school."

Her laughter trailed off. "What do you mean?"

"We can meet *outside* of school," he suggested. "I, really want to see you outside of school."

Marquis sighed quietly. Regardless of her decision, he felt strangely liberated. His affections may have been misguided, but he had to own up to them, as a man. And even if he had read her completely wrong, Nya had no choice but to view him as a man. At this moment.

After what felt like an eternity, she finally responded with a hushed, "Okay."

CHAPTER FIFTEEN
TABOO

To hold you close and kiss your lips
So full
So sweet
So soft
So deep
I can't resist those hips

They met Sunday night at a hole in the wall in Arlington. Nya had never been to the restaurant, and she didn't know anyone in the area. He had chicken fried steak. She ordered a burger. After the food arrived, she wished she had gone with the chicken fried steak.

Marquis sported a long-sleeved collared shirt, untucked, with dark-colored jeans. He wore no tee shirt under the shirt. The exposed flesh about his neck and chest was dark and smooth. His face was clean shaven, say a tuft of hair on his chin. Nya thought he looked young. Young, strong and virile. She wondered what he wanted with a woman like her.

She wore a blue dress. It was the first time Marquis had ever seen her in one. Before they were seated, he took a moment to admire her legs, the way the dress clung to her hips and thighs. Her skin was dark and lovely. Her hair was lightly curled. She moved with the grace of a panther. Her eyes were the only thing that revealed her hesitance.

They discussed Lisa and the team for most of the meal.

Nya finally had to ask, "What's going on here?"

"A date," Marquis said. "I hope it's a date."

"You want to go out with me?"

He nodded. "Yes." His eyes were serious.

"But, why? And no, I'm not fishing for compliments. You're a former football player. You were married to a beauty queen. You're rich and famous—"

"I'm not rich," he said with a smile. "You know I'm not rich. I'm a teacher."

"Some people think you're rich."

"I only played half a season. That was worth about one point seven million."

She shrugged. "That would make me rich. I think I'd still have most of it a few years later."

Marquis chuckled. "You still think I'm that person you read about? Young, rich and stupid, beating up folks and what not, blowing money fast..."

"I don't think you're like that," she said. "But I am curious about it."

He nodded. "I don't mind talking about it."

He told her about his marriage and the glorious home he bought his family in Irving.

"When we divorced, she took half the money in the bank – and the house. I bought another house in Overbrook Meadows, and I'm still paying some serious spousal support. That's how you spend two million in three years."

"Why'd you get a divorce?"

Marquis didn't want to think about Paula, but he wanted to be honest. "I was crazy enough to think she really loved me. The sad thing is I probably would've remained in the dark if I didn't get injured. She would've stayed with me, and I would've gone on believing I had the perfect life. But she couldn't take the idea of life without football money. She couldn't fathom it."

No one told you to quit.

Nya saw the hurt in his eyes. He recovered quickly.

"When I found out what I was married to, I lost it for a minute," he admitted. "I did get involved in some wild nights with the boys. We got into three fights. Somebody got hurt in the last one. I didn't touch him, but I was responsible for that. I understand now. The scenario wouldn't have existed if it wasn't for me. When my ex filed for divorce, I didn't fight it. She got everything she wanted, and she still wants more."

Nya needed to hear that, but she felt guilty for making him discuss it. As with most news articles, his story was deeper than the reporters gave him credit for.

"That must be the hardest thing in the world," she said, "losing your family and your dream at the same time."

He nodded.

"And you ended up teaching girls' basketball."

He smiled. She loved his smile. Marquis had a strong jawline, piercing eyes. He could appear downright intimidating, but when he smiled, she saw his youthful spirit.

"Are you going to coach the football team next year?" she asked.

"That rumor has made it all the way to the parents?"

"It's only a rumor?"

"Yes. Coach Mitchell ain't going nowhere."

"Are you going to leave, to coach football somewhere else?"

"That was the plan."

"Your plan has changed?" she asked.

"Isn't that how the movie goes?" he countered. "I fall in love with the girls and want to coach them forever, right?"

She giggled. "Have you?"

"Maybe," he said. And then he wondered if he'd even be in Texas next year. If Paula managed to relocate to Louisiana, he would have to follow suit.

"Tell me about you," he said. "You don't look old enough to have a daughter who's about to go to college."

"Are you trying to flatter me or find out how old I am?"

"Flatter you, of course."

She rolled her eyes playfully. "I had Lisa when I was sixteen. I was bad and fast, growing up as wild as I could."

His eyes widened. "Really? You don't seem like that kind of person at all."

"I've changed a lot in eighteen years."

"You've always been a nurse?"

"No. I was a dropout for a while. Then I got my GED. I worked a bunch of horrible jobs." She considered that. "Some of them were nice. None of them paid well. I decided to go back to school. I've only been a nurse for two years."

He couldn't hide his surprise. "That's so cool."

"What?"

"You went back to school recently? That's awesome."

"It was hard. I was still working. But I had Daryl..." She caught herself but decided to finish the sentence. "He helped a lot." She hated that Daryl came up so easily in casual conversations. She was with him for twelve years. Like it or not, he was a part of her life story. "Sorry."

"No, it's alright," Marquis told her. "Are you and him still talking about getting back together?"

"No," she said right away. "Not at all."

"That's good," he said and gave her one of those flirty smiles she remembered from the pizza restaurant.

She laughed. "Why is that good? And what's up with all of that you were doing at Mama's Pizza?"

"That was you," he said.

"I did it *once*! The rest of the time it was you. You're lucky no one saw you."

"Or you."

She sighed and told him, "You know Lisa would have a fit if she knew I was here with you."

He didn't have a response for that.

"And the boosters," she said. "They'd hate me for sure. Did you see the way Tenisha looked at us yesterday?"

"They would get over it," Marquis said.

She shook her head. "No. I don't think so."

"It's not illegal, for us to see each other."

"No, just taboo."

"Lisa's basketball season will be over in a few weeks," he said. "It might be over next weekend."

She reached over the table and slapped his hand. "Don't say that!"

He laughed.

"Even when the season ends, you have to deal with her in your biology class," Nya reminded him.

"She graduates in June."

"And thanks to you, she'll be going off to *college*," Nya said. She continued to rejoice in that blessing. "So it's settled."

"What's settled?"

"Us dating would end in *disaster*, so we shouldn't entertain it until Lisa goes off to college."

Marquis was taken aback by her wit and humor. At least he hoped it was humor.

"You're kidding, right?"

"Y'all want anything else?" Their bubbly waitress appeared, seemingly out of thin air. She was a little hood, but her service was great.

"No," Nya told her. "That's it for me." She told her date, "Gotta get home. Got work tomorrow."

Marquis didn't want their time to come to an end, but he had to be respectful of the lady's wishes. "Just the check, please," he said to the waitress.

● ● ● ● ● ●

Outside the moon was high and bright in the sky. The temperature was nippy. Nya pulled her jacket on as she exited the restaurant. Marquis helped her with the garment. His hand rested on the small of her back as they stepped through the doors. The contact was slight, but Nya felt a warm tingle. The heat from his touch rushed up and down her spine.

She thought their date went well. Marquis was not as immature as his age would dictate, but she already suspected that. She'd watched him lead the girls' team like a seasoned captain. She would probably never tell him, but it sometimes gave her chills when he shouted directions down the basketball court. The volume and power in his voice was so commanding. So dominant.

She was aware that she left their dating status in limbo. He didn't seem like he was willing to wait until Lisa went to college. Nya wasn't serious about that, but she didn't have an easy answer for their dilemma. She sensed Marquis was about to further complicate things when he slipped an arm around her waist after she unlocked her car.

Wait.

But he didn't listen, most likely because she didn't issue the warning out loud. She wanted to. But the feel of his hand on her body was startling. She couldn't find her voice. He wrapped his other arm around her. She definitely wanted to protest then. The boy was ten years younger than her. She couldn't let him dictate – whatever it was they were doing. And what on earth were they doing?

Lisa's gonna kill me, she thought as he drew her into his embrace and kissed her so softly, her heart blossomed for him like a blood red rose. She felt it. She felt his large hands caress her back as he deepened the kiss. She lost her breath when he sucked her bottom lip. His grip on her body tightened when she kissed him back.

With her eyes closed, she swam in the moment. Floated weightlessly. She relished his intimacy, his smell, the yearning he conveyed through his touch and his lips. She rocked back on her heels. She felt him support her, and then she felt her backside come in contact with her car. *Oh thank you.* She needed the support of the half-ton vehicle.

Marquis continued to press forward until he pinned her against it. She felt his hard chest against hers. The contact awakened her nipples, until they were hard and bulbous. He stepped closer until there was no space between their hips. His hand slid down her side, caressing her body along the way. A soft moan escaped her lips. Her legs weakened. She felt her clitoris spring to life, and her eyes flashed open.

"Wait."

She said it out loud this time. She was certain of it. Marquis' mouth backed away from hers, but the rest of his body remained hard and tight against her. It was cold outside, but he was hot. Her whole body shuddered. She knew he felt it.

"This doesn't feel like waiting," she breathed.

Their faces were very close. Her breath tasted like a paradise of uncertainty.

"I'm worried I'll never see you again, like this," he said. His voice was hushed yet bass filled. He took a deep breath. Nya felt his powerful chest fill with oxygen. "I don't want to regret not kissing you," he told her.

"This is more than a kiss, Marquis."

"Forgive me," he said, but he didn't unhand her. "If you tell me you'll see me again, I'll feel better about letting you go."

Nya found those terms outrageous. She couldn't make a rational decision while in such a compromising position.

He kissed her again, and her clitoris began to pulsate. She'd be reduced to a puddle of quivering flesh if she didn't give in to him.

"Okay."

"Okay?"

"Yes, Marquis."

He backed away from her. His hands were the last to go. He reluctantly released his grip on her hips. Nya's body wailed with grief the moment they lost contact. The heat from his touch continued to radiate through her chest.

"You're a beauty queen," he told her.

And she was, especially with her lips slightly swollen from their kisses. She wasn't a dainty princess like his ex-wife, but she was a queen, undeniably, glimmering and regal.

"You be careful," he said. He stood watch until she was safely inside her car.

Nya felt her wetness with every move. She felt her walls clench impatiently, for him. She felt him standing between her legs.

It took a bit of concentration, but she managed to make it out of the parking lot without hitting any of the other vehicles.

● ● ● ● ● ●

She called him before she went to bed.

"I forgot to give you your cake."

"Yeah, you did. Are you going to bring it tomorrow?"

"Certainly not. I'll take it to work with me and let my coworkers have it."

He chuckled. "You called to say you're giving my cake away?"

"No, I called to say that *you* forgot it, so you wouldn't think I didn't make it"

"Oh. Thanks for making me a cake – that I'll never taste."

"Thanks for dinner."

"You're welcome. When can I see you again?"

"I'm sure I'll see you at the game on Friday."

"Okay. But I was thinking–"

"Goodnight, Coach."

He grinned. "Alright. Goodnight, Nya."

CHAPTER SIXTEEN
ACTING UP

Marquis had a great day at school on Monday and Tuesday. Their next game would be the regional quarter finals at Abilene Christian University. Overall he only gave his girls a 50/50 chance of winning. But they were confident, and they believed him when he said they could beat James Monroe High.

"They got nothing on you," he told them. "As long as y'all stick to the game plan, we'll keep marching on. We might be able to win the whole thing. What do y'all think about that?"

The girls' eyes danced at the thought of taking home a state championship trophy. It would provide them with a lifetime of bragging rights. And more scholarship offers would roll in for other members of the team.

When Marquis shut practice down on Tuesday, he was surprised to see Nya waiting in the gym. She usually only popped in to let him know she was picking up Lisa. He was careful not to pay her any extra attention, but she crossed the court and headed in his direction.

She wore her blue scrubs, so he knew she had worked that day. He thought she looked more tired than usual, or maybe stressed. Whatever the case, Marquis didn't like to see her that way. He hoped she wasn't upset about something he'd done.

When she was within a few feet, she stopped and looked around, wondering how many parents were watching them. Marquis worried about that as well, but he didn't think anyone was paying them any attention.

"What's wrong?"

"It's Daryl," Nya said, speaking in a hushed tone. "He came to my job today. I had to file a police report. I'm getting a restraining order."

Marquis' mouth fell open. "What? What happened?"

"He showed up on my unit." She folded her arms over her body and shuddered. "Came right to the nurses' station. I couldn't believe it. I walked him down the hall, asking what the hell he wanted. And he, *flipped out*. I never seen him like that. He didn't care where we were or who was watching."

"What did he say?" Marquis features were filled with concern.

"He complained about me pushing him out of Lisa's life," she reported. "The same stuff he talked to you about. But then he started accusing me of seeing..." She looked around again and lowered her voice another decibel before she said, "*You...*"

Marquis eyes widened. "What?"

"I don't know why he said that. I figured he was being his normal, jealous self. He used to accuse me of things like that all the time, any man he saw me talking to. But I don't know why he mentioned you. He said he knew it for a fact."

Marquis fought to control his temper. When he spoke to Daryl last week, he was sympathetic about his situation. Now he wondered if the angry man was stalking them.

"Did, did he follow us?"

"I don't know," Nya said. "I don't think so."

"How would he..." Marquis trailed off when he saw another parent approaching them. It was Ramona Bearfield, Cheri's mom.

"Hey, Coach Berry!"

He forced himself to smile at her. "Hi, Mrs. Bearfield. How you been?"

"Fine," she said. "Can't wait till Friday! We gon' whoop up on Monroe!"

"No doubt," he agreed and held his smile until she turned away. When he returned his attention to Nya, the look in her eyes made him anxious to do something to help her, to protect her. "Did he leave the hospital when you asked him to?"

She shook her head. "No. Not until I told him I was calling security. I did call them, and they said he had left already. If he ever comes back, they won't let him up to my unit. I went to the courthouse and filed for a restraining order."

Marquis nodded. "That's good. When you get it, you need to bring a copy to school and leave it in the office."

"I will," Nya said. "But I wanted to tell you what was going on, in case he came here again and tried to talk to you. I'm sorry about all of this," she said. Her eyes were pained. "I didn't want you to get dragged into my problems."

Marquis frowned. He wondered how he got dragged into this as well. "I don't think he'll come up here again."

"If he does, you should call the police," Nya said.

Before he could respond, they noticed Lisa and a few other girls had emerged from the locker room. Lisa walked to them with a smile that gradually faded as she tried to read their expressions.

"Hi, Mama. What's going on?"

"Come on. I'll talk to you in the car," Nya said and led her towards the exit.

"Bye, Coach," Lisa said before following her.

Marquis waved. His expression remained reflective and concerned.

● ● ● ● ● ●

165

During the drive home, Nya told her daughter about Daryl's latest stunt. She did not tell her about the accusation involving Marquis, because she wouldn't have been able to lie to her if Lisa asked if it was true. When she was done talking, Lisa looked as spooked and worried as Nya felt.

"I had to file a police report."

Lisa's eyes widened.

"I had to," Nya told her. "It's the first step in getting a restraining order."

The girl looked even more troubled.

"Talk to me," Nya said. She reached and took hold of her hand while she drove. "Tell me what you're feeling."

Lisa's eyes glossed over, and gradually the tears began to spill.

"I don't know, Mama," she murmured. "I don't know what to think."

Nya squeezed her hand. "I know this is hard. I didn't want to do that. But things are getting out of hand. I don't know why he's acting like this."

"Is it, is it because you won't let him see me?"

Nya nodded. She sniffled and found her eyes watery as well. "Yeah. That's part of it. But he's still accusing me of being with other people. He doesn't like the idea that we're not together."

"You told Coach Berry? Is that what y'all were talking about?"

"Yeah," Nya said. "I had to tell him, because I don't want Daryl to come to the school anymore. I don't think he should come to your games, either..."

She knew that was a hard pill to swallow. Lisa's sobs progressed until her thin frame was racked with mild shudders.

"Maybe, maybe I can talk to him," she offered.

Nya shook her head. "I can't let that happen, baby. Not right now. I don't trust him."

"He won't hurt me," Lisa assured her. "If he's doing this because he can't see me, I can, maybe I can make it better."

"That's not your place." Nya wiped the tears from her eyes. Her voice was drenched with compassion. "This is between me and him, baby."

"But, Mama..."

Nya shook her head as she stopped at a red light. She turned and stared into her daughter's woeful eyes. "Lisa, you have to trust me on this. I know you're an adult, but this problem is bigger than you. It's good that you care about Daryl. But as you get older and move out into the world, you have to understand when a man has become a problem.

"Right now Daryl is a problem. I don't know what he'll do next. I'm worried about my safety, and I'm worried about yours. I don't want you to talk to him. I don't want you to listen to his side of the story. If he calls, you need to tell him you can't talk right now. If he calls back, then I'll block the number.

"You are not a pawn in whatever game Daryl's trying to play," Nya said. Her voice was stronger now. "You're my daughter, and you're my only priority. I want Daryl to get better. Lord knows I do. But I care about you ten times more. Promise me you won't talk to him until I say it's okay."

"Okay," Lisa said. "I promise."

Nya felt like she was being honest. At this point, she had no choice but to believe her. The light turned green, and they got moving again.

● ● ● ● ● ●

Marquis was on edge as he locked up the gym that night. Since speaking with Nya, he felt an underlying pulse of dread with each one of his heartbeats.

Practice ran from four to six o'clock. It was still light outside when he made it to his truck at 6:30. He paused before entering his vehicle. He looked around, unable to shake an unsettling feeling that he was being watched. But the faculty parking lot was mostly deserted at that hour. There were only two cars left, and he recognized them both. Daryl's truck was nowhere in the vicinity.

Marquis tried to shake off his uneasy feeling as he got behind the wheel of his own pickup. When he started it up, the Ford was quick to remind him that he was low on gas. He knew this already because he got the same warning that morning. He was too busy to stop then, but he had time now.

He didn't notice anyone following him when he left the school. But when he pulled into the parking lot of a Quik Trip five miles down the road, he spotted a familiar Chevy in his rearview mirror.

What the hell?...

A horde of goose bumps sprouted on his forearms. Initially he was freaked out, but Marquis managed to calm himself as he pulled to a stop in front of the pumps. The gas station was heavily populated, so it was doubtful Daryl would try anything stupid there. And it was still light outside. The sun was starting to creep behind a picturesque, pastel horizon in the west, but it hadn't given way to the moon just yet.

Marquis exited his vehicle casually and paid for his gas with a credit card. While he pumped, he looked around the station and saw Daryl parked off to the side, near the air and water pumps. He had backed his truck in, presumably so he could keep an eye on Marquis. They were too far away to read each other's expression. Plus Daryl hadn't exited his vehicle, and his face was concealed behind a glare on his truck's windshield.

Marquis was not a fretful man. Gradually he became more angry rather than frightened by Daryl's intrusion into his life. Who did this asshole think he was, and what was his goal? He considered calling the police but was reluctant to do so without a specific threat to report.

Marquis felt like he may be making the wrong move as he stepped around his truck and walked in Daryl's direction. But he wasn't the 140 pound nurse this creep was accustomed to bullying. He was a bruiser, a workhorse who once ran over bear-sized men for a living. If intimidation was Daryl's aim, he had picked the wrong cowboy.

As he drew nearer, he saw that Daryl's window was rolled down. Marquis felt each one of his steady heartbeats as he approached the open window.

"What's going on?" He took a deep breath, causing his nostrils to flare.

Daryl nodded. He looked him in the eyes. "Evening, Coach."

Marquis didn't think he looked angry. He couldn't tell if the man had been drinking. Daryl didn't have his radio on, but he kept his truck running. The two men stared at each other for over ten seconds.

"Something I can do for you?" Marquis finally asked. His muscles were primed for action, but he had no intention of getting physical. He watched Daryl's eyes, and he also watched his arms. His hands were out of view. Marquis began to wonder if Daryl had a weapon. If so, he would have little chance of reacting in time.

Daryl shook his head, in response to his question.

Marquis' eyes narrowed. "Well, what you following me around for, if you don't want nothing?"

"Who said I was following you?"

Marquis' head tilted slowly to the side. "I just saw you follow me to this gas station. And you're parked over here watching me."

Daryl continued to shake his head. "You got it all wrong, Coach. I came to get some gas myself. This here's a coincidence."

Marquis noticed he slurred the word *coincidence*. He focused on his eyes and was pretty sure Daryl had been drinking.

Why me? Marquis wondered. *I don't need this shit.*

"I notice you didn't get any gas," he said.

Daryl's eyes moved to his truck's dashboard and then slowly back to Marquis.

"Funny thing about that, Coach. My tank's full. I don't need no gas after all."

Marquis sighed loudly and rubbed a spot of tension in the middle of his forehead. "Okay, so why are you sitting here, if you don't need any gas?"

"Free world," Daryl said with a shrug. "You don't own this parking lot."

Marquis' frown intensified. If he wasn't a teacher, he might have considered trying to knock some sense into the man. "Listen," he said, "we're both grown. I think we can figure this out, whatever your problem is. I know you're following me, and I got a problem with it. If it's something you want to say, then spit it out. Otherwise you need to go on about your business."

Daryl grinned, which was not among the reactions Marquis expected.

"You getting mad, boy?"

Daryl looked to be five years older than Nya, which made him fifteen years Marquis' senior. He knew the *boy* comment was meant to disrespect him and piss him off, but he didn't fall for it.

"Get off my back, or I'm calling the police," he said. He turned and headed back to his truck.

"I'm not following you!" Daryl yelled.

"Whatever," Marquis replied with a wave of his hand. "You heard what I said."

"You and Nya got something going on?"

That comment stopped him in his tracks. Marquis felt his temper rising again. He worked to suppress it as he turned and stepped towards Daryl's truck again. When he was close enough to be heard without raising his voice, he said, "What's it to you?"

The question sounded both threatening and confrontational, which was what he wanted. His posture conveyed the same message. He would never attack Daryl, but he decided that he could defend himself if Nya's ex wanted to take it there.

He wanted Daryl to speak his mind and get everything off his chest. He would rather take the brunt of his frustration, rather than worry that he would continue to harass Nya.

But Daryl chuckled, rather than become irate. He didn't respond to the question. Marquis waited a few seconds and then blew him off again.

"You ain't about shit." He disrespected him further by turning his back on him and walking casually to his own truck.

When he got behind the wheel, Marquis glared at Daryl as he started it up. He then rolled out of the parking lot without incident.

But the bastard continued to follow him. Marquis couldn't believe it. He watched his rearview mirror like there was a wild bear chasing him.

"*What the hell?*" he muttered under his breath.

At that point there were two things abundantly clear about his predicament. First, Daryl was an idiot. And second, Marquis needed a restraining order as much as Nya did. According to her, the process would start with him filing a police report. Marquis planned to do that as soon as he got home. But in the meantime, what would he do about the goblin on his bumper?

Did he expect to follow Marquis all the way to his house, so he could stalk and harass him on his home turf? Daryl had to be out of his rabid mind, if he thought Marquis would lead him to his doorstep.

If he was older, or maybe a more experienced teacher, Marquis would've realized this situation had already gone way past his control. Any attempt to handle it himself would surely end in disaster. But Marquis was only twenty-six, and he barely had six months of teaching under his belt. He considered himself a grown, capable individual. It wasn't in his nature to run and tell.

Later he would realize this was the arrogance of youth. But in the heat of the moment, Marquis' annoyance pushed him to make a fateful decision: He turned into the next driveway; it was a heating and AC business that was closed for the day. He exited his truck and waited for Nya's ex to turn in behind him.

Daryl didn't disappoint. His Chevy rolled to a squeaky stop behind Marquis' pickup. He opened his door and stepped out of his vehicle as well.

Marquis stopped in his tracks. He expected Daryl to produce a weapon for sure this time. But Nya's ex-boyfriend was empty handed. He grunted as he stepped in Marquis' direction. Actually *staggered* was a more accurate way to describe it. It took Marquis only one second to determine Daryl was definitely drunk, and he posed no threat at all.

He relaxed his muscles and took a step back. He was irritated with this man for pestering him, but Marquis had a fair amount of empathy. Despite everything that had occurred, he tried to understand what Daryl was going through.

"Alright, man," he told him. "You need to calm your drunk ass down, before somebody gets hurt."

"Who gon' hurt me?" Daryl said as he marched forward. "You? You gon' hurt me, boy?"

Nya's ex-boyfriend was a big guy, bigger than Marquis, but not as toned. Back when he played college football, Marquis would describe players this size as *corn-fed*. But speed was on his side. Marquis knew he could run a full circle around him in the time it took Daryl to throw a punch.

But he hoped it wouldn't come to that. Fighting a parent was a worst case scenario, even if Daryl wasn't technically the parent of any Finley High students. Marquis began to back away.

"No, I don't want any problems," he said. He looked around for a pedestrian or even a hobo. He hoped there was someone around who could intervene. Failing that, he'd settle for a couple of girl scouts who could at least *witness* what was happening and vouch for him later.

"You're drunk, Daryl. You need to go home."

The lummox continued to stalk him. Marquis looked back and then changed the course of his backpedaling. The last thing he needed was to stumble over a curb and let the bull get on top of him.

"You gon' hurt me?" Daryl asked again.

"No one's gonna hurt you," Marquis told him. He held his hands up, to show how passive he was. "Let's just get in our trucks and go home. I won't call the police or nothing."

"You messing with my woman?" Daryl asked, still coming.

"No. I'm not. I don't know anything about Miss. Edmonds. You got the wrong idea."

"*You lying!*"

Marquis didn't know if he had concrete proof of that, but it didn't matter. The important thing was Daryl punctuated his statement with a punch that was very slow and telegraphed. Although Marquis easily dodged it, his eyes filled with panic. If Daryl was stupid enough to throw a punch at a teacher, this shocking encounter wouldn't end until one of them got hurt.

"You told Nya I brought those shoes," Daryl accused. "Now I can't see Lisa no more!"

"No I didn't. I didn't have nothing to do with that."

173

"I talked to you!" Daryl spat. "You said you was cool. You was on *my* side!"

"Man, you tripping," Marquis said. He continued to back away from him. "Let's just–"

Daryl lowered his head and charged at full speed. Given his inebriated state, Marquis didn't think he could move that quickly. He managed to side-step him, but Daryl spread his arms, reaching blindly. Marquis had to push him away with both hands. He winced as the big man went tumbling to the pavement.

"Stop it, Daryl! You gon' hurt yourself!"

The bull scrambled to his feet and looked around indignantly until his eyes found Marquis.

"Kick your ass!" Daryl grumbled, and he charged again. This time he threw a bevy of haymakers as he lunged forward.

Marquis dodged all of the punches, but the last one came so close to hitting him, he felt the wind blow by his cheek. Genuine fear struck him for the first time since this encounter began. He knew that if the punch had landed, he would've been in trouble; either knocked out or dazed long enough for Daryl to get the upper hand.

And then what? Would the drunken fool pummel him to death? Marquis didn't want to believe it, but there was no rationale behind Daryl's hate-filled eyes.

"*Dammit, stop!*" Marquis growled behind his clenched teeth.

Again he looked around for someone, *anyone* to help him. There was no one on foot, but the road had a steady flow of traffic. As a last resort, he waved at the cars speeding by, hoping one of them would stop long enough to offer assistance.

"Help!" he shouted. "*Somebody help!*"

Egged-on by what he assumed was girlish terror, Daryl closed the distance between them. Now he was grinning. His shirt was soiled from his tumble on the concrete, but he hadn't learned his lesson.

"Ain't nobody gon' help you!"

This time the big man came with a burst of speed that caught Marquis off guard. He managed to evade him, but he tripped Daryl up in the process. Marquis was horrified to see his antagonizer stumble towards the pavement, almost in slow motion. He was headed straight for a parking block. Marquis tried to catch him before impact, but he was too late.

Daryl's face collided with the unyielding concrete. The collision was so hard, it sounded off like someone hit a homerun. Marquis cringed, and then he rushed to the fallen man's side. Daryl lay motionless.

"*Aw shit*," Marquis muttered.

Daryl was breathing, deep, heavy breaths. Gradually he began to snore roughly. Marquis rolled him onto his side. The sight of Daryl's injury made the contents of his stomach bubble. The man had a three-inch cut that ran from his forehead to the bridge of his nose. It was already starting to swell as it squirted blood profusely.

"*Shit! Shit!*" Marquis shouted. He rose to his feet and began to pace back and forth. "*You goddamned fool!*" he yelled at the unconscious body.

He had half a mind to leave him there. But with his luck, Daryl would vomit and choke on it, which would make things exponentially worse. Marquis continued to curse his dumb luck and his foolish pride as he dug his phone from his pocket and dialed 911.

CHAPTER SEVENTEEN
REMINISCENT

I was blinded by the signs
All warnings forgotten
And I've gained no deep visions
No keen insight
There's division. There's pressure
There's tension
Handcuffs and detention
This calamity is passionately blameless
I'm tasteless
With each breath I taste death
I'm aimless
I'm wasted

Two policemen arrived at the scene, in addition to an ambulance. Daryl was still out of it when they got there. Fearing possible neck injuries, the paramedics strapped him to a spine board before moving him to a stretcher. Marquis felt sick to his stomach and supremely guilty as he watched them work. Daryl's face was a bloody mess. It looked like he took a tomahawk to the face, rather than a parking block.

The cops were friendly enough. They took Marquis' statement and didn't request that he come downtown for a formal interview.

"There should be a police report on him already," he told the officers. "He went to his ex-girlfriend's job today and started a scene. He's been stalking her, too."

He gave them Nya's information.

"Why is he coming after you?" the cop asked.

"I have no idea," Marquis said. "I'm coaching his step-daughter, and somehow I got dragged into their domestic dispute. He thinks I'm coming between him and his family, but that's crazy. I'm just a teacher."

"He's drunk," the cop commented. "I smell it on him. And there's an open container in his truck."

"You didn't throw any punches *at all*?" the second cop asked.

"I did not throw a punch," Marquis insisted. "I was mad at him for following me, but I didn't want to fight him, especially when I saw that he'd been drinking. I ducked and dodged, and then I pushed him down. I may have tripped him. That's it."

The policeman looked back at the ambulance. When his eyes returned to Marquis, he didn't try to hide his doubt.

"He's pretty messed up," he noticed. "Looks like he got whooped up on pretty bad." He checked out Marquis' muscular physique, thinking he looked like the kind of guy who would do something like this.

"I didn't throw any punches at that man," Marquis asserted. He presented his fists, to show them there were no cuts or bruises. "I swear I didn't hit him."

"That's fine," the first cop said. "We got your information. If something comes of this, we know how to get in contact with you."

"Alright." Marquis was happy they were going to let him go home.

"Think your girls are gonna win this Friday?" the policeman asked as he walked away.

"Yep." Marquis spoke mechanically. "Sure do."

"Go Grizzlies!" the cop said and then laughed.

His partner continued to watch the coach with a critical expression, as if he felt like they should be arresting somebody.

● ● ● ● ● ●

When he got home and bathed and finally felt clean again, Marquis gave Nya a call.

"Hello?"

"Hey. You busy? Are you somewhere you can talk?"

She was watching TV with Lisa in the den. "Hold on." She retreated to the privacy of her bedroom. If Lisa was suspicious of the telephone call, she didn't show it.

"What's up?"

"Daryl followed me from school today. Things went bad. He's at the hospital."

"What?" Nya was shocked. Her heart sank to the pit of her stomach. "What are you talking about?"

Marquis told her about their encounter. She was near tears when he was done.

"That's *crazy!*" A numbing chill enveloped her whole body. "Why would he do that?"

"He was drinking. His ass was drunk."

"That's no excuse. You didn't do anything to him. Why would he take it out on you?"

"I don't know. I think he really thinks we got something going on. Maybe he did follow us." The thought gave him chills.

"Oh my God, Marquis. *I am so sorry.* I never expected him to do anything that crazy."

"It's not your fault."

"I feel like it is. I feel terrible." She wiped fresh tears from her cheeks. "Are you okay? Is, is he okay?"

"He has a cut on his forehead. He'll need stitches, but I think he'll be alright. I hope he will."

"He's trying to control me," Nya cried. "He's been doing it for so long. I should've left him a long time ago. Are you okay?" she asked again. "He didn't hurt you?"

"He never touched me. He was swinging for the fences, but he was too drunk to do any good."

"Are you gonna get in trouble?" She was biting her nails. She got up to close her bedroom door.

"I don't think so. If I was in trouble, the cops would've taken me downtown. I didn't do nothing. It was self-defense."

Nya prayed he was right about that. "Oh my God, this is crazy. I don't, I don't know if I should tell Lisa about this. It'll probably freak her out even more."

Marquis didn't comment on that. It was her call. He sighed. "I'm gonna get something to eat and get ready for bed. I'm tired. Stressed out." It had been a long day. He left the school more than two hours ago.

Nya wished she could be there to comfort him. Marquis was a good guy. He didn't deserve any of this.

"Alright," she said. "I'm sorry."

"Stop apologizing. You can't blame yourself for him being crazy."

Nya disagreed. She knew that she had brought this trouble to his doorstep.

"Let me know if you hear anything," she said.

"Okay. You too."

● ● ● ● ● ●

At work the next morning, Marquis hoped to put his troubles behind him. But when he walked into his classroom, there was a woman there. She was seated behind his desk, looking over some paperwork.

"Um..." He looked around, thinking he'd entered the wrong room. He was definitely in the right place. "Hi," he told the stranger. "May I help you?"

She seemed a little apprehensive but not surprised to see him. "Hi. Mr. Berry?"

"Yes." Marquis approached his desk with a puzzled look.

"I'm Margie Chavis. I'm a substitute teacher."

"But I didn't call-in."

"I don't know what's going on," she told him. "Mr. Walters asked me to give you this."

She handed him a note that was written on the principal's stationary. It simply read: *Come see me when you get here.*

Marquis looked up from the note, his confusion deeper than before.

"I don't know anything," Mrs. Chavis said, shaking her head.

Marquis didn't bother setting his briefcase down before he left the classroom.

● ● ● ● ● ●

When he got to the office, Marquis felt like a hush took over the room. Even Sophia, the talkative clerk, wore a look of foreboding, rather than the smile she usually greeted him with.

"Mr. Walters is waiting on you," she said the moment they locked eyes.

The other office staff remained silent. Marquis felt his breakfast turn over in his stomach as he stared at Sophia.

"Is everything okay?" he asked her.

She pursed her lips and shrugged.

Marquis sighed as he stepped away from the counter, towards the principal's office on the right.

When he walked in, Mr. Walters didn't rise from his chair. He didn't smile as he said, "Have a seat, Mr. Berry."

Marquis did as he was told. He cleared his throat and tried to remain poised, but he didn't feel confident at all. If the principal went through the trouble of bringing in a substitute, then he didn't plan on Marquis teaching that day.

"Have a little trouble last night?" Mr. Walters asked.

Marquis was slightly relieved to know what this was all about. Last night was certainly a problem, but he had an explanation that would vindicate him.

"Yes, sir. There was an incident last night."

"Tell me about it."

"One of my students, her parents are going through a breakup. The guy, he's not the student's father. It's, it's complicated..."

"Sounds like it," Mr. Walters agreed.

Marquis couldn't tell if he was being facetious or not. "The student's mother," he continued, "her name is Nya. She told me she broke up with her boyfriend. She said he was upset about it. He, I believe he was worried about not being able to spend time with the student. Her name is Lisa."

The principal nodded. He didn't respond like any of this was news to him, but Marquis kept talking. "The boyfriend, Daryl, he's had some issues about not being able to pick Lisa up from school and things like that. At some point he decided I had something to do with it. I don't know why he feels that way."

"So you've had issues with this parent in the past?" Mr. Walters asked.

That question sounded loaded. "No, not until last night," Marquis stated. "Daryl came and talked to me last week, but he wasn't upset. I mean, he wasn't upset with me."

"Did you tell anyone at this school that you were having issues with a parent?" the principal asked.

"Um, no I didn't. But like I said, it wasn't an issue."

"Sounds like it to me. Did the mother tell you she was fearful of Daryl? Did she tell you she had to call the police on him or that she was pursuing a restraining order?"

"She did," Marquis acknowledged. "She told me that last night. All of this came to a head less than an hour after I talked to her yesterday."

"Okay, so what happened last night?"

181

Marquis felt like they were merely going through the motions at this point. It was clear Mr. Walters had already formulated an opinion about all of this.

"Yesterday after practice I went to the gas station," Marquis stated, "and I saw Daryl following me."

"You got out of your car?"

Marquis knew he'd be chastised for that. "Yes. I had to pump my gas."

"You didn't have enough gas to make it to a police station?"

"I, um, I didn't think to go to a police station."

"That's what I would've done," Mr. Walters told him. "If someone was following me, and I feared for my safety, I would drive to a police station to see if he'd follow me there."

"I did consider that. I don't know why I didn't follow through. I asked him what was going on. He said he wasn't following me, so I got back in my truck and drove off."

"Did he follow you again?"

"He did."

"You didn't lead him to a police station that time, either?"

Marquis shook his head. His nostrils flared. "No, sir."

"Did you call the police on your cellphone? That's what I would've done, if someone was following me."

"I didn't think to do that, either," Marquis said. He struggled to keep his irritation in check.

"Let me guess," the principal said. "You pulled over again and decided to teach him a lesson."

Marquis' eyes widened. "*No, sir.* That's not how it happened. I did pull over, but I didn't want to teach him a lesson. I only wanted to talk to him."

"And at what point did you go from *talking* to whooping his ass?"

Marquis brought a hand up and covered his mouth. "Sir, you've got the wrong information. It didn't happen like that at all. I never hit that man. The police have the report."

"That's not all they have," Mr. Walters informed him. "They also have a warrant for your arrest."

Marquis didn't think he had heard him right. His mouth went completely dry. "What do you mean?"

"Apparently the victim's version of events is *wildly* different from yours," Mr. Walters told him. "Daryl says you attacked him. And the evidence seems to support that. At least the police think so. He went to the hospital with serious injuries, but you walked away from the fight."

"It wasn't a fight." Marquis was nearly frantic now. "Sir, *he's lying*. If he said I hit him, he's lying."

"They wanted to arrest you in your classroom," Mr. Walters said, ignoring his comment. "Police love to embarrass people; handcuff them and drag them out for all to see. I had to pull some strings, but they agreed to wait for you to turn yourself in. You need to go now, or they'll come looking for you."

Marquis was completely floored. He stared at the man like he was speaking French. His eyes were large, his jaw unhinged.

"Mr. Walters," he managed, "you've got to believe me. That man attacked me. I never touched him!"

"When you sat in *that* chair back in August, I told you what the deal was," the principal reminded him. "I told you that you were coming in with a cloud of suspicion hovering over you. I told you a lot of people thought you were a *thug*. They knew about your past, and I was going to have to explain to them why I allowed you to teach at my school. I told you that."

"Yes, but—"

"And now here we are," the principal continued, "halfway through the school year, and you've got a warrant out for your arrest. For *assault*, of all things. That's the same thing you got arrested for in 2013."

"Okay, but—"

"There's no *buts*, Mr. Berry. I trusted you. I gave you a shot, and *you blew it*. You did exactly what people said you would do. I'm very disappointed in you. Now you need to leave this school – *immediately*. Go take care of your legal troubles."

Marquis had heard that his boss could be a hard ass, but he never thought the principal's venom would be directed at him. None of this felt real.

"Mr. Walters, if you'll just let me explain..."

"There's nothing I can do with your explanation, Mr. Berry. You have much bigger problems than me right now. Now please, leave the building, before you get in even more trouble."

Marquis was devastated, but he knew Mr. Walters was only doing his job. He stood and left the room without another word. The clerks all quieted down again as he began his walk of shame out of the office and out of the school.

● ● ● ● ● ●

Rather than go straight to jail, as instructed, Marquis called his big brother. Omar had hundreds of lawyer contacts at the firm he worked for.

"Hey, what's going on?"

"I'm in trouble," Marquis told him. "I got a warrant for my arrest." Delivering that news to his brother *again* made him feel like the biggest fool ever.

"What? What the hell are you talking about?"

"I got into it with a parent last night. He attacked me. Now he's saying *I* attacked him. The principal made me leave the school. He said I have to go turn myself in."

"What the fuck, Marquis? What the hell's wrong with you?"

"It's not my fault, man. I didn't touch him. I swear!" He was so upset, his voice caught on the last word.

"Whatever. Where are you now?"

184

"I'm leaving the school. On my way downtown, I guess."

"Wait. Don't go yet. Hold on."

Marquis was on hold so long, he had to pull over at a 7-11. When Omar finally came back to the line, he told him, "I want you to meet me at a lawyer's office." He gave him an address in Arlington.

"You're coming?" Marquis knew that his brother worked in Killeen, which was nearly three hours away.

"I'm in Dallas today," Omar told him. "I'll probably make it there before you."

"What about the warrant?" Marquis wondered. "I think the police are expecting me to go straight there."

"What are they gonna do, issue *another* warrant? Do what I say. Damn, man. How the hell did you let this happen again?"

Marquis didn't have an answer for that. It didn't matter, because his brother was no longer on the line.

● ● ● ● ● ●

Omar was not at the lawyer's office when Marquis got there. He showed up twenty minutes later. In the meantime Marquis made the acquaintance of an attorney named Delores Branch who seemed very professional and competent. When Omar arrived, the three of them sat in her office, and Marquis retold the story about how he came to be in a parking lot with an angry parent named Daryl.

Much like the principal had done, Omar and his lawyer pointed out all of the mistakes Marquis made last night that ultimately led to Daryl getting injured. Omar's remarks were a lot more aggressive and condemning than Mrs. Branch's. Marquis was already upset. The last thing he needed was Omar getting on his case, but he had no choice but to listen.

Afterwards, the lawyer began to ask questions that Marquis thought were a lot more helpful.

"Do you know if Nya has a restraining order?"

"Not yet. But she said she filed the papers yesterday. I know she has a police report, from when he showed up at her job."

"Daryl never seemed angry with you before?"

"No," Marquis told her. "He was upset. He talked to me about not being able to see Lisa as much as he wanted, but he wasn't mad at me. He was mad at Nya."

"Why do you think he came to speak to you about that situation?"

"I don't know. I'm still not sure why he did that."

"You stopped at a Quik Trip first, when you initially noticed him following you?"

"Yes."

"They should have cameras there," the lawyer said. "So we'll be able to corroborate that. I have the address where Daryl was injured from the police report. I'll check and see if they had cameras there as well. If they do, then we can get this dismissed in a day or so."

Marquis sighed, feeling hopeful for the first time that morning. "Okay. That would be great."

"If there are no cameras," she continued, "it is your word against his. And since he has all of the injuries, this doesn't look good for you. The police are following the same protocol they would in a domestic dispute: If both parties give conflicting statements, they'll usually go by the evidence and side with the one who's injured."

Marquis' optimism was dashed just that quickly.

"As for your warrant," the lawyer said, "I'm afraid you do have to turn yourself in today. Let me find out what your bond is, and hopefully we can do a quick walkthrough."

A walkthrough?

Marquis hung his head in despair. That meant he would be arrested and they'd throw him in jail, at least for a little while.

"Excuse me," the lawyer said as she picked up her phone.

"We're gonna step out and talk for a second," Omar told her.

She nodded.

Omar left his seat and gestured for Marquis to follow him into the hallway.

When they were alone he asked, "Is this *Nya* lady the one you were telling me about, the mother of your star player?"

Marquis did not want to confirm that. But his brother was trying to help him out of a jam. Plus he always had trouble lying to him.

He nodded. "Yeah, but this doesn't have anything to do with whether I like her or not."

Omar shook his head. "Have you gone out with her?"

Marquis sighed and nodded.

"Why would you do that?" his brother wanted to know.

"It's not illegal," Marquis insisted. "We're both grown. I don't see what the problem is."

"Does Daryl know you went out with her?"

Marquis frowned. "He said he did, but I don't think so."

"Why?" Omar asked. "Why do you think he said he knew, if he doesn't really know?"

"Because he was bitching about a lot of stuff. He sounded like he was fishing, hoping I would tell him something."

"Are you listening to yourself right now? Why are you making excuses?"

"I'm not making excuses. I don't need to make an excuse. I wasn't in the wrong, Omar."

"But this never would've happened if you had listened to me. We talked about all of the things that could go wrong if you went after that woman. Didn't I tell you there would be a scandal?"

"That man does not have the right to follow her around and start shit with whoever she's dating. Why aren't you saying anything about that?"

"I don't give a damn what he does," Omar growled. "*You're* my brother." He accented that statement with a stiff finger in Marquis' chest. "I only care about *you*. I told you going after that woman was nothing but trouble. Now look at you. Look what you got yourself into this time. You're about to lose everything – *again*. You think she was worth it?"

Marquis didn't have an immediate answer to that. Omar didn't wait for him to figure it out. He returned to the lawyer's office. Marquis cursed under his breath before he followed him.

● ● ● ● ● ●

The trio left the office a few minutes later. They arrived at the downtown branch of Overbrook Meadows Police Department half an hour after that, and Marquis turned himself in for assault. He knew it would only be a walkthrough, but that knowledge didn't make him feel any better when the police handcuffed him and led him away from his brother.

They took him to a holding cell that was miserably reminiscent of his 2013 arrest. Marquis didn't think he did anything wrong that time, either.

He was only in the cell for about an hour before he was arraigned and allowed to post bail. That hour felt like an eternity. Marquis had a lot of time to think about what his brother had asked him.

Was Nya worth it?

He knew that he may feel differently when he got out of jail. But as he sat on a cold, concrete bench, staring at a toilet with a sink built into it (he'd be damned if he used either), he had to say no, she wasn't worth any of this.

CHAPTER EIGHTEEN
WHERE'S COACH BERRY?

Nya was a bundle of nerves when she went to pick up her daughter after practice. She had the day off, so she was able to follow up on her restraining order against Daryl. And she checked the local hospitals – first to confirm Daryl didn't get checked into Jackson Memorial, and then to find out if the idiot was okay. She couldn't get any information about his condition, but she learned that he'd been discharged from Saint Peters that afternoon.

Nya encountered a crowd of parents and booster moms when she arrived at Finley High. There was still ten minutes left in practice. As she pulled to a stop near the gym's entrance, she noticed the women were animated and upset about something.

Rather than get out of her car and mingle with them, she rolled down her window, hoping to eavesdrop on their conversation. What she heard made the blood drain from her face. Her eyes were wide as she stared at her steering wheel, rather than at the women who were talking. She thought she looked nonchalant, but she was anything but.

"I heard he got arrested," one of the ladies was saying.

"Who told you that?" another asked.

"I got a friend who works in the admin building."

"Why would he get arrested? Your friend couldn't have been talking about Coach Berry."

"Well, where is he then?"

"Hell, I don't know. He could be sick. He could've taken a day off, for all you know."

"He got arrested before," a third woman chipped in.

"When?"

"It was a while back, when he played for the Cowboys."

"Arrested for what?"

"They say he beat somebody up."

"He looks like he could whoop some ass."

"Nuh uhn, girl. You lying."

"No, for real. You can look it up."

"Maybe he had an old warrant that came up. It's probably nothing serious."

"If Coach Berry is in jail, I'll go down there and break him out myself!" That was Bridgette, the woman who had given Marquis a cake, a casserole and a batch of cookies since the season started. "The girls got a game this Friday. They can't play without Coach Berry!"

Nya was sick to her stomach by the time the players began to emerge from the building. When she saw her daughter, Lisa looked to be in the same shape. The Grizzlies' star player took a seat next to her mom and shuddered involuntarily. Nya was shocked to see tears in her eyes.

"Baby, what's wrong?"

"*Coach Berry's not here,*" Lisa cried. "No one knows where he is. They won't tell us nothing!"

"Who coached y'all today?"

"Coach Mitchell. He's the football coach, but he doesn't know anything about basketball. We're gonna lose our next game, Mama! Our season's over!"

Nya unbuckled her seatbelt, so she could lean over and put an arm around her. "Baby, don't say that. I'm sure it'll be alright."

"People are saying he went to *jail*, Mama. They said Coach Berry got arrested."

"I don't think he got arrested," Nya said. "I talked to him last night. He said he was alright."

Lisa was surprised to hear that. "You, you talked to him?"

Nya nodded. "Yeah. I, I know a little bit about what happened..."

• • • • • •

During the ride home, she told her daughter what Marquis said occurred between him and Daryl. As she spoke, Lisa's emotions ranged from depressed to angry to heartbroken and finally miserable again.

"Why would Daryl do that, Mama?"

"Baby, I don't know. I told you he came to my job, and I had to call the police on him. I hate to say it, but I think he's losing it. Coach Berry didn't have anything to do with what's going on between us. He had no reason to follow that man around."

"But why would they arrest Coach, if Daryl started it?" Lisa's tears flowed thick like oil. They pooled on her chin and dripped onto her tee-shirt.

"Baby, I don't have all the answers. I promise, as soon as I do, I'll tell you."

As luck would have it, the ladies got some concrete information the moment they got home. They made it in time to catch the tail-end of the six o'clock news. The sports' anchor, Neil Coulson, was the same reporter who had interviewed Marquis and Lisa when they were on TV. He looked solemn as he delivered the latest news:

"... The police aren't revealing the name of the victim at this time, but according to reports he suffered what police are calling '*serious injuries*' at the hands of Marquis Berry. We're told Berry posted bail shortly after his arrest, so he's a free man tonight. As for whether he'll return to his teaching or coaching position at Finley High School, that remains uncertain.

"Of course this arrest is eerily similar to another incident in 2013, when Berry was arrested following a bar brawl that left one patron seriously injured. Those charges were later dropped, and after a two year hiatus, it appeared Berry was ready for a fresh start.

"If you recall, we had Berry here at the studio a few weeks ago with one of his players from Finley High. Here's what he had to say then..."

The view changed to Marquis and Lisa's pre-recorded interview. Nya and Lisa were standing in the living room staring wide-eyed at the television; both of them too tense to sit down. Nya had a lump in her throat as she watched her daughter and her coach smiling and laughing with the reporter, in what were clearly happier times.

"Why do you think the team is so good this year?" Coulson had asked in the interview. "You remember those old Nike commercials, where they said, '*It's gotta be the shoes!*' Well, a lot of people in Overbrook Meadows are saying, '*It's gotta be the coach!*'"

On TV Marquis laughed politely at the joke. Even as her eyes filled with tears, Nya thought he looked very handsome that day. She remembered when she straightened his tie for him before they started filming. That was the first time she had ever touched him. She recalled how nervous she became when she realized what she was doing, and he smiled at her.

"It's *not* the coach," Marquis said in the interview. "Remember, I just got here. These girls have been playing together for *years*. I wish I could take credit for the magic that's happening right now. But, honestly, I don't think I'm that good. This team was destined to have the season they're having. Take me out of the picture, and I'm sure they'd still be winning."

The shot cut back to Coulson in the newsroom. He paused for a moment to let Marquis' last comment sink in.

"Well, I hope that's the case," he said at length, "because it looks like the girls at Finley High *will* have to continue their season without Coach Berry. This is a sad day for girls' basketball. But, as we all know, the show must go on. The Lady Grizzlies will face the Spartans of Clover Valley this Friday at Abilene Christian University. With or without Coach Berry, this game promises plenty of fireworks. Good night folks."

Lisa hurried to her room with fresh tears in her eyes as they went to commercials.

●●●●●●

Nya retreated to her own room and worked to get her emotions under control before she called Marquis. She could hear the stress in his voice when he answered.

"Hey."

"Hey," she said. "Are you, how are you feeling?"

"Pretty bad," he revealed.

Nya felt so guilty her heart ached. She couldn't stop her tears from falling. "What happened?" Her voice was soft and hopefully comforting. "I saw on the news that you got arrested."

"The *news*?"

She winced. She thought he knew about that already. "Yeah. It was just on."

"Dammit," he breathed. "Here we go again."

"What happened?" she repeated. "I thought everything was okay because it was self-defense, and you didn't hit him..."

"He lied," Marquis growled. "He woke up and told the police I attacked him, like he was totally innocent. It was my word against his at that point. And since he was the one with the bruises, they sided with him."

"Daryl told them that?" Nya didn't have the best opinion of her ex-boyfriend, but she didn't think he would stoop this low.

"Yeah. That's what they said."

"But, but why?" Nya wondered. "Why would he do that?"

"We've been trying to figure that out," Marquis told her. "Our guess is that he wants to get me arrested and fired. He succeeded at that."

Nya's sorrowful eyes widened. *"You got fired?"*

"They're using the word *suspended* for now, but that's where we're headed. If I get convicted of this assault, I won't be back at school. And it could take over a year before this case gets settled."

Nya brought a hand to her face to cover her mouth. She tried to force herself to stop crying, for his sake.

"But why?" she wondered. "Why would Daryl do that to you? He doesn't even know you."

"He sees me as a threat," Marquis guessed. "He thinks I'm interfering with his relationship with Lisa, and I'm interfering with him getting back with you, too."

"But I don't want him back. I told him that."

"Some guys don't ever wanna give up. I'm just glad he didn't shoot me or something. That guy's crazy. And he's hurting. There's no limit to how far people like that will go."

She couldn't believe he was holding it together so well, while she felt like her whole world was crumbling around her.

"This is all my fault," she wailed. *"I'm sorry, Marquis. I'm so sorry."*

"It's okay. It's not your fault."

"Yes it is. How can you be so calm about this?"

"I'm not calm," he said. "It's taking every bit of will power I have to stop from screaming and punching holes in the walls. I wanna find Daryl and strangle the shit out of him, drag him down to the police station and make him tell the truth. I've been here before. I've been in this *exact same spot*. I can't believe it's happening again." He took a deep breath and let it out slowly. "How's Lisa doing? Does she know about any of this?"

"Yeah," Nya said. She wiped the tears from her eyes, but they filled just as quickly. "We watched the news together. Everybody at the school knows something is wrong. The boosters are about to start a riot."

"What did you tell Lisa?" he asked.

"I told her everything – except about us going out."

After a pause he asked, "Are you gonna tell her?"

"I have to," Nya breathed. "If she finds out from anyone but me, she'll hate me forever."

"Tell her to keep her head up," Marquis said. "She has to be strong. The team will depend on her now more than ever."

"Okay," Nya said. She was a mess. She had to pull it together before she talked to her daughter. "I'll talk to you later."

● ● ● ● ● ●

The hallway leading from Nya's bedroom to her daughter's room seemed ten times longer than usual that day. With each step her sense of guilt deepened. She knew she hadn't done anything wrong, but on a moral level, maybe she had. Dating her daughter's teacher felt like dating her best friend's ex. She believed their attraction had cost Marquis everything.

She found Lisa lying on her bed. She was curled up, crying softly, with her favorite pillow squeezed close to her chest. Nya took a seat on the mattress. She didn't know what to say, but she needed to purge very badly. Beating around the bush or trying to work up to the revelation would only drag out the inevitable, so she took a deep breath and got it over with, the same way she used to pull her daughter's Band-Aids off when she was smaller.

"Me and Marquis went out."

Lisa's sobbing came to an immediate stop. She didn't sit up right away, but she opened her eyes and looked in her mother's direction.

"Wh, what?"

"We went out," Nya repeated. "He told me he liked me, and I liked him too. He asked me out on a date, and I went. It was last Sunday. When Daryl came to my job yesterday, he said he knew me and Marquis were dating. I don't know if he really knew that, or if he was just jealous of him. But either way, he was right. Daryl told Marquis that too, when they got into it."

Nya blew out a pent up breath. There. It was over. She told the truth, and there was nothing left to do but wait for a reaction.

Lisa stared at her for a few seconds. The girl looked like a stranger had just sat on her bed. Finally she said, "Are you serious?"

"Yes," Nya said. She didn't feel strong at all, but she made sure her voice and posture was.

"*Why?*" Lisa cried. Her features were set in a scowl.

"I didn't want to at first," Nya told her. "I knew it would upset you."

"Then why'd you do it?"

"Because I..." She wasn't sure how to answer that. She felt like she had made a selfish decision. "Its..." She sighed. "Ultimately the decision didn't have anything to do with you. Marquis and I are both adults."

"But he's my *coach*," Lisa said as she sat up.

"Him being your coach doesn't have anything to do with the fact that we like each other."

"That's not right, Mama," the girl cried. "You could've been with anybody. Why *him*?"

"Lisa, I know you have a romanticized idea about how love and relationships work, but we don't always get to pick and choose like that. When he asked me, I tried to think of every reason why I shouldn't go out with him. But you were the only one that mattered."

"Then why didn't you say no? He went to jail because of you!"

"No." Nya was struggling to convince herself otherwise. She didn't want to go back to that line of thinking. "He went to jail because of *Daryl*."

"But Daryl only did that because you went out with Coach."

"Lisa, I know you're upset. But by that logic, I should never go out with anyone else, because of what Daryl might have to say about it. I'm not gonna let that man ruin my life or run it, either."

"But it didn't have to be *Coach Berry!*"

Tears squirted from her eyes. Lisa's face was already red and puffy from crying so much.

"That's fine," Nya said. She decided to absorb her daughter's pain, rather than push it back at her, even if Lisa was wrong. "I'm sorry I hurt you." She rose to her feet and left the room to give the girl time to process her emotions.

She thought Lisa would be a little better by dinnertime, but when she summoned her, she didn't respond. She went to her room and found her lying in the same position she left her in.

"Dinner's ready."

"I'm not hungry."

Lisa had her back to her. Nya didn't try to establish eye contact.

"You need to eat something, before you go to bed."

"Leave me alone, Mama. I don't wanna talk. I don't wanna eat. I don't want nothing."

Nya took a step towards her but thought better of it. She retreated to her own room and found solace in her bed. She didn't have much of an appetite, either.

In the morning she found her pot of spaghetti cold and forgotten on the stovetop.

CHAPTER NINETEEN
QUARTER FINALS

Nya did not want to go to work on Thursday. After a troubled night's sleep, she managed to convince herself that she and Marquis had done nothing wrong. But Lisa made her second guess herself. She continued to give Nya the silent treatment when she woke her up for school. As a mother, she always put her child's needs above her own. But she didn't do that with Marquis. The aftermath of her decision had affected the whole community.

When she got to the hospital, Nya found that Marquis was a hot topic. The Overbrook Meadows Telegram ran a story about the shamed former football player who could never seem to get right. It seemed like everyone was talking about him, even some of her patients.

The break room on her floor had as many gossips as any other unit. When Nya went there at lunchtime, she found two of her colleagues sitting at the table with the morning paper spread out between them. Their eyes lit up when they saw her. They knew Nya's daughter was the star player on Finley High's team and wanted to know what she had to say about Coach Berry's new scandal.

"Hi, Nya," a seasoned nurse named Gwen called. "What the hell's going on at your daughter's school?"

Nya had dark lines under her eyes from troubled sleep. She put her Rubbermaid container in the microwave and stood next to it while her food heated.

"I don't know any more than what's in the paper," she told them.

"How's your daughter taking this?" the other nurse asked. Her name was Ellen.

"Pretty bad," Nya told her. "About what you'd expect."

"I saw Lisa on the news yesterday," Gwen told her. "They showed a clip from when she did that interview with her coach."

"Yeah," Nya said. "I saw it."

"I heard he got into a fight with one of his student's parents," Gwen said.

"I heard that too," Ellen said. "I heard he was messing around with somebody's mama, and he got into it with the dad."

Nya's mouth hung open. A chill rushed through her chest. "Where'd you hear that?"

"That's what people are saying," Ellen told her.

"I heard it from James in respiratory," Gwen offered.

Nya was stunned by how quickly the rumors were gaining momentum. The newspapers didn't mention anything like that. The smell of her lunch began to fill the room. But her stomach squeezed uncomfortably, and she didn't want it anymore.

"What have you heard?" Gwen asked.

She shook her head absently.

"What are the other parents at Lisa's school saying?" Ellen wanted to know. "I know those booster moms are always gossiping."

Nya almost told her no one was gossiping more than the two of them, but she didn't want to sound defensive. As far as they knew, she was on the outside looking in.

"If I hear anything, I'll let you know," she said and hurried out of the room.

"Wait. What about your food," Ellen called.

"I gotta go to the restroom."

When she got there, she turned the water on and allowed herself to cry for a minute or so. She washed her face and went back to the break room to retrieve her meal. The nurses were still there. They noticed her emotional state and gave each other wary looks.

"What's wrong, honey? Are you worried about what's going to happen to your daughter's team?"

That was mostly true, so Nya ran with it. "Lisa loves her coach. She got a scholarship offer because of him. If they lose tomorrow because he's not there, she'll be devastated."

"It'll be okay," Ellen assured her. "They're not gonna take her scholarship away if they lose. She still made it to the playoffs."

"And it's probably for the best," Gwen added. "If that coach beat up somebody's daddy so he could get his freak on, he doesn't need to be around children..."

• • • • • •

Nya couldn't wait to get home after that, which made the day drag on miserably. Eventually it was time to clock out. She knew she would encounter more gossip when she went to pick Lisa up from practice, but she was surprised by how focused the booster moms now were.

Six of them had congregated outside of the gym when she arrived. Whatever conversation they were engaged in paused when Bridgette saw Nya pull into a parking spot. Bridgette said something to the women, and they all glanced at Nya before resuming their hen party.

Nya frowned, thinking they were just curious about who had pulled up. But a couple of the women looked her way again as she turned off her ignition. Nya's eyes narrowed. There was no doubt they were talking about her. Not only were her ears burning, but her face heated as well.

She considered ignoring them, but the longer she sat there, the more frustrated she became. She didn't deserve this, and neither did Marquis. She got out of her car and walked to them boldly. Every one of them turned and watched her.

"What's going on?" she asked Bridgette.

Bridgette looked around with a snotty expression, as if she couldn't believe Nya had singled her out.

"Why don't you tell *us* what's going on?" she replied. "You're the one with the secrets."

"Oh yeah. And what might that be?" Nya asked, giving back as much attitude as she was getting.

"You can save the innocent routine," Bridgette said with a roll of her eyes. "We know all about you and Coach Berry."

Nya had never liked Bridgette. Not only was the woman loud and obnoxious, but she was jealous and catty. And the way she threw herself at Marquis when he first came to the school was disgusting.

"What do you think you know about me and Coach Berry?"

"What, you gon' lie and say you ain't fucking him?" Bridgette said.

The rest of the hens had eyes as big as quarters. They were eager for the scoop and glad that Bridgette was finally putting Nya in her place.

"No," she said. "I'm not seeing Coach Berry. You got bad info."

"Quit lying," Bridgette said with a smack of her lips. "Tenisha saw y'all on your little date last week."

Tenisha Burns, the woman who ran into Nya and Marquis at the bookstore, nodded her head in agreement.

"Y'all were at Barnes & Noble," she confirmed.

"Me and Coach Berry just happened to run into each other that day," Nya insisted. "We told you that when you talked to us."

"Whatever," Bridgette said. "And I guess your boyfriend *Daryl* ain't a part of this..."

Nya was caught off guard by the new information the ladies had. She didn't think her face registered surprise, but she wasn't able to respond right away.

"And that's not the same *Daryl* who Coach Berry got in a fight with?" Bridgette continued. "Bitch, you ain't gotta lie. We know what's going on."

Nya might not have been ready to counter those allegations, but she was always prepared to stand up for herself.

"Call me a bitch again," she dared her. "Trust me, you don't know me like you think you do."

The two women stared each other down with venomous eyes while Bridgette considered it. Nya wasn't skinny, but she wasn't fat either. She looked like she could defend herself, and apparently she didn't have a problem with being the aggressor.

"You ain't even worth it," Bridgette decided.

"You right," Nya agreed with a victorious nod of her head. She stepped past the women and entered the gym to retrieve her daughter.

• • • • • •

On the way home Nya found that although Lisa was still upset with her, they were able to band together to battle a mutual foe: Bullies.

"How was practice?"

"Sucked," Lisa told her. "Everybody's depressed. They were crying."

"What about Coach Mitchell? He's not doing a good job?"

"I don't know," Lisa said with a slump of her shoulders. "Nobody's really listening to him. We all want Coach Berry back."

"I know," Nya said. "I've been hearing that all day."

"They're saying it's my fault," Lisa revealed.

Nya frowned. "How is any of this *your* fault?"

"They said Coach got into a fight with Daryl because of you."

"The girls on your team told you that?" Nya found it astonishing how many people were talking and spreading the story. When this was all said and done, she knew she'd be a pariah.

"They know everything, Mama."

"But why would they blame *you* for it?" Nya's expression was drenched with concern.

"Who else can they blame? You know they're not gonna say anything to you."

Nya shook her head. "I wish I could say the same about their parents."

"What do you mean?"

"I just got into it with Dalia's mom. They all know me and Marquis went out. They know about Daryl, too. They said everything that happened is my fault."

Lisa felt the same way, but her heart softened. Up till then she never considered how any of this was affecting her mother. She couldn't be part of the mob.

"What are you gonna do?" she asked.

"What can I do?" Nya pondered. "People are talking about me. They're talking about you. They're talking about Coach Berry. We can't control people talking."

Lisa was quiet for a moment as she let that fact of life sink in. "I just want them to shut up."

Nya took hold of her hand. "You can shut them up by winning."

Lisa shook her head. "We can't win without Coach Berry."

"Yes you can," her mother said. "And Tricia is playing the best she's ever played. I talked to Marquis last night. He said you have to stay strong and lead the team."

"So he's not coming back?" Lisa was on the verge of tears again.

"I don't know, baby. I hope so."

● ● ● ● ● ●

Marquis was not back at school on Friday.

The Lady Grizzlies only had to attend classes until lunchtime. At 12:30 they boarded a school bus that would transport them to Abilene Christian University for their regional quarterfinal game against the Clover Valley Spartans.

Nya arrived at the school in time to give her daughter a word of encouragement. She also spoke to the bus driver to let him know she would be following him to Abilene in her car.

She could've ridden the bus with the other booster moms, but after yesterday's incident, she didn't think it was a wise move. The two hour drive to Abilene was sure to be filled with more gossip and tension. She and Bridgette might duke it out after all, if they were forced to share cramped quarters for so long.

When they arrived at the venue, Nya sat by herself and cheered her daughter on with the same enthusiasm she'd been exhibiting since Lisa joined her first team in the sixth grade. But from the first play, she knew the Grizzlies were in trouble. The Clover Valley girls were not very tall, but they were swift and scrappy. Their point guard had a jump shot that was so accurate, it looked mechanical. She rushed down the court and didn't bother to work the ball around. Lisa gave her a little cushion at the top of the key, and number 12 took advantage. She took a step back behind the three-point line and threw up a perfect rainbow.

Swish.

The bleachers were packed with fans. The crowd went crazy. Several Finley High players were noticeably shaken as the scoreboard reflected they were already down three to nothing. Nya hoped the first shot was a fluke, but it didn't take long to realize number 12 was the real deal. She shot two more three-pointers in the first half and made both of them. The Spartans also had a chunky center who refused to let Tricia bully her out of the paint.

By halftime Finley High was down by an insurmountable 15 points. They marched to the locker room with their heads down, their spirits low. To make matters worse, the booster moms let their frustration get the best of them. Rather than rally around the interim coach, who was doing a decent job, they began to chant, "**WE WANT COACH BERRY! WE WANT COACH BERRY!**" which had to be a blow to Coach Mitchell's pride.

As Nya sat watching them, she felt embarrassed for Finley High for the first time in four years. She wondered if she had ever participated in mean-spirited chants like that when she was sitting with the booster moms. She didn't think she had. She knew God wouldn't bless their team because of all the spite and gossip and bad blood between them.

But things took an unexpected turn in the third quarter. The Spartans' star player went up for another one of her perfect jumpers, and Lisa moved in to contest it. The shot was nothing but net, but the shooter landed on Lisa's foot when she came down. Her ankle rolled so severely, everyone in the building cringed. The girl fell to the floor, crying out in pain. The game was halted for five minutes while trainers assessed her and then helped her off the court.

When the game resumed, Lisa was a totally different animal without number 12 there to hound her up and down the court. Nya watched anxiously as Finley High slowly narrowed the lead. She didn't think they would pull it off.

She expected the Spartans' star to rush from the locker room at any minute to reclaim her title as the best player on the court. But that never happened.

When number 12 did return, she was on crutches with a heavy walking boot strapped around her ankle. She was crying, and by the end of the fourth quarter, several girls on her bench were crying with her. At the final buzzer, Finley High was up by four points.

Nya was ecstatic about the win. She was extremely proud of her daughter for persevering in what had been their most challenging game. But Nya, as well as other fans she overheard, had to put an asterisk next to this one. No one believed Finley High would've been victorious if not for number 12's injury.

But in the world of sports, a win is a win. Finley High advanced to the regional semifinals. That game would take place next Saturday. The venue was the luxurious Alamodome in San Antonio. No one thought they would make it that far. The girls had tears in their eyes as they celebrated.

● ● ● ● ● ●

Before they boarded the bus for home, Nya found her daughter and gave her a big hug.

"Baby, I'm so proud of you!"

"I didn't hurt her on purpose, Mama," Lisa said, shaking her head.

"I know you didn't."

"We wouldn't have won if she was still playing," Lisa told her. She was elated, but the asterisk bothered her too.

"You can't let that get you down," her mother said. "You won fair and square. You did an awesome job!"

"Do you want me to ride home with you?" Lisa asked.

Nya did want that, but she didn't want to pull Lisa away from her friends. "No, baby. You need to go celebrate with your teammates. I'll be at the school when you get there. Don't worry about me."

Lisa might not have taken her advice if not for the fake smile Nya painted on.

"You sure, Mama?"

"Yes, baby. I'm fine. Go. Go be with your teammates."

"Okay," Lisa said, her smile big and bright.

She ran to catch up with her friends as they boarded the bus. Before Nya turned to head for her car, she heard them chanting their war cry. Today the song gave her a bit of gloomy nostalgia, because she wasn't part of the crew any more.

We from the dirty south!
Yah! Trick! Yah!
Grizzlies all in yo mouth!
Yah! Trick! Yah!

● ● ● ● ● ●

The ride home was long and lonely. Nya called Marquis to cut into the monotony of highway exits and billboards.

"Hey. You coming from the game?"

"Yeah," she said.

"Are you on the bus?"

"No. I'm in my car, by myself."

"You didn't ride with the team? How come?"

"Me and Bridgette got into it yesterday. I didn't think it would be a good idea for us to be that close to each other."

"What? Why y'all get into it?"

"Over you," she said. She told him about the argument.

"I'm sorry you had to go through that."

"It's not your fault."

After a pause he said, "I heard the girls won..."

"Yeah, they did. They should get an asterisk, though."

"Why do you say that?"

"You didn't hear about the injury?"

"No. One of our players?"

"No. It was one of theirs. She was the best player on the court. Twisted her ankle. Real bad. We were gonna lose until that happened."

"Damn," Marquis said. "Well, you know, a win is a win."

"Yeah. That's what I told Lisa."

"How'd she do?"

"She got seventeen points. I couldn't keep up with her assists."

"Seventeen points? That's great. So Coach Mitchell did a good job?"

"Oh my God, Marquis, I feel so sorry for him."

"Why? What happened?"

"The boosters. They treated him bad. They were yelling, '*We want Coach Berry.*' I know he was embarrassed."

"That's messed up," he agreed. "Donovan's a good guy. That would've been a hard job for anybody to step into."

"We're going to the Alamodome next Saturday."

"I know. That's amazing."

"Are you gonna go?"

"Yeah. Hopefully I'll be coaching, but I'll be there either way."

"You haven't heard anything about your case?"

"No."

He didn't elaborate on that, and Nya didn't ask him to. If he didn't have good news, thinking about it might upset him.

"Are you okay?" he asked.

"It's been a hard couple of days," she said. "I know it's worse for you, so I don't want to complain."

"No, it's okay. Tell me what's going on."

She shook her head. Her eyes filled with tears as she followed the school bus' taillights. "It's a lot of stuff. I got problems with Lisa. The people at work are gossiping. All of the boosters know about you and me and Daryl now. Even Lisa's teammates are trying to blame *her* for what happened to you. It's so much. Too much."

Marquis' heart bled for her. "Can I come see you tonight?"

Nya shook her head as she said, "Wha – *no*. That wouldn't help at all."

"It might. I think it will."

"Marquis, everybody hates me because of *one date* I went on with you. Even Lisa says I shouldn't have done it."

"I don't care what they think. I mean, I do care about Lisa. But you said you talked to her. She knows about us."

"Her knowing about it doesn't mean she's okay with it. She's still mad at me."

"You don't have to tell her you're seeing me. We can meet at the same place in Arlington."

"No, Marquis. I can't run around behind her back anymore."

"She's your child – not the other way around. You don't have to tell her anything."

"You don't understand."

"Okay. Maybe I don't," Marquis conceded. He knew that his relationship with the twins didn't have the complexities of Nya's bond with Lisa. "But what about us?"

"Marquis, you're my daughter's teacher. You're her coach. I don't think it's a good time for us to try to... I don't even know what we're trying to do."

"What are you saying?"

"You don't think we should chill? If we see each other, it would only add fuel to the fire," she reasoned. "I want it all to go away. I want you to get your job back. Don't you want that?"

"Of course I want that. But we're not doing anything illegal. I don't care what people think about what we have going on."

"We only went out once."

"I felt something with you. Are you saying you didn't feel anything? You don't think it's worth pursuing?"

"I did feel something," she admitted. "But is it worth pursuing despite all of the trouble we caused?"

He sighed. "Nya, after all I've been through – *after all I've been through* – I don't feel like leaving you alone would be the solution."

Her face flushed with heat. His passion made her pulse race. "Okay. I'm sorry."

"So I can see you tonight?"

She knew he was getting upset. She didn't want to make things worse by telling him no.

"Okay."

He didn't think he heard her right. "Really?"

"Yeah. Text me your address. I'll come by after I take Lisa home."

● ● ● ● ● ●

By seven o'clock Marquis began to wonder if she'd changed her mind, but Nya knocked on his door a few minutes later. When he answered, he saw that her eyes were filled with indecision. She looked totally drained, physically and mentally.

He longed to wrap his arms around her, to absorb her pain, so she could be happy again. But her expression was guarded. He wasn't sure if his affection would be welcomed.

They sat in the living room and talked. She declined food or wine, but she accepted a glass of iced tea. Gradually, as the sun descended in the west, blessing Overbrook Meadows with a picturesque, purple skyline, she began to relax. Marquis moved closer to her on the sofa, and she leaned into him.

He put his arm around her, and she rested her head on his chest. He nuzzled the top of her head, savoring the smell and the feel of her hair on his face. Nya enjoyed their closeness, too. Marquis was a mountain of strength and courage. Without words, he managed to alleviate a lot of her stress. He made her feel as though they could take on the whole world, just the two of them.

But it was foolish to think like that, considering they had only gone out on one date. Nya understood that she was falling in love with him. Unfortunately the inner joy that should accompany those feelings was missing. Instead she wondered if their union was cursed.

Her heart stirred when she felt him kiss the top of her head. She looked up at him, and his next kiss found her lips. Her eyes slipped closed. Her body sang in appreciation. His kiss awakened every part of her. Her heart began to drum with hope and happiness for the first time that day.

As she returned his kisses, she couldn't help but consider how defining this moment was. Marquis made her feel like he'd always be there for her, which was conflicting because they weren't even in a relationship. For all she knew, she was nothing more than a conquest to him. When the dust settled, he might leave her high and dry, left to pick up the pieces of her life all by herself.

And Nya had yet to get over the fact that he was nearly ten years younger than her. Regardless of how mature Marquis seemed to be, he had a lot of growing up to do. If they were in a relationship, Nya knew that she would have to be submissive at times. She didn't think she could do that for someone so young.

She hesitated and then pulled away. When she opened her eyes, he was watching her. The intensity of his gaze compelled her to stay with him, but she knew she couldn't. She shouldn't have come in the first place.

He took hold of her hand as she rose from the couch. "Don't leave."

Her countenance was pained when she told him, "I have to."

He didn't rise from his seat. He didn't let go of her, either. "Why?"

"Lisa's at home," she managed. "She's worried about me."

Marquis didn't believe that was the case. Lisa hadn't tried to contact her mother since Nya arrived. He reluctantly let go of her hand and watched as she backed away from him. She looked as unsure of herself as she did when she first arrived. Marquis hated to see her like that. He hoped this visit would bring them closer. It was clear that it hadn't.

"Why does it feel like you're walking out of my life?"

It was a bold question, but Marquis felt their time for pretense was over.

"I'm not," she said.

Her voice wasn't strong or convincing. He could've stopped her before she left his home, but Marquis remained seated. His mother once told him that any woman who wouldn't stand by him when he was down was not worth having.

Marquis was at the lowest point he'd been since his divorce. Nya knew that, and she proceeded to open the front door and walk out of the house.

CHAPTER TWENTY
SYCAMORE PARK

Marquis felt stressed the moment he opened his eyes on Saturday morning. He had absolutely nothing to do. No papers to grade. No lesson plans to go over. And he hated it.

He called his brother at 9 am.

"What's up, bro?"

"What's the word?" Marquis asked. "You heard anything from the lawyer?"

"No. Nothing since yesterday."

"Does she work on Saturdays? Can you call her?"

"I don't know if she's in the office," Omar said. "But I can call her. How you holding up?"

"I'm pissed," Marquis told him. "I wanna go find Daryl and make him tell the truth."

"That doesn't sound like a good idea."

"I know. I'm just saying."

"Your girls won yesterday. You not happy about that?"

"I am. Of course I am."

"You didn't go?"

"No. Didn't want to be a distraction," Marquis replied. "But I'm going next week, whether I'm coaching or not."

"That's the one in San Antonio?"

"Yeah, the Alamodome." Even in a state of irritation, Marquis was afforded a moment of pride for his team's accomplishments.

"What about that woman?" Omar asked.

"What woman? Lisa's mother?"

"Yeah."

Marquis' chest squeezed uncomfortably at the thought of Nya. "What about her?"

"You still pursuing that?"

"Not right now," Marquis said. He didn't tell him this was her choice. "She's taking a lot of heat from the other parents."

"They know about y'all?"

"Yeah."

"What's done in the dark…"

"We didn't commit any sins," Marquis said. "We never even had sex. I don't care what people have to say about it."

"What about her daughter? She okay with it?"

"I haven't talked to her. But Nya says she's not."

"I guess you're okay with that, too?"

"It doesn't even matter right now," Marquis stated. "Can you call the lawyer and find out what's going on with my case?"

"Yeah," Omar said. "Gimme a sec'."

He called back ten minutes later.

"Yo. What'd you find out?"

"I have Mrs. Branch on the line," Omar told him.

"Morning, Marquis," the woman said.

He changed his lingo effortlessly. "Hi. Good morning, Ma'am."

"I'm afraid I don't have any progress on your case," the lawyer said. "Daryl is holding strong to his story."

"What is his story exactly?" Omar asked.

"He says he ran into Marquis at the Quik Trip gas station, and it was a coincidence. There are cameras at the location that captured the encounter. Daryl says Marquis approached him and started an argument."

"About what?" Marquis interrupted. "What did I supposedly start an argument about?"

"He says you confronted him about his ex-wife," the lawyer informed them. "Daryl says you're currently dating the woman, Nya Edmonds, and you were upset because he visited her at work earlier that day."

"That's a lie," Marquis stated. "And she's not his *ex-wife*."

"Are you dating this woman?" the lawyer wanted to know.

"We went on *one date*," Marquis acknowledged.

The lawyer didn't respond. Marquis didn't think that was a good sign.

"What about Nya calling the police on him when he went to her job?" Marquis asked. "She's getting a restraining order against him."

"Unfortunately that plays into his hand," the lawyer stated. "If he created a scene and upset Nya at work, and she told you about it, then it would make sense that you were angry with him when you saw him at the gas station."

"I wasn't mad about that." Marquis struggled to keep his cool despite this calculated character assassination. "I was mad because he was following me. He followed me *to* the gas station, and he followed me *out*. The cameras don't show that?"

"Yes," she confirmed. "But it could've been a coincidence."

"What about that other place we went to?" Marquis asked. "They don't have any cameras there?"

"The second encounter occurred at a heating and A/C business that was closed for the day," the attorney said. "And no, they don't have exterior cameras."

"What did he say about how we got there? If he wasn't following me, how'd we end up in another parking lot together?"

"Daryl acknowledges that he'd been drinking that night. He says he doesn't remember how he came to be in that parking lot. He also attributes the trauma he sustained at your hands as another reason for his memory loss."

Marquis fumed. "That's bull!"

"It's your word against his."

Marquis found himself growing more hopeless and desperate. He knew there were plenty of people in prison based solely on the complaint of one person. But that always seemed like something that would happen to someone else.

"So what's next?" he asked. "Can we take lie detector tests, or something?"

"I doubt he'd agree to that," the lawyer said. "Even if he does, the results aren't admissible in court, and they wouldn't be enough to get the case tossed. I've hired an investigator to dig up some dirt on Daryl. He's spending a lot of time in the area of the incident; looking for evidence the police might have overlooked. He's searching for any witnesses who have not come forward. Hopefully he'll find something that will corroborate your story."

"What if he doesn't?" Omar asked. "What are our options then?"

"I'll try to talk the D.A. down to simple assault," the lawyer said. "Marquis can plead to that, get probation and avoid jail time. Daryl will probably sue in civil court. He may be willing to settle for twenty, twenty-five thousand, plus his attorney fees and medical bills."

Marquis couldn't believe the lawyer wanted him to accept responsibility for the whole thing.

"I won't get my job back unless we get this case dropped," he told her. He spoke with a defeated tone.

"We're doing our best," she promised.

● ● ● ● ● ●

After fretting for most of the morning, Marquis was desperate for a release. He wanted to call Nya. But it was Saturday afternoon, and she was most likely with Lisa. Plus Nya didn't want to stay with him last night. Marquis was upset with her because of the rejection.

He dressed in shorts and a tee-shirt and decided to get some exercise. Strengthening his body had always been his best stress reliever. He had a treadmill in his spare bedroom, but he laced up his sneakers and hit the streets instead. It was a pleasant 57 degrees outside. He was tired of being cooped up and disparaged by the community. He'd be damned if he spent another day at home with his head down.

Marquis was never on a track team, but running was essential to basketball and football. He was fairly sure he could still run a five-minute mile. But he didn't try today – not with the unpredictability of the landscape. He lived in a good neighborhood where the sidewalks were smooth and clean of debris. But he wasn't sure where his run would take him.

When he left his house, his only thought was the warm sun on his dark skin and the pleasing feeling of fresh air in his lungs. The rhythmic sound of his sneakers clapping the pavement was music to his ears. He only slowed to check for cars at busy intersections. Before long, his momentum and a thin layer of sweat caused his tee-shirt to cling to his chest and biceps. Marquis accumulated a few smiles and even more stares from pretty drivers who were happy to see a fine, young, healthy black man.

About an hour into his run, he was happy to see Sycamore Park looming in the horizon. When he was younger, the area was gang-infested. The park was soiled with graffiti and pollution. But a decade ago the city initiated an effort to save and restore the park. The landscape was now well-kept and rich with vegetation. Marquis entered the property and diverted his route to a biking trail. A minute later he was lost in a sea of trees, mostly sycamores, which had not recovered their greenery from the winter months.

At the top of the trail, Marquis encountered a large community center. There were a dozen vehicles in the parking lot, so he knew it was open. He decided this would be a good place to take a break. He jogged up the steps and wiped the sweat off his brow as he entered the building. He was pleased to spot a water fountain near the front desk. As he headed for it, Marquis heard something that made his heart skip a beat, filling him with a myriad of emotions.

Someone was playing basketball.

His reaction to the sound of dribbling and shouts for someone to play better defense was bittersweet. But he wasn't dissuaded from exploring further. He drank from the fountain and then approached the main desk. He was greeted by an attractive woman who had fair skin and curly hair.

"Hi. Y'all have a gym in here?"

She looked him up and down and liked what she saw. Marquis' run left him winded and sweaty. The muscles in his chest and shoulders were primed and swollen. The clerk took a deep breath and muttered something that may have been *Oh my goodness* before she responded.

"Yes, we have a gym. But you gotta have a membership before you can play. You want a membership?"

Marquis didn't think he'd frequent the community center, but he asked, "How much is it?"

"Twenty dollars a month." She smiled. Her lips glistened with a coat of raspberry lipstick.

"Do y'all have a fitness center?"

"We have a weight room," she said.

Twenty bucks was a lot to pay for a gym he may never return to, but he agreed to the terms. After filling out an application and paying the fee, he descended the stairs, following the sound of tennis shoes squeaking on the court.

He came upon a decent gym with hardwood floors and regulation-size goals. There were eight people playing a full-court game and a few people shooting on another hoop off to the side.

Marquis approached the court to check out the action. The players ranged from teenagers to men in their forties. The teams were divided into shirts against skins. It looked like the shirts were only a few shots away from winning. All of the players gave Marquis the once-over as they finished their game, but none of their stares were antagonizing. He was pretty sure no one there recognized him, which was great.

When the shirts won, they were ready to run another one.

"You playing?" one of them asked Marquis.

"Yeah."

"You any good?" someone else asked.

"Haven't played in a while, but I used to be."

They looked him up and down.

"Alright, you're with the skins," the first one said.

When Marquis peeled off his shirt, the man added, "Hey, y'all got *muscle man*!" He laughed.

"It might all be *fluff*," his teammate joked dismissively. But it didn't look like he believed that.

● ● ● ● ● ●

Marquis hadn't played ball in months, other than practicing with the girls, but it all came back to him in no time. He had a jump shot that was money eight times out of ten, and he could handle the rock, too.

Down by five, the best player on the shirts' team declared, "Hell naw! Y'all got a ringer! Muscle Man used to play for the *Mavericks!*"

But it was all in good fun. Marquis liked the crew he was playing with, and they seemed like regulars. He thought he might get his money's worth from the community center's membership after all.

After a dominating victory, he decided to sit the next one out.

"Aww. Come on, man. You just got here," one of his new teammates complained.

"I've been running since noon," Marquis told him. "I ran all the way over here. Might have to take a cab home." He laughed, but that only served to deepen his new friends' curiosity.

As he watched the next game from the sideline, Marquis noticed an older man pushing a mop bucket. The man stared at him with an inquisitive expression and began to roll the bucket in his direction. The closer he got, the wider his toothy grin became.

When he was close enough to speak without having to yell over the sounds of the game, he said, "*Marquis Berry.*"

Marquis was not happy to be recognized. So far the gym had been a safe haven. No one there knew him or judged him.

"Hey, how you doing, sir?" he told the man.

"I'm doing fine. What are you doing here?" the custodian asked. He couldn't stop smiling.

"Just happened to stop by."

"I'm Otis," the man said. "I been working here for, going on six years. I retired from the post office in 2009, got bored and needed something to get me out the house – and out of my wife's hair," he said with a wink. "They let me sweep and mop. Give me a little money for it, too."

Marquis decided he liked Otis. He reminded him of his deceased grandfather.

"Can I have your autograph?" the custodian asked.

"Autograph?" He tried to laugh it off. "I'm nothing special." If he signed an autograph, the guys he played against really would think he was a ringer.

"*Nothing special*?" Otis said. "Yeah right. Son, I've been impressed with you since you played for *Castleberry*. My daughter's a teacher over there. She never had you in any of her classes, but she used to talk about how special you was. I checked out your games a few times. I thought you'd go to college for hooping, but you always had that football on lock, too."

Marquis was impressed by how much he knew about him. But the stranger wasn't done.

"You tore it up at LSU," Otis said. "They started calling you *Trucker*, 'cause of the way you ran them boys over. Couldn't nobody stop you. Got drafted by the Cowboys. I thought you would've went second or third round, but it didn't matter. When the season started, you made a name for yourself right off the bat.

"And *then*," Otis said, raising a finger in the air, "you come back to Overbrook Meadows and damned near take the girls to the state championship your first year. So don't tell me you ain't nothing special," he said with a grin.

Marquis was humbled and embarrassed for initially denying his request. If anyone deserved his autograph, Otis surely did.

"Now, I might not have kept up with your Finley High games if not for my great niece," Otis stated. "She plays on your team."

"Really? What's her name?"

"It's Dalia. Dalia Young."

"Wow. Small world," Marquis said. "If you can find a pen, I'd be happy to give you my autograph."

● ● ● ● ● ●

He played two more games before he decided to take another break. He wasn't sure how long he'd stay at the community center, but he thought he had at least one more game left in him. He was at the water fountain upstairs when he heard a young voice call his name.

"Coach Berry!"

He turned and was surprised (but not totally) to see Dalia and her mother Bridgette entering the building. Dalia had a look on her face like she never expected to see him again.

"Hey," Marquis said when she rushed to him. She threw both arms around him and hugged him tightly. Marquis didn't expect that, and he was a little uncomfortable, despite the fact that her mother was standing there.

"Whoa, I'm all sweaty," he said, reluctant to return the affection.

"It's okay, Coach. What are you doing here?"

"Just came to shoot some hoops," he said. "Did your Uncle Otis call and tell you I was here?"

"Yeah!" She stepped back nodding, grinning brightly. And then she frowned. "Coach, what happened? Are you coming back? We need you! Everybody misses you!"

"I'm working on it," he told her. "I didn't do what they're saying I did."

"We know you didn't do it," Bridgette said as she stepped closer. "It's all *Nya's* fault. She's the one who got you in this trouble."

Her disdain for Nya was palpable.

"No, it's not her fault," Marquis said. "Y'all shouldn't give her a hard time. The trouble I'm in is *my* doing. But it's still not what it looks like."

"I believe you, Coach," Dalia insisted.

Marquis was surprised by how good that made him feel.

"Thank you, Dalia."

"Can I come play with you?" the girl asked.

"Well, I don't think–"

"*Please, Coach*! Tricia lives around the corner from me. We can bring her, too. I just gotta go home and change right quick. And I can call Latavia. She lives close by." Her eyes lit up. "Ooh! We can practice here!"

"No, we definitely can't practice here," Marquis said, shaking his head. "That's against the rules. I'm still suspended."

"Can we at least come and play with you?" Her eyes were big and hopeful.

"I don't mind bringing them," Bridgette said. "They just wanna spend some time with you, before the season ends."

Marquis couldn't say no to that. He missed his girls terribly. And nothing in his suspension paperwork indicated he couldn't see his team away from school.

"Alright."

"*Yay!*" Dalia squealed.

"But I won't be here much longer. How long will it take for y'all to get back?"

"We're only five minutes away," Bridgette told him. "It might take another ten minutes to get the other girls, if they wanna come."

"Alright," Marquis said. "I'll wait for y'all. But *we won't be practicing*," he reiterated to Dalia. "You could get the whole team in trouble, if people think I practiced with you today."

"Okay. I'll tell them it's *not* practice," Dalia promised. She hurried to the exit and turned back when she realized she'd forgotten her ride. "Come on, Mama! *Hurry!*"

● ● ● ● ● ●

Marquis was shooting around by himself when the girls returned. As promised, Dalia had Tricia and Latavia with her. All three students were decked out in their shorts and high-tops. Seeing them filled Marquis' heart with love. He saw that Latavia's mother had come as well.

"I didn't think you were really here!" she said, smiling broadly. "We sure hope you can come back before their next game."

"Me too," Marquis replied. "But I'm going to San Antonio either way. I wouldn't miss it for the world."

He shot around with the students for another forty-five minutes, playing friendly games of two-on-two, until the community center closed at six. Marquis had to admit it felt great to be with his team again. Their smiles and laughter made him forget about his worries for a while.

As they left the building, Dalia asked him, "Can we come back and play again tomorrow, Coach? I'll try to get the whole team to come."

That sounded delightful, but he told her, "The community center's not open on Sundays."

"We can play over there," Tricia said, pointing to another basketball court outside of the building. These goals didn't have nets, but they appeared to be in good shape.

"It might be too cold," Marquis said. "And what if it rains?"

Bridgette pulled up a weather app on her phone while they walked to the parking lot. "It's supposed to be 59 degrees," she told him. "And no rain."

Marquis was surprised she was so willing to make this work.

"Okay," he decided. "I can be here tomorrow at two o'clock. If y'all can get in touch with the other members of the team, and their parents say it's okay, you can invite them. I'm not sure how long we'll stay, but it should be fun. Make sure they know it's not practice, though."

"Alright, we got it," Dalia said with a giggle.

"How are you getting home?" Latavia's mother asked him. "Where's your truck."

"I jogged over here," Marquis said. "I was planning on running home. But I wouldn't mind a ride."

"I'll take you," Bridgette and Latavia's mom said at the same time.

"Thanks. I appreciate it," Marquis said. He headed for Latavia's car, because it was closest.

"See you tomorrow!" Dalia shouted.

"Alright," Marquis told her.

He'd be there, but he was doubtful about how many of his girls would come. All of their mothers couldn't be this forgiving.

CHAPTER TWENTY-ONE
NOT PRACTICE

On Sunday morning Marquis woke up fresh and energized. He didn't get upset when Paula called and asked him to take the twins unexpectedly.

"I tried to get them Friday," he reminded her. "You said you wanted them all weekend."

Although his official child support order indicated Marquis was to get the boys each first and third weekend, he rarely adhered to it. He typically picked up his kids every Friday, unless Paula had plans that weekend. That worked out fine with her.

"Sorry. I changed my mind. Is it okay?"

"Yeah, it's fine," he said. He didn't have anything to do today except meet his team at Sycamore Park. "What time do you want me to get them?"

"I'm about to leave in five minutes," she stated. "I'll drop them off."

Marquis grinned, thinking that was a little presumptuous of her.

"Okay. I'll be here."

When she arrived less than an hour later, Marquis thought Paula was dressed rather fancy for a Sunday morning.

"You going to church?" He was kidding. He knew that she rarely attended services.

She surprised him by saying, "Yes."

"Really? With who?"

"A friend," she replied vaguely as she helped the boys out of their car seats.

"Must be special, if he's got you going to church," Marquis said.

"We'll see," she quipped. "Do you want to bring them back tonight, or can you–"

"No. I'll take them to school on Monday. You have a nice day."

"You, too."

Lately it was rare for them to have a conversation that didn't end with arguing, especially with their new court date looming. Marquis hoped the rest of his day would be as pleasant.

● ● ● ● ● ●

At noon he dressed in basketball gear and tossed three fairly new balls into the bed of his truck. He took the boys to Rosa's Café for lunch. They left an hour later, all of them happy and full. Marquis hoped a few of his girls would actually show up at the park, because he needed to work off what turned out to be a king-size meal.

When he arrived at the community center, he was happy to see three vehicles in the parking lot and seven people milling around the basketball court. Dalia was there with her mom Bridgette. Tricia and Cheri brought their mothers too, and one of the girls' little brother had tagged along. The group converged on Marquis' truck as he unloaded the boys.

"Hey, Coach Berry! We were starting to wonder if you were coming."

"And I was worried that y'all *weren't* coming," he told them.

"Please tell me you brought some balls," Dalia said.

229

"I did. They're in the back of the truck."

The girl climbed in and tossed them to the other players.

"Who are these handsome young men?" Cheri's mom Ramona asked.

"That's Carl, and this is Omar," Marquis said as he hefted the boy from his seat.

"Hey, boys!" Ramona smiled, leaning down to greet the twins.

"Hi!" they responded.

"Ooh, they're so precious!" Bridgette exclaimed. "We'll keep a good eye on them, while y'all are playing."

"There's a playground right by the basketball court," Ramona said. "It's shady, too."

"Oh, and I brought a couple of coolers," Bridgette said. "I should have enough drinks for everybody – and we made some sandwiches too."

Marquis was surprised and grateful. He didn't think of that himself.

"Thank you," he told her. "I'm sure everyone will appreciate that."

Bridgette beamed. Marquis thought she'd be resentful because he rejected her advances all year, and he came to Nya's defense yesterday. But it didn't appear that she had any hard feelings.

"I told you from day one that the boosters would be here for anything you needed," she reminded him.

"You did," Marquis said as the group headed for the court. "It's nice to see that you really meant it."

Her eyes twinkled with delight, much like his students did when they got good grades back on tough assignments.

● ● ● ● ● ●

The atmosphere at the community center was unlike anything he'd experienced with the team before. Without the requirements of practice, they were able to enjoy a few leisurely games of basketball. And the group continued to grow. By three o'clock Tamika had come in addition to Michele, Maria and their lively center Tricia. Most of the parents remained at the park, rather than drop the girls off.

The outing had the feel of a family reunion. With all of the negative press Marquis was getting, these parents could've opted to side with the school administrators and turn their backs on him. But they trusted him enough to bring their daughters to him on a Sunday afternoon, even while Overbrook Meadows' district attorney was working to get him locked up.

That was the kind of support you couldn't pay people for. Marquis got a lump in his throat every time he saw another vehicle pull into the parking lot.

The most notable absence was Lisa, but Marquis was not surprised by that. He hadn't spoken to Nya since Friday night, after the girls beat Clover Valley. He doubted if any of the other parents had invited her to the park. As far as he knew, they were still giving Nya the cold shoulder because of her involvement in the coach's troubles.

While the girls played a game of three-on-three, he went to check on the twins in the playground area, where the mothers were congregating.

"Good afternoon, ladies."

"Hi, Coach Berry!"

"Thanks again for bringing the girls. This feels real good."

"Are you gonna be back by Saturday?" Michele's mom asked. "They really needed you for the last game."

"Yeah, that new coach they got ain't about *nothing*," Tricia's mom agreed.

"Thanks for bringing that up," Marquis said. "I heard some troubling news about the way you ladies behaved during the Clover Valley game..."

Half of the women looked confused. The other half wore guilty expressions.

"Did y'all start chanting, '*We want Coach Berry,*' at halftime?"

They grinned sheepishly.

"She started it," Michele's mother said, pointing at Bridgette.

"Snitch," Bridgette muttered.

They all laughed.

"Coach Mitchell is a friend of mine," Marquis told them. "He's been helping me out since I started working at the school. I talked to him a couple of days ago. He never complains, but I know how hard it was for him to take over my position without any warning. I'm sure it's even harder, with you ladies disrespecting him."

"We didn't disrespect him," Bridgette said. "We were just playing."

Marquis gave her a side-eye.

"Well, if you're back by Saturday, we won't have no problem," she stated.

Marquis could do nothing but smile at that.

"Please tell us you'll be back by Saturday," another woman said.

"I'm working on it," he assured her.

"Why'd you get in a fight?"

"I didn't. I promise you that. I never threw a punch at that man. The problem is I'm having trouble proving it. But once I do, I'll be back. Don't worry."

"We believe you," the mother said.

They all nodded in agreement.

Again Marquis was moved by such unconditional support. These women didn't know him on a personal level. He wondered what it was that made him so trustworthy in their eyes. Was it because the Lady Grizzlies were having such a great season? That might have been it, but he felt it was something more. It was deeper than basketball.

• • • • • •

Marquis joined the girls on the court, and they began to rotate the players, to make sure everyone got their share of game time. They all tried to show off for him, but the spirit of fun and togetherness outranked competitiveness.

At three-thirty Marquis heard cheers coming from the parking lot. When he looked in that direction, he was delighted to see their star player marching up the hill. He hoped Nya would stay, too, but he saw her car leaving the area. He noticed Lisa looked a little wary, even as her teammates crowded around and welcomed her to the event.

"Good to see you!" Marquis said when she drew nearer. "How you feeling?"

She shrugged and half smiled.

"Can I talk to you for a second?" he said and led her away from the group. As they walked down the sidewalk, he asked, "You mad at me?"

She shook her head, but he saw that she wasn't making eye contact.

"It's okay if you are," he told her. "I know my problems are affecting you and your mother."

She met his eyes then. She was so tall, she barely had to look up at him.

"You went out with my Mama?"

Marquis's eyes widened. "Umm... Okay. We can talk about that, if you want."

"I already know you did," she said. "I wanna know why."

"I, um, I'm not sure what you want to hear. I like her. I mean, you know that, right?"

She shrugged.

"I do like her," he said more definitively. "I think your mother is beautiful and smart. We get along well. We didn't do it to hurt you. You understand that?"

233

She sighed and nodded.

"Does it bother you?" he asked. "If so, can you tell me why?"

"Because you got in trouble."

He nodded. "Yep. I did. But I didn't get in trouble because of the way I feel about your mama."

"I thought that's why Daryl got mad at you."

"I'm sure that's part of it," Marquis conceded. "But you know that's not cool. Your mother has the right to go out with whoever she wants. Daryl doesn't own her. He can't and shouldn't threaten her or me. He needs to move on."

"I know," Lisa said. "I hate him."

As much as he despised the man, Marquis didn't want to hear that from her.

"Don't say that."

"Why?"

"Because Daryl raised you since you were six years old. You told me yourself he's the closest thing you have to a father. It's okay to be mad at him, but don't say you hate him."

"Mama said he lied, and you didn't hit him."

"That's true," Marquis confirmed. "But I understand what he's going through. It would be hard enough to lose Nya. To lose her and you at the same time – that's enough to drive any man crazy. I know he loves you very much. Once he gets over this little hump in his life, he'll go back to being the same guy you grew up with. You'll see."

She grinned. Marquis was happy to put a smile on her face.

"As far as me and your mom," he said, "are you okay if we go out?"

"No."

Surprised he asked, "Why not?"

"Because you're my coach," she pouted.

"Only for a few more weeks," he said with a chuckle.

"You're still my teacher after that."

234

"If I'm dating your mom, you'll make straight A's."

Her eyes lit up. "Really?"

"No. Not unless you earn it. But I'll be able to help you with your work any time you need me."

She grinned. "Alright."

"Whew." He wiped his brow comically. "I was afraid we'd have to sneak around behind your back. Your mom said she wouldn't do that, but I could've talked her into it," he joked.

"I would've found out."

"Yeah. Probably," he said.

They turned and headed back to the others.

● ● ● ● ● ●

By five o'clock the girls were getting tired, and the twins were too. Before they left the community center, the team gathered in the playground to eat the snacks Bridgette had brought for them. Marquis didn't notice when Nya arrived to pick up Lisa, but some of the other parents did. They greeted her with suspicious, unwelcoming eyes. Nya regretted not calling her daughter from the parking lot. These women were not her friends anymore.

When Marquis saw what was happening, he stood and got everyone's attention.

"What's going on? Everyone was cool a minute ago."

Nya waved at her daughter from the outskirts of the group. Lisa hopped to her feet and headed her way.

"Wait," Marquis told her. "Everybody, hold on for a second."

When all movement in the area stopped, he walked to the middle of the crowd and told them, "I don't like this at all. Why are y'all giving Nya a hard time?"

Her face flushed with heat. She didn't expect him to call attention to her. The other ladies didn't want to say what their problem was.

235

"Look," Marquis told them, "I already told you she's not the cause of the trouble I'm having. She needs your support right now, not your animosity."

Nya's body grew even warmer as she stared at him. It was a different kind of heat this time.

"If we're going to act like family," Marquis continued, "then we have to discuss things like a family. And the truth is I like Miss Edmonds a lot. But now she won't go out with me, in part because of the way you ladies are treating her."

Nya's jaw dropped as the students grinned at her.

"So I was hoping y'all would forgive her for whatever you think she did wrong," Marquis said. "Yes, you too, Bridgette." He looked her way.

She gave him a *Who me?* look and smiled.

"Because if you don't forgive her," Marquis continued, addressing the group again, "I don't think she'll ever go out with me, and that's something I would like a lot..."

He turned and regarded Nya. Her mouth fell open. She was overcome with emotions as she stared into his dark, brown eyes. Every girl wants a man who'll stand on the tallest mountain and profess his love for her. This was the closest Nya had ever come to such an experience.

"How about it, Miss Edmonds?" Marquis had never done anything like this, either. It felt good to clear the air and make his intentions known.

Nya couldn't stop a smile from spreading her lips. "Marquis, stop. You're embarrassing me."

"I'll be embarrassed too, if you say no."

She looked around and saw that everyone was waiting for her to reply. "I never said I wouldn't go out with you."

"So that's a yes?" he asked. "I can call you?"

The girls on the team tried to suppress their giggles as they watched them with bright, amused eyes.

"Girl, you better let that man call you!" Bridgette advised her.

"Yes," Nya said with a laugh. "You can call me. Now would you please stop?"

The crowd cheered for them, as if she'd accepted his hand in marriage.

Nya gave Marquis a playful roll of her eyes before she and Lisa continued on their way.

CHAPTER TWENTY-TWO
BETTER DAYS

Marquis and Nya had their first non-secret date the following Tuesday. She invited him to her home for dinner. That was perfect for him, because he continued to worry about how Lisa felt about them going out. She said she was okay with it on Saturday, but they were only talking about it then. Her reaction might be different when the scene played out in front of her.

Thankfully his concerns were unwarranted.

Nya made meatloaf with mashed potatoes and corn. The threesome enjoyed the meal amicably. Marquis asked Lisa how things were going in biology class and basketball practice.

"The sub doesn't do anything but give us worksheets," she complained. "She tried to give a lecture the other day, but no one listened to her."

"I'm surprised she tried," Marquis said. "When I was in school, we didn't give substitutes any respect. Sometimes when we'd see we had a sub, we'd turn around and skip the class."

"Don't tell her that," Nya said.

Marquis saw that she was smiling. "Oh, you don't have to worry. Lisa never skips."

"I don't," the girl agreed.

"It's been the same sub since I left?" Marquis asked.

238

She nodded.

"I'm gonna have to give her something nice when I get back."

"When are you coming back?" Lisa asked.

"We're still working on it." He kept the conversation moving, before Daryl's name came up. "What about practice? Is it getting any better?"

"We're being nice to Coach Mitchell," she said, "because you told us to."

He chuckled. "How about being nice to him because it's the right thing to do?"

"You pushing it, Coach. He better take what he can get."

"*Okay,*" Marquis said. "Sounds like I owe him a nice gift, too. Are you excited about the Alamodome?"

The girl's face lit up. "Yes. I've never been to San Antonio!"

"It's a beautiful city," Marquis told her. "If we have time to do some touristy stuff, we should check out the River Walk."

"I hope you can make it," Lisa said.

"I'll be there," he promised her. "I may be watching from the stands, but I'll be there."

She appeared to accept that.

"What's going on in your world?" he asked Nya. "How was your day at work?"

She smiled. It felt good to have a man ask her that. It was nice to have Marquis at the table with her and Lisa. She hoped for something like this but didn't think they could pull it off.

"I had a long, hard day," she said. "I don't want to bore you with it."

"I don't know about Lisa, but I won't be bored," he assured her. "Tell me about it..."

● ● ● ● ● ●

By nine-thirty the dinner plates were in the sink, and the dessert plates were scraped clean. Marquis was stuffed and content. He didn't want to leave, but he knew that Lisa and Nya had to get up early in the morning. Because of her no-good ex-boyfriend, Marquis was the only one who could sleep in.

Nya walked him to the door, and the couple lingered there. For their date, she wore a peach-colored blouse with a black, pencil skirt. She knew the skirt hugged her hips and thighs. The way Marquis stared at her curves, now that they were out of Lisa's sight, made her feel sexy and vivacious.

He wore khakis with a blue button-down. The shirt fit him perfectly. He had an undershirt on, so the sexy crease between his pectorals wasn't on display. But his clothing couldn't conceal the bulges of his arm and shoulder muscles. Nya thought he was sinfully sexy. The fact that he had eyes for her made her feel amazing.

At the moment those eyes were low and beckoning. The way he watched her reminded Nya of their kiss in the restaurant parking lot. She remembered how heated she was that night. She had no intentions of allowing it to happen again today – not with Lisa on the premises.

He reached for the door and then turned and told her, "Thank you for a wonderful evening."

"You're welcome." She beamed like a happy homemaker. "I'm proud of you."

His head tilted slightly. "Why's that?"

"You got to spend quality time with your team this weekend. You got them to stop hating me somehow. And here you are, having dinner with me and Lisa."

She smiled. He did too. Nya thought his lips looked perfectly kissable. Marquis felt the same way about hers. He reached for her hand and pulled her to him. Nya almost gave in, to whatever he wanted, but she placed her other hand on his chest and pushed back at the last moment.

God, why did I do that? she wondered. She could feel his sculpted pecs, which seemed to tighten beneath her fingers. She longed to run her hand across his bare skin, to feel his nipples and his hard stomach. The thought alone made her own nipples stiffen beneath her blouse.

"What's wrong?" Marquis asked, wondering why she stopped him.

"We can't do that." She spoke with a hushed voice. "Lisa will hear us."

He frowned. "She can't hear a kiss."

"Stop it."

She reached and placed her fingers over his mouth. His lips were warm and full, his breath moist. He licked his lips. Nya pulled her hand back when his hot tongue came in contact with her fingers, though a naughty part of her wanted to leave her hand where it was.

"Boy, stop," she said and pushed him again.

He looked over her shoulder. "Lisa's not in here." His voice was low and deep. "And you don't have glass walls."

"Trust me, she's around," Nya assured him.

"What about a hug? I miss you."

Even if she wanted to refuse the request, Nya couldn't refuse those eyes – and those lips. She gave in to his charms and stepped into his arms. She felt paradise when he wrapped his powerful biceps around her. She squirmed when he buried his face in the crook of her neck. His cologne was faint but alluring. She closed her eyes and smiled as she inhaled his scent. She wanted to kiss him from his earlobe to his navel, and then some.

"I'm not going to grab your ass," he whispered close to her ear.

Nya's eyes fluttered open. The thought hadn't entered her mind, but now she worried that he might. She felt his hands on the small of her back. One of them inched lower, towards her waistline.

"That's good," she managed, "because Lisa–"

"Yes, I know," he said. "I said that because I want you to know how much self-control I have. I've been admiring your body since October, and I want to – grab it. I really do. Next time I hold you like this, I will."

His confession made her legs weak. She wanted to jump into his arms and have him carry her away. She didn't care where they went, so long as they could take their time peeling each other's clothes off when they got there.

But she was grateful when he released her and backed away.

"Goodnight, Miss Edmonds." He turned and quietly exited the house.

Nya barely had a moment to compose herself before Lisa rounded the corner.

"You should've kissed him."

"I knew you were somewhere close," her mother said with a frown.

"I wasn't spying on y'all," Lisa said. "I was headed to the kitchen, but I stopped because I didn't want to interrupt anything."

"That's fine," Nya said. "You didn't interrupt anything. What did you need from the kitchen?"

"I forgot," Lisa said, then, "Why didn't you kiss him?"

"Because I'm not going to make out with some man while my daughter is in the hallway eavesdropping."

"Do you know how many women would love to be in your shoes?" Lisa asked her. Her eyes were bright and surprisingly mature. "I bet they would've kissed him."

"Maybe that's why he chose me instead of them," Nya said and walked past her with her head up high.

"Ooh, *sassy*!" her daughter noticed.

Nya laughed at that.

● ● ● ● ● ●

The next morning Marquis got a call from his lawyer.

242

"Mr. Berry, I have good news."

His whole body froze. "Yes?"

"The police have dropped the charges against you. You've been exonerated."

Relief hit him like a tsunami. He closed his eyes and took a deep breath. "Okay. How? What happened?"

"My investigator uncovered video of the incident from one of the neighboring businesses. Seems the police never checked with them."

Marquis was not happy to hear that. "Really?"

"Yes. The video captured the entire incident. It shows that Daryl followed you, and you tried your best to avoid the fight. You never threw a punch."

"I told you."

"Yes, you did."

"I can get my job back now?" He was pacing the room. He couldn't sit still.

"I would think so, but that's up to the school district. Not my deal."

"Alright, Mrs. Branch. Thank you so much."

When he got off the phone, he screamed into the air. *"Thank you, Jesus!"*

He wanted to call the principal immediately, but it was only nine o'clock. Mr. Walters may not have gotten the word by then. Besides, once the police told them what really happened, the principal would be the one to call him.

Marquis tried to enjoy a normal day, but as the hours went by with no word from Finley High, he got antsy. He knew his mom would settle him down, but she couldn't return his call until she got a lunch break at the electric company.

"Do you think that man doesn't want you back?" she asked.

"It's 12:30," Marquis complained. "Why is it taking him so long to call me? And I watched the news. They didn't say *anything* about my charges being dropped. If they're

243

gonna make a big story about it the first time, they should make a big story now."

Kendra grinned, but she knew her son was serious, and frazzled, by the sound of it.

"They don't have to put you on the news again," she said. "When you go back to school and keep winning, that'll tell the story."

"What if they don't take me back?"

"Why wouldn't they?"

"You know how it goes; sometimes negative publicity is enough, even if you didn't do anything. Plus I did make some mistakes with that dude. I should've told the principal what was going on from the beginning. And I never should've stopped my truck."

"You live and learn," his mother said. "You gotta take your bumps. If they don't want you back, then go somewhere else. You done built a name for yourself, Marquis. You could probably get a job coaching *college*, if you want to."

"You think so?"

"Yes. Of course I do. And you know it's true."

Kendra believed in him unfailingly. When Marquis found a companion who had this much faith in him, he would marry her.

"So what's this I hear about you getting fresh with the mother of your star player?"

He grinned, his face growing warm.

● ● ● ● ● ●

Mr. Walters still hadn't called by three p.m.

Marquis couldn't take it anymore. This was torture. Today was Wednesday. If he expected to return to teaching on Thursday, the principal would've called him by now.

He called the school and was greeted pleasantly by the clerk. When she transferred him to Mr. Walters' office, the principal was pleasant as well.

"Good afternoon, Mr. Berry."

Marquis frowned. He didn't expect cheeriness. "Hi. Good afternoon. I was, um, I was wondering if you had heard anything from the police, about my, um, situation."

He hated that he was stammering like one of the teenagers who was sent to the principal's office. He tried to shake off the nerves.

"Yes," Mr. Walters said. "I got a call from the superintendent this afternoon."

And...

Marquis waited, but he didn't elaborate on that. "So, you know they dropped the charges?"

"Yes, Mr. Berry. We've been informed. Congratulations."

And...

"So, um, I get to come back to school – soon?"

"Oh, most definitely, Mr. Berry. To be honest, I'm sick of my phones blowing up because of you. Everybody and their mama wants Coach Berry back."

Marquis thought his heart would burst. His eyes watered, but that was his allergies. Surely.

"However..." the principal said.

That one word brought Marquis halfway back down to earth.

"... there are certain things you did that go against district policy. You will face some sort of reprimand. At the very least you will have to attend relevant training courses and maybe some lessons online. You're a first year teacher, but that does not excuse your actions; the part you played in this."

"Yes, sir." Marquis was floating again. His career was so much bigger than a few black marks in a folder. "When can I come back?"

"We have to take care of some administrative stuff," the principal told him. "Shouldn't take more than a few days."

Marquis' eyes widened. "But the girls play this Saturday."

"I'm sorry, but I don't think anyone at the district office will work any faster because of that. I'll give you a call when it's okay to come back to work."

"Okay," Marquis said. "Thank you, sir."

He was between highs again. He sighed. He knew he had to let it go. It was out of his hands at this point. If he was meant to coach the girls this Saturday, fate would align it as such. If not, he'd make the five hour drive to San Antonio on his own.

Maybe Nya would ride with him.

The thought made him smile.

CHAPTER TWENTY-THREE
THE FINAL CHAPTER
THE BEST OF THE BEST

On Friday, March 4th the girls' team was fortunate to have another day out of school. During the morning announcements, the principal asked everyone to show their support for the Lady Grizzlies, who would be travelling to San Antonio for their regional semi-finals match.

"They've done an extraordinary job this year," he boasted. "Just a few more games, and they'll make it to the state championship! We're very proud of them and their coach. If you see the team in the hallway before they take off, please take a moment to wish them luck. Make Finley High proud, ladies. Go Grizzlies!"

The girls headed for the bus after first period. Their classmates lined the hallway and cheered for them as they left the building. Lisa and her teammates had the swagger of rock stars. Regardless of the outcome of the game, their popularity would be at an all-time high for the rest of the school year.

When they got outside, there were more students and faculty waiting to see them off. The crowd had banners and streamers like the ones they used at the pep rally. The players didn't expect so much support. Even the principal was there to give each one of them a pat on the back.

When they boarded the bus, they met up with the four booster moms who would be traveling with them. Nya was among them. Their game against Lincoln Academy wasn't until Saturday, but they would arrive in San Antonio a day earlier. This would give them time to watch the other semifinal game, which featured Corliss against Dunbar. Finley High would face the winner of that bracket next week, if they were successful against Lincoln.

The girls would also have time to take in some of the sights of San Antonio. They were all thrilled about spending the night in a hotel. In less than two weeks, the booster moms had managed to come up with enough funds to pay for their rooms.

The obvious downside to all of this was Coach Berry. It had been two days since he was cleared of any wrongdoing. But the powers that be were dragging their feet on getting him reinstated. It was enough to cause a riot. Marquis had to call the booster moms personally and implore them to keep cool.

"I'll be there regardless," he had promised them. "This game is all about the girls. Don't make it about me. That's unfair to them."

When everyone was seated, and they were ready to hit the road, Coach Mitchell stood at the front of the bus. He quieted them down and prayed for traveling grace.

When he was done, he said, "I know this isn't how any of you thought it would go. You've had a tumultuous season. No one expects to lose their coach this late in the game. But what you ladies did this year is what matters most; how you persevered, despite the setbacks.

"I won't ask you to pretend I'm Coach Berry or even to treat me the same as you would treat him. I only ask that you keep your eyes on the prize. I'll do my best coaching you. If you give your all on the court tomorrow, we can't lose."

He didn't get any applause for his pep talk. That was fine, because he didn't expect any.

He took a seat, and the bus began to roll out of the parking lot. They didn't make it twenty feet before a boisterous roar began to build in the crowd outside the school.

One of the girls on the bus shouted for the driver to, "*Wait!*"

Her teammates looked around but didn't see anything.

"Over there!" she said, pointing.

By then some of their classmates were chasing the bus, waving their hands in the air. When the players saw the familiar truck pulling up behind them, everyone began to shout.

"Stop the bus!"

"It's him!"

"*Wait! It's Coach Berry!*"

Nya didn't believe it. The last time she talked to Marquis, his plan was to drive to San Antonio and meet them there. He would leave his home around the same time the bus left the school. But when she looked out the window, there was no mistaking his heavy duty pickup. The sight of it filled her belly with butterflies. Marquis had his hazard lights on, and he was blowing his horn to get their attention.

Nya didn't know what to expect from this, but her eyes were wide and hopeful. Her heart began to knock at the same rate of the hurried feet that rushed to the front of the bus as the driver came to a stop.

"Open the door!" they pleaded.

The driver looked to Coach Mitchell who shrugged.

He opened the doors, and half the passengers burst from the vehicle like an agitated wasp nest. The booster moms watched the girls converge on Marquis as he exited his truck. He had a travel bag in one hand and a briefcase in the other. He said something to them, and everyone outside erupted in cheers. Marquis headed for the bus with the girls flocking him like ducklings.

"Sorry I'm late," he said as he climbed aboard. His smile was sheepish. His massive chest rose and fell with his quickened breaths. "Coach Mitchell," he said, addressing his replacement, "I believe I can take it from here, unless you wanna ride with us..."

"They said you can coach?" Bridgette asked. She was on the edge of her seat.

"Yes, I'm officially back on duty!" Marquis announced. "Just got the word from Mr. Walters."

More excited screams filled the bus. So many people wanted to hug and congratulate Marquis, Nya didn't bother trying to fight her way through. She watched from her seat with delightful tears in her eyes.

Coach Mitchell gave him a hardy handshake.

"As much as I'd like to see y'all whoop up on Lincoln, I think I'll sit this one out," he told Marquis. "And the next time you need a replacement, count me out! This is definitely *your* team."

Everyone laughed at that.

A minute later the bus got moving again, sans Coach Mitchell. He stood in the parking lot with the rest of the students and faculty. They all waved as the Lady Grizzlies belted their fight song. They were so loud and hype, everyone could still hear them as they turned onto the main thoroughfare.

We comin' to your town!
Yah! Trick! Yah!
We gonna shut you down!
Yah! Trick! Yah!

● ● ● ● ● ●

The five hour drive to San Antonio was long but not boring. Everyone was excited to hear the tale of Marquis' last minute reprieve.

"I was about to leave the house," he told them. "I was packed and ready to go. When Mr. Walters called, I thought he had more bad news. No way was he going to wait till the last second and say I could go. But he told me the word just came in, and I was cleared for the trip!"

"This has got to be *fate!*" Tricia's mom decided. "We made it this far your first year coaching. And after all the trouble you been through, you made it back just in time. This is God, y'all!"

Nya believed that too. This season had been a miracle. She didn't think they had come this far, only to lose it all.

When they made it to San Antonio, they went straight to the Alamodome, rather than check into their hotels first. The stadium was a humongous structure located in the southeastern portion of downtown. The girls felt like they'd made it to the finals already as they emerged from the bus and stretched their travel-weary limbs.

Once inside, they saw that nearly 10,000 seats were filled with fans of girls' basketball. Lisa and her teammates headed for the concession stands to grab snacks before the Corliss/Dunbar game. Marquis and Nya hadn't spoken much during the bus ride. He sidled up to her as they looked for their seats.

"Hey, Miss Edmonds."

She offered him a quick smile. "Hi, Coach Berry."

"You looking mighty fine today," he commented.

Nya didn't think so. She wore jeans and a teeshirt, and she felt unkempt after the long ride.

"You're easy to impress," she noticed.

"Who you bunking with tonight at the hotel?" he asked.

Her eyes widened. She smirked. "I don't know. I can tell you who I'm *not* bunking with."

"Oh, no, I didn't mean me," he said. His smile was playfully wicked.

"Mmm hmm." Nya thought he looked gorgeous, even though he wasn't dressed to impress either. His shorts were baggy. It was his tee-shirt, exposing his powerful, dark arms, that made her stomach tighten.

"I'll be the only one with a room all to myself," he told her. "If you find yourself bored in the wee hours of the morning... I'm just saying."

"Thanks for sharing," she said, "not that I need that information."

"Of course not," he agreed. "I'm just saying..."

"Mmm hmm."

● ● ● ● ● ●

The game against Corliss and Dunbar was outstanding. It was do or die for both teams, and the players left everything they had on the court. The teams were neck and neck throughout all four quarters until Dunbar hit a crucial three-pointer with less than a minute to go. Corliss was left with no choice but to commit fouls that would stop the clock during Dunbar's last few possessions. It didn't help. Dunbar sealed the deal by making five of their six free throws.

The Lady Grizzlies remained excited about the venue and tomorrow's game, but Marquis could see they were a little spooked after watching that match. Next weekend they would face Dunbar's scrappy Wildcats, if they managed to get past the Rams of Lincoln Academy.

They boarded the bus and made it to the Embassy Suites thirty minutes later. The hotel was beautiful. All of their rooms were on the same floor. By then it was five o'clock. They made plans to eat dinner together at seven-thirty at a nearby restaurant. In the meantime, the ladies wanted to check out an outlet mall they spotted during the bus ride. It was within walking distance, and the booster moms were going, so Marquis okayed the venture.

They implored him to go with them, but he declined.

"I'm too tired," he complained. "Plus I have to go over our game plan for tomorrow. I'll be ready for dinner when y'all get back."

The team headed downstairs with their chaperones while Marquis settled into his room and unpacked some of his belongings. He brought a few bottles of water, but they were no longer cold. He grabbed an ice bucket, thinking he had seen an ice machine down the hall.

When he opened his door, he spotted a straggler on the floor. He stood in his doorway and waited for her to pass by as she headed for the elevators.

When Nya saw him, she stopped short.

"Oh. Hi."

Marquis leaned on his doorframe like a gigolo. "Hello there."

She giggled. "You're about to get some ice?" she asked, noticing his bucket.

"I was," he confirmed. He stepped out of his room and looked up and down the hallway. "Where is everybody?"

"Down in the lobby, waiting on me," she replied.

She had her hair pulled away from her face, not a dab of makeup on. Still, she looked remarkably beautiful to him. She recognized the *come hither* look in his eyes and took a step back.

"Do you have to go with them?" he asked.

She nodded, grinning. "If everybody goes except me and you, we'll have more rumors spreading than we already do."

"Yeah," Marquis agreed. "You probably right."

She started to walk away, but his stare was enchanting. She could see the outline of his chest beneath

253

his tee shirt. All of his muscles looked primed, as if he'd been working out. Nya wanted to bathe in that sea of black skin, but she knew better.

He turned slightly and placed his bucket on the counter. "Come here."

"Uh-uhn." She shook her head.

"A quick kiss," he said. "For luck."

"No, Marquis. What if one of the girls comes back?"

"Comes back for what?" he asked. "You haven't been gone that long."

She laughed. "You don't know that." She shook her head. "It's too risky. You're gonna get fired."

"I don't think so," he said. "Come here." He reached and took hold of her hand.

"Marquis, no..." But she allowed him to pull her into the room, into his embrace.

Just for a second, she told herself.

The moment he wrapped his strong arms around her, her body melted, hot and fast. It felt so good to touch him, to have him touch her. She started to complain when he reached and closed the door, but his lips brushed her cheek and then reunited with her mouth, and her ability to speak was momentarily hindered.

He kissed her softly, but his hands were more anxious. More demanding. Nya remembered that he'd told her what would happen the next time he had her in his arms. She knew this wasn't the right time or place, but she couldn't bring herself to stop him as his hands slid down her back and claimed her ass as a prize.

"*Uhn*."

She moaned against his mouth, and he squeezed harder and pulled her hips closer to his. He deepened the kiss. Nya saw pink and white clouds behind her eyelids. When her lips parted, he licked her tongue and sucked it. Nya felt a sensual stream flowing between her thighs. She felt the insistence of his hands as he fondled her. She felt the hot hardness between his legs.

Her eyes flashed open just as he released her. He took an uneasy step back. Her heart was hammering. Her nipples were hard and visible beneath her tee-shirt. Her clitoris was throbbing, singing a glorious melody of illicit longing. She still felt his hands all over her ass, though she could see they were no longer there.

She saw the hardness she felt a moment ago. Marquis' basketball shorts did little to conceal a powerful erection. The sight of it made Nya's eyes dilate. The blood drained from her face, and she forgot to breathe for a moment.

Marquis' voice was low and animalistic when he told her, "Yeah, you should go. I don't know why I thought I could handle that."

His eyes were darker than midnight. He stepped past her. His movements were stiff. She stepped aside, and he opened the door slightly and peered down the hallway.

He cleared his throat and told her, "The coast is clear."

Nya knew she had no choice, but she didn't want to leave. She considered sending her daughter a text message, saying she decided to stay behind. Of course that would be a crazy move. She could expect thinking like that from Marquis, but she was ten years his senior. One of them had to be the mature one.

As she stepped past him, she couldn't stop herself from reaching for the bulge in his shorts. She knew she was wrong. She didn't want to be a tease. But *damn*. She had to. He sucked air between his teeth when she squeezed slightly.

"Why?" he moaned. His eyes were half closed. His body was scorching.

"I'm sorry," she whispered.

He opened his eyes and stared into hers. She still had his dick in hand. She leaned forward and kissed him again.

She felt his manhood pulsate beneath her fingers. She knew it was communicating with her. She forced herself to let him go.

He said, "The next time we're in a room alone, you're not leaving me in this condition."

The comment made her feel guilty for grabbing his erection, but that didn't mean she regretted it.

She checked the hallway herself before she made a smooth escape. When she got downstairs, everyone was too excited about the trip to notice she was as hot as a ghost pepper.

● ● ● ● ● ●

On Saturday the Lady Grizzlies lost to Lincoln Academy by a final score of 78-71. It was one of the highest scoring games in the team's history. The girls did their best. Lisa brought them back from the brink of defeat several times before they finally succumbed. She finished with a season high 22 points, 11 assists and 5 rebounds.

Later, in the locker room, Marquis stood before his vanquished warriors. Their exhaustion and disappointment was so palpable he could taste it. They were scruffy and battle-weary.

The girls expected their coach to point out all of the flaws that lead to their defeat. They thought he'd tell them how they'd get them next time, even though they all knew that was a lie. Most of them were seniors, and this was the last high school game they would play.

For some, it was the last time they would ever play basketball for an official team. Their tears weren't only for the game they loss. They cried because the team that sat in that locker room would never exist again.

Instead of laying into them, Marquis surprised them by smiling. "Y'all did your damned thing out there."

They looked up at him with wet, inconsolable eyes.

"I'm sure all of you know I never wanted to coach basketball," he said. "If I had to coach basketball, I didn't want to coach *girls*, because, in my opinion, girls can't play basketball. But, over the course of the season, you ladies did something I never would've thought possible: Not only did you play basketball *well*, but you did it with heart and passion. You made me fall in love with a school and a team and a bunch of your crazy mamas, too."

The girls giggled at that, despite their heartache.

"You made it all the way to the *Alamodome*," he told them. "You're one of the best teams in the state. You played better than I could've ever hoped for. You played better than the boys did. You played better than every school in Dallas, Arlington and Overbrook Meadows. *You did better than all of them*. And that's major. Despite what happened today, don't ever forget that what you did this season is *major*.

"Some of you are going to graduate this year and go off to college. Some of you will forgo college and start a family. No matter where life takes you, you will all remember this day and this season. The lessons you learned about teamwork, comradery, leadership and sacrifice will stay with you *forever*. It may not feel like it now, but you are all stronger and smarter because of what we did this year, because of what *you* did.

"As I watched y'all hustle for the ball today and crash the boards and set up picks that left the other players flat on their backs, I realized something: You were all playing like *girls* – and it was absolutely beautiful!"

He stuck his hand out and said, "Come on, y'all. Bring it in!"

The girls rushed forward to put their hands together. Most of them were smiling now. They were content and inspired.

"*Grizzlies on three!*" their coach barked. "One, two three..."

"***Grizzlies***!"

"One, two, three…"
Grizzlies!"
"One, two, three…"
GRIZZLIES!!"

• • • • • •

When they returned from the locker room, they were greeted by a barrage of applause from the booster moms and other fans who had remained in their seats.

"Go Grizzlies!"

"Way to go ladies!"

"We're proud of you!"

Overcome with emotions, most of the girls started to cry again as they were embraced by their loved ones.

By then the crowd had thinned enough for Marquis to notice a troubling face on the sidelines. It was Daryl. The sight of him made Marquis apprehensive, though Nya's ex didn't look drunk or antagonistic today. As a matter of fact, he looked awkward as he made his way across the court to where Marquis was standing.

"I wanted to apologize for what I did to you," Daryl said.

He could barely make eye contact. Marquis saw that the bruise on his forehead was still pronounced. The swelling had gone down, but the cut and stitches were obvious.

"I acted like a fool, and I lied on you," Daryl continued. He had his hands stuffed in his pockets. "Ain't no excuse for what I did. I don't deserve your forgiveness, but I wanted to apologize." He looked up at him. "I wanted to tell you that you did a helluva job this year. You're the best coach I ever seen. I…" He nodded. "That's it," he said and turned to walk away.

"Wait," Marquis said.

When Daryl turned back to him, Marquis offered his hand.

"I do forgive you. I understand what you were going through, and I wish you the best."

They shook hands while most of the players and booster moms watched. When Daryl turned away again, he saw Lisa and Nya standing together. It was clear he wanted to approach them but was afraid to do so. Lisa turned to her mom, and they had a brief exchange. Nya had a smile on her face as she nodded.

Lisa left her side and met Daryl near the center of the court. He tried to say something, but his joy and regrets left him tongue tied. Tears spilled from his eyes as he reached for her. Lisa hugged him so tightly, no one in the stadium could doubt that he was her father.

• • • • • •

The group brought all of their belongings to the game, so there was no need to return to the hotel. Before they bid adieu to the beautiful city, they spent a couple of hours at the River Walk. It was as beautiful as the postcards in the hotel's gift shop depicted.

Nya and Marquis took a picture with the breathtaking waters as a backdrop. They hoped it would be the first of many wonderful memories they shared.

All of the Lady Grizzlies were back to their happy, goofy, electronic-addicted selves by the time they boarded the bus again and headed home.

EPILOGUE
ONE MONTH LATER

When you're not here
I grope with my hands and my mind
Reaching for slippery memories
Of our mingling flesh
I wonder if you know that
When I smell your fragrance on my shirt
I think of you with such intensity
I can feel you

"Sorry," Marquis told Nya. "I gotta take this."

She nodded as he left the room with the phone.

Marquis stepped in to the dining room before he answered it. The table was cleared, but the scent of the burgers they had for dinner lingered pleasantly. Nya joked that she expected a more elaborate meal when he invited her for supper. But Marquis wasn't a great cook, and he told her so. Besides, his burgers were delish.

"What's up?" he said to Paula.

"I wanted to let you know that I'm not going to fight your little court thing on Monday, so you don't have to waste your money on a lawyer."

The news surprised Marquis, but it also made him suspicious. For the past couple of weeks, their impending court date had been a constant worry. Would the judge let her take the twins to Louisiana? He didn't think so, but even Omar believed Paula had a compelling argument.

"Why is that?" he asked.

"I've been seeing someone," she told him. "We're getting married."

A smile brightened Marquis' features. Now he believed her. He'd still take his lawyer to court with him, but this made sense.

"He must be pretty rich," he guessed.

"He's doing well," she confirmed.

"Well enough for you not to need my money anymore?"

"I still want the child support."

"I'm talking about the spousal support."

"That's up to the judge," she said. "Whatever they decide is fine with me."

"The most they can take is half my check," he warned. "I get paid $4,300 a month."

"That's sad," she commented. "But whatever."

He chuckled. "Damn. He must be loaded. What does he do for a living?"

"Stocks," she said vaguely.

"So he could lose it all at any minute," Marquis ventured. Always two steps ahead of her, he worried about Paula threatening to leave again if her and her new hubby one day went broke.

"I already have my dowry set aside."

"*Dowry*? What the hell?"

"I learn from my mistakes."

Marquis knew she was referring to him as the mistake. She thought she had a winner, but he'd cost her millions when he quit football.

He wondered what kinda of chump Paula had sank her teeth into this time. It was hard to believe a man would give her money up front, just to marry her trifling ass. But Paula was fine. And she could pretend to be sweet.

Marquis figured he'd find out who her next sponsor was soon enough. The important thing was she wasn't trying to take his boys out of state.

"Alright, well, I guess I'll see you Monday," he said.

"Okay, bye."

When he returned to the front room, Nya was standing, looking at family photos he had over the fireplace. She wore a skirt with a sleeveless blouse. She was springtime fresh. Marquis took a seat on the couch. He loved to watch her from the back, but he liked the view even more when she turned and smiled at him.

"You were such a cutie," she said, referring to a picture of him and his brother when they were toddlers.

"I'm still a cutie."

Nya agreed with that wholeheartedly. Marquis wore jeans with a designer, V-neck tee. His skin was dark and smooth. She loved his strong jawline. He had the most perfect set of lips. She wanted to kiss him every time she laid eyes on him.

"Sorry, that was my ex-wife," he told her. "It could've been about the boys."

Nya understood. She nodded.

"Anyway, I got good news," he said.

"What's that?"

"Paula's getting married. She said she's not gonna fight me in court on Monday."

"Really? That's great!" She knew how worried he'd been.

"Yeah. I told you it was all about money with her."

"What does her fiancé do for a living?"

"She didn't say exactly, but it has something to do with stocks. She said he gave her some money to put aside."

"Good for her."

He nodded. She came and sat next to him.

"Guess I won't be moving to Louisiana," he told her.

"That's nice," Nya replied. She liked the way he was staring at her. She leaned over and kissed him. He kissed her back, slowly. Nya felt a rush of heat flow from her face to her chest.

"What school did Lisa pick?" he asked. His eyes were low and relaxed.

"She wants to go to UCLA."

His eyebrow rose.

"I don't want her to go that far," Nya admitted. "But if that's the one she chooses, I won't ask her to stay." Her eyes were reflective. "It will be the first time I've ever been alone."

"You won't be alone. I'm still here."

Nya didn't respond to that. She knew Marquis sometimes said things he didn't mean. He wasn't a dishonest person, but he couldn't possibly know where the future would take them.

"What about you?" she asked. "Where are you going to coach next year?"

In addition to several high schools, he'd also gotten offers from TCU and Oklahoma State.

"Not sure yet," he mused. "I said I'd be here with you, so I know it won't be Oklahoma."

"Don't be silly," she countered. "We've only been dating for a couple of months. I shouldn't have anything to do with your decision."

"Now *that's* silly," Marquis said.

He seemed so sincere, it made her heart flutter. She reminded herself that he was ten years younger. And they had yet to make love. Men are expected to say anything to get to the sweet spot.

"Maybe I'll stay at Finley," he offered.

"Why would you do that?"

"Money's not everything." Marquis realized the irony of his comment, considering his brother was holding nearly half a million dollars for him.

He kissed her this time. She closed her eyes and gradually leaned back on the cushions. He reached and touched her breast, sliding his thumb back and forth over her nipple. She felt a jolt flow through her chest as the bud hardened. Marquis brought two fingers together and squeezed it slightly. The sensation caused a clap of lightening to shoot down her body. It came to a stop between her legs and hummed softly.

They took turns sucking each other's lips. Marquis' skillful hand slid down her frame and came to a rest on her hip then moved again, down to her thigh. While sitting, her skirt was well above her knees. Marquis caressed her bare flesh. His hand slipped between her legs, coaxing her thighs open.

Nya knew he wouldn't stop this time. There were obstacles before; never the right time or place. But they were home alone now. His fingers disappeared beneath her skirt, and her breath's became heated. He touched her panties. Nya inhaled sharply. She was very wet. She didn't want him to know, but then again, a part of her did.

He stopped kissing her. Immediately she missed the delight of his lips. His hand moved further beneath her skirt. She had to spread her legs even more to accommodate him. There were three fingers on her panties now. They stroked her, up and down.

Marquis felt her glorious heat. His manhood sprang to life. She had brought him to this state of arousal a dozen times in the past, but his was not a drill. Tonight he would swathe himself in her heat. Her wetness.

She opened her eyes and saw that he was staring at her. His eyes were drunk with passion. As they watched each other, his fingers slid under her panties. She gasped. In one swift motion he had her, all of her, in the palm of his hand. Her lips lightly trembled. Her chest rose and fell unevenly.

He caressed her, and then his longest finger invaded her. It slipped between her labia and found her slippery oasis.

"*Oh.*"

Her legs squeezed around his hand. The way he watched her was intimidating. She may be older, but Marquis was definitely a man. She knew that he would be dominant.

He removed his hand and took hold of hers. As he helped her to her feet, Nya wondered if he realized he was using the same hand that touched her, penetrated her. Her essence was transferred from his fingers to hers.

He led her to the bedroom, and gestured for her to take a seat on his bed. Marquis stripped off his tee shirt as he stood before her. Nya was mesmerized by the sight of his bare torso. His chest was massive. His stomach was smooth, broken by the creases of his six-pack.

Nya was so enthralled, she barely noticed when he reached under her skirt to remove her panties, even though she had to lift her hips to assist him.

She had never been with a man with a body like Marquis'. She knew he was in superb shape. She could see that even when he wore long-sleeved shirts. But with no top at all, she understood that he was a work of art. A biological masterpiece.

She wanted his chest in her hands. She wondered if he read her mind when he stepped closer and began to suck her lips again. She reached for his pecs with both hands. The feel of his hard muscles made her moan in gratitude. She ran her hands over his soft nipples, groped him freely. Her fingers went up and down his torso as Marquis nibbled her lips.

His hands were busy, too. He found the zipper on the side of her skirt and pulled it all the way down. Nya helped him remove the garment. He stepped away and placed it on the dresser. Nya was removing her blouse when he turned back to her. His eyes remained on hers as he slipped out of his pants and boxers. Seeing his dick made the muscles between her legs clench anxiously. He was completely engorged.

He left his pants on the floor but took her blouse and placed it on the dresser with her skirt. Nya's eyes swam up and down his frame as she removed her bra. Marquis was a mountain of nude, muscular flesh. His physique was toned and sculpted for athletics, but tonight this raw power was all for her. She couldn't help but feel a little overwhelmed.

Marquis was in a similar state of amazement as he watched her disrobe. Nya's body was perfect. He loved every one of her curves. He knew she was dieting, but as far as he was concerned, she didn't need to lose any weight. He didn't want her thighs to get any smaller. He wanted to dive in to her pillowy breasts. He longed to drown in them.

She dropped her bra on the bed. He retrieved it and placed it on the dresser. She smiled at his diligence. She was further impressed when he retrieved a condom before she requested it. She watched him open it and slide it down his shaft.

She lay back as he crawled onto the bed and on top of her. He paused midway up to explore her nude breasts for the first time. With an arm planted on either side of her, he used only his mouth to bring both nipples to a state of erection.

Nya's eyes were closed, her mouth ajar. The feel of his tongue was captivating. Every sensation rolled down her stomach and excited her clitoris, causing it to throb at the same rate as her pulse.

Her legs squirmed beneath him. The friction between her walls gave her a wonderful pre-orgasm. She felt her body creating more juices. Her labia glistened. Her stomach clenched spasmodically. She wanted him inside her so badly she almost demanded it. But Marquis had his fill of her breasts, before he began to crawl again.

Nya spread her legs, and he settled between them. Every cell in her body yearned for him. Finally she felt the head of his manhood pushing her slick opening. She cried out as he slid in slowly ensuring she felt every inch as he filled her. She was not surprised to find her orgasm building the first time he stroked her G-spot. Her walls squeezed, urging him to go deeper.

Marquis had never been with a woman whose body responded to him like she did. He felt his climax rising, but he was determined to please her for as long as she wanted. When he pushed in to the hilt, every muscle in her body replied. She wrapped her legs around him. His dick jumped inside her, and she moaned next to his ear.

"Oh. Oh yes."

Marquis felt lightheaded. He backed out, and his hips began to pump rhythmically. He slid in and out of her slowly, but forcefully. Nya reached and gripped his flanks. She had to hold on to something as the speed of his strokes increased. He reached with one hand to grip her hip as he stroked, faster now.

Nya's eyelids fluttered as her orgasm bubbled with volcanic heat. Marquis coaxed it from her with hard, demanding patience. His black skin flowed all over her. Through her. She saw bright pink passion behind her closed eyelids. She screamed with delight, and he grunted with satisfaction, and she marveled at the wonderment of them coming together. It was poetic.

She felt every throbbing pulse of his dick as he spilled his seed, and he felt the constant, fist like grip of her walls as she coated him with her essence.

Above them their spirits coupled.

Beneath them the earth trembled.

KEITH THOMAS WALKER

ABOUT THE AUTHOR

Keith Thomas Walker, known as the Master of Romantic Suspense and Urban Fiction, is the author of nearly two dozen novels, including *Life After, The Realest Ever,* the *Brick House* series and the *Finley High* series. Keith's books transcend all genres. He has published romance, urban fiction, mystery/thriller, teen/young adult, Christian, poetry and erotica. Originally from Fort Worth, he is a graduate of Texas Wesleyan University. Keith has won or been nominated for numerous awards in the categories of "Best Male Author," "Best Romance," and "Author of the Year," from several book clubs and organizations. Visit him at www.keithwalkerbooks.com.

www.ingramcontent.com/pod-product-compliance
Lightning Source LLC
Chambersburg PA
CBHW020719130726
47899CB00011B/464